Praise for the Lords of Vice novels

Till Dawn with the Devil

"*Till Dawn with the Devil*'s romance is first-rate with unusual characters and an underlying mystery that will intrigue readers."
—Robin Lee,
Romance Reviews Today

"A terrific second book in this series. I had it read in a day and then bemoaned the fact it was over."
—Sandra Marlow,
The Good, The Bad, and The Unread (A+)

"You will devour every sexy and intriguing morsel of this divine read."
—Christine Morehouse,
Romantic Crush Junkies (4 ½ stars)

"Hawkins cements her reputation for bringing compelling, unique, and lush romances to fans eager for fresh storytelling."
—*Romantic Times BOOKreviews*
(4 ½ stars)

All Night with a Rogue

"Sizzling, smart, and sophisticated."
—Gaelen Foley, *New York Times*
bestselling author of *My Wicked M...*

St. Martin's Paperbacks Titles
by Alexandra Hawkins

All Night with a Rogue

Till Dawn with the Devil

AFTER DARK
WITH A
SCOUNDREL

Alexandra Hawkins

St. Martin's Paperbacks

AFTER DARK WITH A SCOUNDREL

Copyright © 2011 by Alexandra Hawkins.

Cover illustration by Jim Griffin

For information address St. Martin's Press, 175 Fifth Avenue, New York, NY 10010.

ISBN: 978-0-312-38126-4

Printed in the United States of America

St. Martin's Paperbacks edition / February 2011

St. Martin's Paperbacks are published by St. Martin's Press, 175 Fifth Avenue, New York, NY 10010.

10 9 8 7 6 5 4 3 2 1

I prefer a pleasant vice to an annoying virtue.

—Molière [Jean Baptiste Poquelin],
Mercury in *Amphitryon*, Act 1, Sc. 4

Chapter One

London, August 1, 1817

"What say you, Regan: red, white, or green fire?"

Fifteen-year-old Lady Regan Bishop pursed her lips together as she studied the open book. "Why settle for one when we could have them all?" She tapped the left page with a grimy finger. "However, according to the book we should focus on making each skyrocket in a separate batch. There will be less risk of a disastrous outcome or some such nonsense."

"Utter rot," Christopher Courtland, Earl of Vanewright, said cheerfully. "I have done this dozens of times, and I still possess all of my limbs."

Eight years older, Vane, as he was called by family and friends, treated Regan as an equal and fellow member of the Lords of Vice rather than a troublesome younger sister who always seemed to be underfoot. It mattered little to her that her older brother, Frost, Earl of Chillingsworth, was the true member of Nox, the notorious gentlemen's club situated at 44 King Street between Covent Garden and the clubs of St. James.

With the exception of Frost, the members of the Lords of Vice were the closest thing Regan had to family. Her father had perished in a hunting accident when she was a mere babe, and her eccentric mother had abandoned her young children several years later when she ran off with her lover.

"Why do you encourage her?" Hunter, the Duke of Huntsley, demanded, observing Regan's and Vane's efforts from a respectable distance. He bit into the crisp flesh of the apple in his hand and chewed. "Frost will happily murder you if you blow up his sister."

"No one wants your surly opinion, Your Grace," Regan said loftily.

She cast a glance in Hunter's direction and stifled a giggle. Nicolas Towers, Duke of Huntsley, was a handsome devil with his long dark hair and amber eyes. If a lady was unaware of the duke's wicked appetites, she might foolishly have mistaken him for a chivalrous knight. However, Regan knew the gent better than most. Hunter was no fair lady's knight, but rather a sorcerer who seemed to seduce women with his voice alone.

Unimpressed with such skills, Regan sniffed. Long ago, she had decided that she preferred white knights over sorcerers. "You are welcome to join us if you like."

"I must respectfully decline your generous offer, my dear girl." Hunter gestured with the apple toward the two wooden buckets of water at his feet. "I am merely on hand to put out any fires. The last time I assisted the mad chemist, his antics burned the hair off my left arm."

Regan laughed, recalling the incident. "You singed your fine frock coat and eyebrows, too," she reminded him gleefully.

"Best you remember my fate." Hunter waggled his dark eyebrows at her. "You would look like a plucked goose without all that pretty hair on your head."

"Do not listen to him," Vane said, delivering his sneer over his right shoulder before his attention returned to the canisters arranged on the table. "What color should we start with, Regan?"

She dismissed Hunter's snort with a graceful wave of her hand. "Red," she said decisively to Vane.

"Sticks or without?"

Regan glanced up from the array of canisters and bowls scattered on the table and met Vane's clear blue-green gaze. "What do you recommend?"

"Sticks," he said, reaching for the canister of powdered sulfur. "Less work and it will keep His Grace from pissing his drawers."

Hunter tossed his apple core at his friend, hitting the young earl on the right shoulder. "You should have a care with your language, Vane. You are in the presence of a lady."

Regan fluttered her lashes at Vane. She raised her voice an octave and said, "Almighty hellfire, Lord Vanewright, do have a care. Such coarse language will cause me to collapse with a fretful case of vapors!"

Both Regan and Vane laughed. Even Hunter smiled ruefully at the outrageous suggestion that a few impolite words would cause Regan to swoon. She was made of sterner stuff than most of the silly ladies of the *ton*. With Frost as her reluctant guardian, Regan had been practically raised by the members of the Lords of Vice.

While her upbringing might be considered unconventional by most, Regan had reveled in her freedom. She had learned something from each gentleman. From Frost, she had learned much about the world. He had also taught her how to articulate her views in a forthright manner that would make most ladies blush. Hunter shared his appreciation of prime horseflesh, and Vane, his love of chemistry and his penchant for playing with fire. Sin, the Marquess of Sinclair, taught her to fence. Reign, Earl of Rainecourt, taught her how to avoid a fist, which he often teased her was likely to be a regular occurrence because of her cheekiness, while Saint, the Marquess of Sainthill, honed her gaming skills. And finally, there was Dare, or Lord Hugh, as he was called by his family. The second son of the Duke of Rhode had shared his afternoons with her, teaching her how to fish and swim when she was younger.

To her great disappointment, Dare had abruptly ended their private adventures two years earlier after he had declared her a proficient swimmer.

Regan discreetly glanced down at the gentle curves of her breasts beneath her drab brown dress, and hid her knowing smile. As much as she missed those lazy afternoons by the lake, she was secretly pleased that Dare had finally noticed that she was no longer a little girl.

Or a sister.

Unfortunately, she was uncertain how to proceed with the stubborn gentleman. How could she entice Dare into courting her, if he was deliberately avoiding her? With her thoughts centered on Dare, Regan absently reached for the marble pestle.

"Regan . . . watch out!" Hunter shouted, stirring from his slouched position.

The warning came too late, as Regan's hand collided with the glass-and-brass lamp. Hot oil and flame splashed into several bowls, creating a brilliant, blinding flash of white.

Regan screamed, staggering backward away from the shriveling heat as the table became engulfed in flames. Her throat closed up on her as the black smoke threatened to steal the remaining air from her lungs. She felt strong hands catch her and drag her away from the building conflagration, while Vane and several servants frantically tried to extinguish the fire before it destroyed Nox's kitchen.

"Are you hurt?" Hunter shouted at her, sliding his hands roughly over her as he searched for hidden injuries. He lightly tapped her on the cheek when she did not respond to his queries. "Regan!"

"I am well," Regan snapped, attempting to untangle her arms from his unyielding hold. "I am—odds bodkins!" Her words were slurred as she swayed.

To Regan's utter dismay, she slumped into a very ladylike faint.

Dare stuck his head out the coach window and eyed the commotion on King Street with impatience. He withdrew and pounded on the trapdoor to get his coachman's attention. When the small door slid open, he asked, "What can you see from your perch, Cager?"

The coachman coughed. "A fire, milord. The air

is fouled with smoke, and I just caught sight of the fire brigade's pump. It appears we've missed most of the excitement. A damn shame if you ask me."

Bloody hell! It was the perfect ending to a spectacularly awful day. Always the dutiful son, Dare had paid his respects to his father as was expected of him, and the afternoon had quickly disintegrated into a debacle with the appearance of his older brother and his wife.

"Can you tell which building was ablaze?" His friends were going to be disappointed if Madame Venna's brothel had been burned to the ground by a careless patron.

The coachman's face filled the opening. "I daresay it might be Nox, milord."

With a muttered oath on his lips, Dare kicked open the door and leaped from the coach. He pushed his way through the crowd that had congregated on the street. As he approached Nox, he noticed the narrow black column of smoke that was sluggishly rising from the back of the building.

Dare broke through the crowd and circled until he saw what remained of Nox's kitchen. What had happened during his absence?

Where the hell is everyone?

"Dare!"

His head snapped to the left, and there he saw Vane, Hunter, and Saint crouched down with Frost's sister sitting on the ground between them.

Regan.

As he hurried toward his friends, his blue-gray eyes narrowed on the slender young lady, noting the charred holes in her ugly dress and the caked soot marring her too-pale complexion. "What happened?"

Regan's vivid blue eyes gleamed with unshed tears. "It is my fault," she said, her voice husky from the smoke. "I was careless."

"Oh, someone was careless, indeed," Dare said, shooting an angry glance at his friends. "What started the fire?"

"A slight mishap with fireworks," Vane said, the casual, almost amused tone in his voice attaching little importance to the seriousness of the incident.

Dare grabbed Vane and backed him against the nearest tree. "You call this a slight mishap? Christ, man, you almost blew up Frost's sister!"

Behind him, Regan slowly climbed to her feet with Saint's assistance. "Dare, leave Vane alone. He was not responsible for the fire. If you feel the need to throttle someone, it should be me. I was the one who knocked over the oil lamp." She covered her mouth with her dirty hand and moaned.

At the faint sound of distress, Dare released Vane and walked toward Regan. The misery in her eyes was eloquent as her tears cut muddy tracks down her face. When he gently pried her hand away from her mouth, she cried, "Oh, God, Frost is going to kill me!"

"Do not fret, sweet. If you are unhurt, your brother will only maim Vane for his foolishness."

Dare caught Regan in her arms as she swayed. He swept her up and held her slender body tightly against his chest. "How bad is the damage?" he asked, directing his question to Hunter.

The duke gestured at the partially burned kitchen.

"Not as bad Vane deserves for his recklessness. The kitchen will have to be rebuilt, but the rest of Nox is solid. The gambling resumed the moment the smoke cleared from the main rooms."

Dare gave his friends an exasperated look. "Then why is Regan sitting in the mud?" He whirled about and headed for the front of the club. "Has anyone sent word to Frost?"

"I asked them not to," Regan murmured into his coat.

Dare grunted at the news. His friends would have ignored Regan's request and sent for Frost. Regan would not appreciate the men's high-handed actions, but Frost was her guardian. He deserved to know what had happened.

Dare nodded to Berus as he walked through the front door and headed for the stairs. If the steward of Nox had thought it odd that Dare was carrying Frost's sister, he was polite enough to keep his mouth shut.

"Do you require assistance, milord?"

Find Frost, Dare mouthed silently to Berus. "Lady Regan requires some privacy while she recovers from her mishap," he went on aloud for Regan's benefit, ignoring the steward's raised brows as he strode by the servant. "See to it that we are not disturbed."

All of the doors and windows had been opened to clear the smoke. However, Dare was confident that no one would follow them upstairs to the private rooms that only the founding members of Nox used.

"Very well, milord."

As he entered the large drawing room, Dare

bumped one corner of the billiards table with his hip while he made his way to the nearest sofa.

"You can put me down, Dare," Regan said as she brought a hand to her hair and pushed the unkempt mess from her tearstained face. "I vow never to faint again. It was a humiliating exercise."

His grip tightened at her confession. "You fainted?"

Regan sighed. "A momentary weakness. If I have a say in the matter, it shall never happen again."

Dare froze at her horrified gasp. "What is it?"

"I cannot sit on the sofa!"

"Of course you can." He ignored her protest and dropped her on the sofa. "See? You're sitting."

Her eyes seemed to glow as his actions sparked her temper. "Have you noticed that my dress is covered in soot, mud, and other things that I dare not contemplate too closely?" she demanded. Her arms opened, encouraging him to inspect her ruined dress.

Dare crossed his arms over his chest and brought a fist to his mouth to conceal his grin. Poor Regan. She looked like a bedraggled waif who had never been intimate with soap and water. He knew from experience that she was a fetching little minx when she was scrubbed clean.

Dare scowled at the unbidden thought.

He walked over to the small cart and concentrated on the glasses and several crystal decanters. "You need something to calm your nerves."

"My nerves are just fine."

Dare poured her a small glass of brandy anyway. Picking up his own glass, he tossed back the contents and winced as the brandy burned a path down to his gut. He poured more brandy into his glass, and picked up Regan's before he returned to her side.

His gaze strayed to her dirty skirt. Hot embers from the kitchen fire had burned a dozen holes into the fabric. There were large smears of soot across her bodice as if Regan had used the front of her dress to clean her grimy hands. The delicate features of her face looked like they had been painted in soot. Only her eyes and ears seemed untouched by today's mischief. Much of her thick black hair had been freed from the long braid that she preferred to wear. The uneven lengths suggested that she had been close enough to the fire to scorch some of the strands.

"Christ, you're a mess, Regan." He handed her the glass of brandy. "Drink it."

Regan took the glass and sniffed suspiciously at its contents. "I do not particularly care for brandy."

"Now, that is a shame. Drink it anyway." Dare sat down next to her on the sofa. "You're going to need some false courage when you face Frost."

Regan managed a baleful glare as she sipped the brandy. After several generous swallows, she took a ragged breath. "Why? Do you think he will be very angry with me? Turn me over his knee?"

Dare cupped his glass with both hands and studied the amber liquid. "So that is why you begged everyone not to summon your brother. You are worried he might paddle your backside for this mischief, eh?" When she did not reply, he added, "Regan, Frost indulges your every whim. Mayhap more than he should. Vane has more to worry about than you."

His heart clenched when Regan squeezed her eyes shut in a futile attempt to stem her tears. "Ho, what is this?" Dare set his glass on a side table and pulled her onto his lap before he recalled that she was too old to be comforted in this manner.

Regan was no longer a little girl whom he and his friends could coddle and spoil. Two years ago, when she stepped out of the lake dressed only in a wet chemise molded to her body, Dare had realized that his thoughts about Frost's sister were not innocent or brotherly. From that day forward, he had tried to put a respectful distance between him and Regan.

Until now.

Regan seemed oblivious to Dare's inner conflict or the possibility that anyone could enter the room at any moment. Like a cat, she curled against him, pressed her face into his shoulder, and shuddered.

"You can talk to me," he said, his body noting how perfectly she fit against him.

"Do you know why I have been spending my days at Nox?" Regan straightened and took another sip of brandy. "Lady Karmack. She has taken an interest in me, of late, and has been badgering Frost endlessly."

Dare rubbed Regan's back. "What does she want from Frost?"

Regan grimaced. "My brother will not say. Needless to say, Lady Karmack is a disapproving old biddy. Can you believe that she actually lectured me when she caught me wearing breeches?"

The outrage in Regan's hoarse voice made Dare chuckle. He could not stop himself. Regan could be as outrageous as her brother when she put her mind to it. "And why do I suspect, my darling Regan, that you deliberately sported your scandalous togs in front of the lady?"

Regan huffed and shifted on his lap. Dare stifled a groan. "Frost would not let me slip a beetle in Lady Karmack's teacup so I had to do *something*!" Almost nose-to-nose, their gazes met. "Oh, Dare, I fear that Lady Karmack hopes to convince Frost to send me away."

Her lip quivered.

Dare swallowed thickly as he concentrated on Regan's lower lip.

"Rubbish. Frost is not sending you away from us." He gave her a reassuring smile as he tenderly stroked her hair. "Nor will he bow to a stranger's opinion."

"Lady Karmack is a distant cousin," Regan corrected. "Very distant. My father's side of the family, I believe."

"Well, the details hardly matter since you belong to us," Dare said before he could stifle the words. His stomach muscles clenched as the fear he saw in Regan's expression faded and was replaced with a sly, very shrewd look that he never expected from her.

"Do I?" she asked, a small smile teasing her lips. "Will you be my faithful white knight, Dare?"

Dare stiffened at the innocent question. He doubted Frost had told his sister about Dare's pathetic attempt to play a fair lady's white knight, and the bitter betrayal that still managed to turn his stomach when he dwelled on it. "I refuse to play the chivalrous knight for any lady."

"Even me?"

Instead of feigning hurt feelings, Regan had tossed the words at him like a taunt. The question heated his blood faster than the brandy. After the afternoon he had endured with his difficult family, the lady was playing with fire.

"Chivalrous knights care little about being rewarded for their good deeds." The corner of his mouth quirked at her crestfallen expression. "I, on the other hand, thoroughly enjoy claiming my rewards whether or not I deserve them."

As far as Dare was concerned, he had earned a hefty reward for resisting Frost's tempting little sister. Two years ago, he had managed to keep his hands off her, had he not? He had kept his distance, even when a part of him had longed for the chase.

Now Regan was sitting on his lap with a mouth that was just begging to be kissed. Covered in soot and grime, she should not tempt him in the slightest.

Unfortunately, his unruly body did not seem to care.

"And what reward do you deserve, Dare?" she whispered.

Lust coiled in his gut. "This . . ."

Regan's eyes widened as Dare claimed her mouth. It was not the tender kiss a man gave an innocent such as Regan. His lips glided over hers with the purpose to claim and dominate. Dare expected her mouth to taste of sweet innocence, but instead he tasted brandy and the slight bitterness of the soot. With a murmur of encouragement, he used his teeth to nip her lower lip. Regan parted her lips in surprise. Dare ruthlessly took advantage of the reaction and pulled her closer as he deepened their kiss.

In the distance, he heard the sound of a glass breaking. Dare almost smiled. Regan had dropped her glass of brandy. His body hardened as he felt her tentatively touch his arm. She tilted her face toward his, and tried to mimic his sensual ministrations to her willing mouth. The hesitant touch on his arm quickly became a restless caress. Minutes later, Regan had brazenly slid her hands up Dare's arms and wrapped them around his neck.

A not-so-discreet cough from across the room was as effective as a bucket of cold water dumped on the couple.

Dare avoided Regan's startled gaze when he ended the kiss and glanced toward the open doorway. He was not surprised to see an expressionless Frost. Dare did not recognize the older woman standing beside Regan's brother, but considering his luck of late, he assumed the woman gaping at them was Lady Karmack.

"Frost is going to kill me," Regan whispered so softly, Dare doubted anyone else had heard her.

Dare kissed Regan on the forehead and gently nudged her off his lap. He had been aroused by their kiss, but the scowl Lady Karmack was giving him should wither the rigid flesh soon enough.

Dare stood and waited for Frost to challenge him. He did not have the heart to tell Regan that if her brother was going to kill anyone this evening, it was likely to be him.

Chapter Two

"I am being banished for a kiss? A *kiss*?"

Hurt and baffled by her brother's astonishing announcement, Regan sat on the sofa where fifteen minutes earlier she had shared said toe-curling kiss with Dare. After witnessing Regan's shameless display, Frost had ordered Vane and Hunter to escort Lady Karmack downstairs to one of the informal parlors below. At Frost's insistence, Dare had remained in the room, though he did not seem inclined to participate in a family squabble.

"Banished? The word is a tad dramatic for sending you off to a respectable school for young ladies, my dear child. Do you not agree, Dare?" Frost cast an amused glance at his friend.

Her brother had been subtly taunting Dare into defending Regan, as if he was seeking just one more reason to put a bullet into the man. Dare had not taken the bait. He leaned against the wall across from her and silently drank his brandy.

Regan refused to acknowledge Dare with a glance. "Do not be so patronizing," she said to her brother. "Lady Karmack put this maggoty notion in your head, did she not? You were perfectly content for me to receive my lessons at home—"

"And that has been going so well for us, has it not? You have frightened off seven tutors in the past five years. I suspect that your latest mischief—setting fire to Nox—is not precisely the education our father and mother would have desired for you."

Regan sprang to her feet, her hands curled into impotent fists at her sides when Frost mentioned their parents. "Why should I care? Our father is dead. I barely remember him. And our mother might as well be since she has not bothered to post a single letter in all the years that she has been gone."

Frost sighed. He rolled his shoulders as if he were facing an opponent in a prize ring. "Not very sentimental, is she?" he said to Dare. "Beneath all that fire is a cold, ruthless heart. Our mother would be proud."

Regan gasped at her brother's callous assessment of her character. "Take it back!" Forgetting about Dare, she charged at her brother and seized the front of his dark brown coat. "I am nothing like her. You have no right to judge me. If anyone does not have a heart, it is *you*! Over the years, I have watched you dally with the affairs of the heart, and that is not the organ that you exercise with any regularity!"

Dare choked on his brandy. "Christ!" He wheezed as he tried to fill his lungs with air.

Both Frost and Regan ignored him.

"You cheeky little monkey." Frost shook his head, his turquoise-blue eyes glowing with admiration at her daring. "If you had been born male, I would have recommended you for membership at Nox in a few years. However, neither you nor I can change your sex, my dear sister. You are not meant for this life, and it is past time that I do right by you."

Regan sagged against Frost as she struggled to keep her stinging tears from falling. "If this is about the kitchen, I will gladly pay for the damages done."

"Oh, Regan, the kitchen should be the least of your concerns."

She swiped at a traitorous tear on her grimy cheek. "I knew it. This *is* about me kissing Dare."

Frost cupped her cheek and tipped her face until her gaze met his. Regan expected anger, even frustration. It was his pity that shamed her. "You have been around Nox long enough to learn that a kiss has no more importance than scratching an itch. None of the Lords of Vice is worthy of your affections."

"Even you?" she said.

"Especially me," Frost countered, dropping his hand. "As your guardian, I have been remiss in my duties toward you, Regan. It is something I intend to rectify with Lady Karmack's assistance."

Regan took umbrage at the mention of the meddlesome woman. This was all Lady Karmack's fault. She had ruined everything. "You cannot make me go with that woman. I will run away before I surrender myself to that tiresome creature."

Frost tossed his head back and laughed. With his wavy dark hair loose around his lean, handsome face, he looked like a fallen angel. "My darling sister, have a care with your childish threats. You would be astounded by what I can do when I put my mind to it."

Unimpressed, Regan shoved her brother away from her and stalked toward Dare. The man's silence annoyed her almost as much as Frost's casual threats.

Her brother was about to banish her from London. She wanted someone to come to her defense.

"And what say you to all of this?" she demanded, slowing at the lack of interest she noted on Dare's face.

"Forgive me, I must side with your brother on this," Dare said, straightening from his slouched stance. "You are too old to be running about like an unkempt hoyden. Certain things are expected of you, Regan, and the ladies of the *ton* can be cruel."

Regan felt each word like a barb to her heart. "And the kiss?" she asked in a hushed whisper.

"Idle curiosity. Nothing more." Dare walked over to the small table and picked up a decanter. He poured more brandy into his empty glass. He did not even glance her way.

Scoundrel.

Turning her back on Dare, she swallowed several times, fighting down the misery and betrayal she was feeling from the two gentlemen in her life she loved the most.

"Very well," she said, her voice wavering with suppressed emotion. "Banish me from London. Send me to some damn school of bloody refinement. I hope it beggars you, Frost!"

"Tut-tut . . . do not worry about the family coffers. You will be looked after properly."

Regan resisted kicking her brother as she passed. "Why be coy about the true reasons you are sending me away? You never wanted me underfoot, and Lady Karmack has provided you with a respectful excuse to abandon me."

I will not cry . . . I will not cry . . . I will not cry . . .

"You know me so well," Frost said mockingly. "I will mourn you when you are gone."

Her eyes dried as outrage and despair consumed her. "And I hope it rots off!"

It did not take much imagination to figure out which "it" Regan was referring to.

"Regan!" Dare called after her, but she was too angry to reply.

She marched out of the room, her head held high. Frost's laughter kept the indignation in her belly churning as she stepped out into the corridor.

Frost might be able to send her away from the only family that she knew, but she was not going to let anyone turn her into one of those fluttering butterflies the *ton* idolized.

Never.

Frost sobered as Regan's footfalls faded. His sister had been too upset to notice that Frost's laughter had been for her benefit alone.

There wasn't a hint of amusement in his friend's light blue gaze when it finally settled on Dare. "How long do you think it will take for her to forgive me?"

Weeks, months, or maybe years.

Dare tossed back the rest of his brandy. Exhaling loudly, he shook his head and said, "She does not understand the real reason why you are sending her away."

"And you do?"

"More than she does, I wager." Dare set down his glass with a decisive *clink* against the half-empty decanter. Palms forward, he extended his hands from his sides in a manner that could have been interpreted both as an invitation and surrender. "Now that your sister is gone, perhaps we should discuss what happened earlier before the others return."

"There is nothing to discuss."

Dare's forehead furrowed. "Nothing?"

He did not quite believe his good fortune. While Frost possessed some rather flexible scruples, he was protective of his younger sister in his own way. At the very least, Dare expected a bruising punch to the jaw for kissing Regan.

The humor Dare thought doused flared to life in Frost's gaze. "Did you expect me to challenge you over a kiss? Of all the Lords of Vice, you are the last man I would accuse of wrongdoing when it comes to my sister."

Now Frost was being outright insulting.

Some of the annoyance Dare had been feeling must have been visible on his face, because Frost chuckled.

"Why are you so certain?" Dare demanded.

"Why? Because I am aware that another lady claims your heart."

Dare's gaze narrowed at his friend's observation. Frost was pushing his luck by bringing up Allegra.

"And while none of your friends would accuse you of taking a vow of chastity over your brother's wife, we all know that cunning bitch owns you heart and soul."

Dare wanted to lunge at Frost and pound his denial into his friend's smug face. Allegra belonged to his older brother. The lady had made her choice, and Dare had come to terms with their marriage. It was not his fault that family obligations kept pushing them together.

Frost was wrong about Allegra's hold on him.

The fact that he wanted to kiss Regan was proof of that.

Still, it chafed Dare's pride that his friend could look into his eyes and deduce the unspoken desires that he kept buried so deep, even he had forgotten that they existed.

"Your sister is lovely, Frost, and ripe for seduction," Dare softly taunted. "Why are you so convinced that I would not take advantage of her innocence?"

"Old habits, my friend," Frost replied without any hesitation. "My sister is not fair sport. That is why you and I both know that Regan is more to blame for what I witnessed than you are."

Dare glanced away. Frost was wrong. He had wanted to kiss Regan. He had even enjoyed it. Regan had, too. If Frost and Lady Karmack had not disturbed them, Dare could not swear that he would have been satisfied with just a kiss.

Perhaps it was for the best that Regan was being sent away to school.

During her absence from London, Regan's affection for him would wane. She would go on to find some other gentleman on whom to practice her feminine wiles. Perhaps she would even marry him.

Dare gritted his teeth in frustration.

His thoughts were going to make him daft. He was already haunted by one lady who could never be his.

Dare unquestionably did not need another.

We take no pleasure in permitted joys,
But what's forbidden is more keenly sought.
                              —Ovid, *Amores*, 2.19.3

Chapter Three

"Is Lord Chillingsworth pleased that you will be able to join him in London this season?"

Regan blinked, distracted by the innocent question. All she wanted to do was rend the paper in her hand into dozens of illegible pieces and scream. Instead, she carefully folded Frost's letter and smiled demurely at her friends' expectant expressions.

"Of course." Her fingers tapped the paper lightly. "While it has only been four months since I last saw Frost, I have not had the pleasure of visiting London in almost five years."

And if Frost has his way, another five years will pass before he grants me his consent.

"Our first social season in Town!" Nina sighed.

Miss Tyne was nineteen and possessed an overly optimistic view on life. The daughter of a baron, Nina was expected to make a good match for her family. It was a laudable goal, and the young woman was amenable to her family's wishes. Regan was confident that Nina would soon have a dozen suitors vying for her affections.

Perhaps some of Nina's optimism had rubbed off on Regan while they were in school, after all.

"Well, I say it is high time Lord Chillingsworth does his duty by you, and gives you a proper season, Regan. I will have you know that Mama agrees as well."

She did not have the heart to remind Thea that her mother was the person responsible for Regan's banishment from London in the first place. Frost would have never thought to send her away to school if it had not been for Lady Karmack's meddling. He had been too busy pursuing his own amusements to be bothered with giving his sister the education and polish befitting an earl's daughter.

Lady Karmack, on the other hand, had taken one look at Regan and feared that under the care of her notorious brother, she was destined to become a famous courtesan or, worse, the wife of one of the Lords of Vice. As a distant cousin, the older woman felt it was her Christian duty to remove Regan from her brother's ghastly influence.

It still hurt that Frost had not fought harder to keep her.

In the beginning, Regan had not appreciated Lady Karmack's keen interest in her welfare. She had been disrespectful, outrageous, and oftentimes deliberately obtuse when it came to her lessons. The first year away from Frost and the men she considered her family had been the worst, and Regan had not been shy about displaying her anger toward the people who sincerely believed that they were saving her from a life of depravity. It was at Miss Swann's

Academy for Young Ladies that she gradually became friends with Thea and Nina.

Instead of looking down their noses at Regan's outlandish behavior as many of the other girls had, the two young women had been in awe. No one dared to challenge Miss Swann or speak her mind, yet Regan often did both. The trio had banded together by the end of their first year, and had been nearly inseparable. When Regan had not been sequestered at school, she often spent her summers visiting her friends. If Frost was in residence at the family's country seat, she joined him. However, their weeks together were usually strained, and, in hindsight, Regan acknowledged that she was often to blame.

In those early years of what she had come to view as her banishment, she had written her brother dozens of letters, begging him to relent and come for her. She missed her old life. She missed Nox and the Lords of Vice. She had often wondered if Dare might kiss her again if she returned to London.

Frost never gave her a chance to satisfy her curiosity.

He always denied her requests. Not one for sentimentality, the only time her brother wrote to her was to tell her that she could not return to London until Miss Swann had transformed the hoyden into a lady. His casual rejections had taken their toll on their relationship, and Regan could not quite forgive Frost for sending her away.

However, she was willing to let bygones be bygones if her brother was willing to be reasonable.

She intended to spend the entire season in London with or without his blessing.

With Lady Karmack on her side this time, Frost

was going to find it difficult to dismiss her polite request.

"Will you be remaining at our house or will you join Frost at his town house?" Thea asked.

"My brother undoubtedly will want me to reside with him," Regan brazenly lied. "However, it might be prudent to remain here until I have had a chance to speak to him."

Nina shut the book that she had been reading and placed it on her lap. "Good heavens!"

Regan tried to appear innocent. "I beg your pardon?"

Her friend rolled her eyes heavenward. "I cannot believe your audacity. Now tell us the truth, is your brother aware that you are in Town?"

Thea gasped. "But you told Mama—"

Regan gave her friends an exasperated look. "Be sensible. Our recent travels have added to the delays in my correspondence with my brother. While Frost is looking forward to seeing me"—she crossed her fingers behind her back and prayed that her words were true—"he most likely has not received my last letter."

There was no reason to tell Thea and Nina that Frost was expecting to see her in August when he returned to the family's country estate.

Her arrogant brother had not mentioned London at all.

Thea thought Regan's explanation was sound. "Should we send a messenger to his town house?"

Unconvinced, Nina glanced at Thea and then Regan. She nodded, silently agreeing to whatever plan Regan had concocted. "Or that club he frequents. Oh, what is it called?"

"Nox," Regan absently replied, rising from her chair. With Frost's letter in her hand, she gracefully strolled over to the small fireplace. "I do not believe that will be necessary, ladies. Some messages are best delivered in person."

Regan bent down and dropped Frost's letter onto the burning coal embers. The folded paper quickly caught fire, the flames greedily destroying the letter.

Her banishment was finally over.

Dare smoothed his hair back before he pulled the crimson drapery aside and entered the private theater box that Hunter had rented for the season. His late arrival would likely provoke a few comments from his friends.

Frost did not disappoint him.

With his chair positioned at an angle to accommodate his long legs, the earl grinned up at him. "Why, a good evening to you, Lord Hugh!"

Dare stepped over his friend's legs and nodded to Hunter and Saint, who had yet to take their seats. "Keep your nasty wit to yourself, Frost. I know that I am late. It could not be helped."

Frost pivoted, pulling his legs in as he faced Dare. "How kind of you to join us this evening. I must confess when I espied Lady Pashley sitting alone in her box, I feared that your honorable nature might rear its ugly head and put an irreparable blight on our promising evening."

"If true, Dare's honor might not be the only head rising this evening," Saint muttered to Hunter as he nudged the duke.

Dare acknowledged his friend's ribald comment with a low chuckle. He peered out into the sea of private boxes in search of his brother's marchioness. He spotted her one tier down. Another couple had joined Allegra, and with luck they would remain at her side for the evening.

"Unlike you, Frost, manners and duty may dictate me to stop by Lady Pashley's private box to pay my respects. Nevertheless, I have no inclination to tarry."

Frost snorted, making his disbelief apparent.

"While you may find this difficult to believe, another lady has engaged my attentions this evening." Dare was in too good a mood to be annoyed with Frost. "Mrs. Randall has invited me to call on her after Lord and Lady Quinton's ball."

Frost's eyebrows slid upward as he nodded with begrudging approval. Hunter and Saint offered their congratulations. The lovely twenty-eight-year-old widow had come out of mourning last season. She had rejected all suitors and, as far as anyone knew, all potential lovers. The young widow had even been impervious to Frost's charms.

"I assume you expect us to join you at Lord and Lady Quinton's ball?" Frost said, casting a sly glance in Lady Pashley's direction.

Dare braced his palm against the back of his friend's chair and stared directly into Frost's turquoise-blue eyes. "Mrs. Randall never mentioned me joining her at the ball. Nor would she approve of me bringing the likes of you along to her town house."

"Widows are daring creatures. She might be agreeable with the proper enticement," Frost said, bringing his gloved hand up to the apex of his trousers to make his vulgar point.

All four men laughed, earning them several curious looks from the nearby boxes. Dare sat down beside Frost. He was looking for another subject to distract his friend when Saint came to the rescue.

"Has anyone heard from Reign or Sin this evening?"

Hunter slid into the seat in front of Dare. "Sin will join us later. His wife decided to sit with her mother and sisters this evening."

A noncommittal noise rumbled in Frost's throat. He did not exactly approve of Lady Sinclair, and the lady did not hide the fact that she was merely tolerant of Frost for her husband's sake.

Hunter gave their friend a bemused glance. "Show some respect, Frost. Lady Sinclair is expected to deliver the Sinclair heir sometime in September. Sin is just protective of his lady."

"And Reign?" Dare prompted.

"Worse than Sin, now that he is a father." Saint crossed his arms across his chest and braced his stance by bending his left knee. "He left London five days ago to collect his wife and infant daughter. Reign did not want them traveling alone."

Dare could not blame Reign. He had never seen a gentleman so besotted. Last season, when Reign had encountered Lady Sophia Northam at a ball, he had fallen hard for the demure blonde. Reign had the lady wedded, bedded, and with child before the season had ended.

"Another good man . . . ," Frost mumbled, the rest of his sentence unintelligible, but his meaning was clear to his friends.

Frost enjoyed ladies as well as any other gent. He

just did not view them as anything permanent in a man's life. As far as the earl was concerned, marriage had ruined Sin and Reign.

To some degree, Dare silently agreed with Frost. His older brother's marriage to Allegra was a miserable union, and Reign's first marriage to Miss Roberts had been an unmitigated disaster. Still, both Reign and Sin seemed happy in their recent marriages. Dare did not begrudge his friends their newfound bliss.

While Saint regaled them with Vane's latest mischief, Dare idly observed the lords and ladies from private box to private box. He immediately spotted Lady Sinclair. Seated beside Lady Harper, the marchioness was engrossed in a discussion with one of her sisters. Sin was nowhere in sight.

Dare moved on to another private box, recognizing some of the patrons as he let his gaze continue to wander. It meant nothing if his attention lingered on Allegra. After all, she was a beautiful woman. If his heart ached, it was his own damn business. Before his older brother had stolen her from him, Allegra had been his.

Frost often teased him about Allegra, but his friend did not understand Dare's inner conflict. While a part of him would always love the lady, he also hated her. His familial obligations kept him tethered, and he seemed doomed to never be quite free from her.

And his brother enjoyed Dare's torment.

Before he could dwell further on his dark thoughts, a glint of amber caught Dare's eye, distracting him from Allegra's private box. One tier up and two boxes to the right, a dark-haired lady in an amber evening dress presented him her elegant profile. Captivated, he watched as the silken fabric of her dress gleamed like the sun while the candlelight from the chandeliers played across the angles of her puffed sleeves and skirt. Her dark tresses had been pulled high, and only a few curls near her hairline had escaped. The lady's pale creamy complexion was untouched by the sun, yet even in the dim interior of the theater, her skin glowed with health and vitality.

Dare watched as she extended her gloved hand to a gentleman who had slipped into their private box to pay the woman and her female companions his respects. Slightly envious that the gent had discovered the lady in amber before he had, Dare leaned forward as he watched the silent courtship play out for his eyes. The young woman smiled and gestured as she formally introduced her friends. The gentleman bowed, his eyes remaining on his amber prize.

Arrogant bastard.

The gentleman was older and possessed a weak chin. Possibly two. A lady of wealth and beauty could do better. The three gentlemen entering the crowded box must have thought the same thing.

Dare stood when the young woman brought her hand to her heart, and then practically threw herself into the arms of one of her would-be suitors. His gaze narrowed as recognition flooded his envious heart.

"What the devil—is that *Vane*?" Dare said, his voice infused with such fury that Frost, Hunter, and Saint ceased speaking and stared at him with varying degrees of amazement.

He could not blame them for their curiosity. Dare did not understand his reaction himself. A small part of him was still tempted to leap from box to box until he reached Vane so he could have the pleasure of tossing the rogue headfirst into the pit.

What spared him was that the woman in amber released Vane and stepped back. At Vane's urging, she looked across the interior of the theater. Dare inhaled sharply as his hungry gaze drank in her beauty. Familiarity tickled his senses, but it was elusive. Unexpectedly their gazes locked, and the dark-haired beauty seemed almost as startled as he was by the impact.

Recognition popped in his head like miniature fireworks.

The last time Dare had seen her endearing face, it had been sullied by soot and grime.

"Gents!" Sin said, bursting through the closed curtains at the back of their private box. He was grinning from ear to ear. "Why did no one tell me that our little Regan has come home?"

Chapter Four

The confrontation was inevitable.

From across the theater, Regan could have sworn she felt the invisible undercurrents of her brother's surprise and growing fury that she had ignored his dictates.

Then there was Dare.

Regan had not expected to encounter him on her first night in London. Nor had she thought her face would warm and her heart race at the mere sight of him. When Frost had sent her away, she had written Dare and begged him to appeal to her brother on her behalf.

His response had been swift and brief.

Behave yourself, mon cocur.

Dare had not offered her words of love or regret. Regan had burst into tears when she had read his note. She had gone on to appeal to the other members of the Lords of Vice, but they had all abandoned her.

Regan allowed Vane to lead her away from the front of the theater box where Lady Karmack, Thea, and Nina were seated to give them a small measure of privacy, which amounted to very little in a crowded theater.

"You are causing a spectacle, my dear," Vane said, his eyes twinkling with charm and merriment.

Her right brow lifted coquettishly. Her brother and his friends would ascertain soon enough that she had learned more than housekeeping and genteel arts at Miss Swann's Academy for Young Ladies.

"How so?" she said, her senses humming pleasantly under Vane's admiring regard.

"Your beauty will stir speculation. Everyone will want to be introduced to the dark-haired beauty in the amber dress." He clasped her gloved hand and brought it to his lips.

Regan tipped her head to one side. She was enjoying Vane's flirtation. "So you like the dress? Good. I hope my brother will appreciate it as well, since I told the dressmaker to send all my bills to him."

Vane squeezed her hand affectionately before he released it. "It's stunning. I almost swallowed my tongue when I realized that the lady in amber used to be my eager assistant. However, Frost's reaction to your low-cut bodice is not the spectacle you should worry about."

"Then what?"

"The gossip, of course," Vane said in a cheerful tone. "Before the *ton* deduces exactly who you are to Frost, I'll wager that what happens next will pique everyone's curiosity."

"Vane, what are you—"

The crimson curtains at the back of the box flew open with a dramatic flourish. In a nervous gesture, Regan touched the citrine necklace that adorned her neck. The swag front was composed of flower-head clusters and pear-shaped drops. It had been a gift from Frost on her nineteenth birthday.

Sin, Hunter, and Saint walked through the opening, followed by Frost and Dare. The five of them together made an impressive entrance. Her throat tightened with emotion at the sight of them. Good heavens, soon they were going to have to start tossing the chairs off the balcony to accommodate everyone.

Regan glanced at Vane. "You did warn me," she said lightly.

Sin was the first to embrace her. "Lady Regan. You clean up well, my girl." Not caring if they had an audience or not, he passed her on to Hunter.

"I hear no lady will have you," Regan teased when he kissed her hand.

"Perhaps I was waiting for you to grow up, imp," Hunter quipped, earning a snort from Frost. His Grace winked at her brother and nudged her toward Saint.

"It is good to see you again, Saint," Regan said, her eyes misting as she realized she had her family back. "I never had a chance to thank you for that lovely French soap that you sent me."

Saint pinched her chin playfully. "I was not certain you would use it."

Regan was aware that Nina and Thea were likely wide-eyed and speechless at the sheer number of handsome males that had invaded Lady Karmack's private box. Introductions were expected, and she would get to them as soon as she greeted her brother.

And Dare.

Neither gentleman had moved closer. Ignoring the butterflies in her stomach, Regan stepped away from Saint and approached her brother. He and Dare stood like watchful sentinels on either side of the closed curtains, waiting for her to come to them.

Regan was not fooled by their bland expressions. Halting in front of Frost, she curtsied. "Good evening, brother. You look well." Feeling like a brave mouse that was about to pull the hungry cat's whiskers, Regan leaned in and kissed him on the cheek.

Her brother turned his head slightly, and she felt his warm lips brush against her cheek. "Regan," Frost drawled. "What are you about?"

Regan pulled back. "Did you not receive my letter?" she asked, feigning innocence.

"Meaning you have been planning this mischief for some time" was his dry reply, his turquoise-blue eyes staring into hers as if he could peer into her soul.

Since it appeared Frost was not prepared to embarrass her in public, Regan touched her brother lightly on the arm. "Brother, pray forgive me for my atrocious manners." She raised her arm in a gracious sweeping motion to include the two ladies behind her. "I have neglected to introduce you to my dear friends, Miss Tyne and Miss Bramwell. And, of course, I would be remiss in forgetting our gracious chaperone, Lady Karmack. You do remember our cousin, do you not?"

"Regan," Frost said, the growl in his voice alerting her that he was not oblivious to her mockery. "Why do we not leave the introductions to Vane since he seems to be enjoying himself?"

Regan looked over her shoulder to discover that Vane and the other Lords of Vice were chatting amiably with Thea and Nina under Lady Karmack's quiet scrutiny. Both of her friends appeared flustered by all the attention. Later, she would explain to them that her brother's friends were the sort of gentlemen Miss Swann had told them to avoid at all costs.

Every last one of them was a scoundrel.

Including Frost.

Of course, during her absence, two quick-witted ladies had managed to leg-shackle Sin and Reign. Frost had been rather sullen about the marriages. Nevertheless, Regan was looking forward to meeting the women. She hoped they would welcome her friendship once she made it clear that she was nothing like her brother.

Regan stepped away from Frost, only to find her wrist encircled by his fingers. She raised her hand to catch the viscountess's eye. "Lady Karmack, I shall return shortly. My brother wishes to continue our tender reunion on the other side of the curtain where we might not disturb the other patrons."

"Lady Regan, I do not believe—" Lady Karmack began as a frown creased her forehead.

"Indulge me, madam," Frost said, gifting the older woman with a guileless smile. "I have not seen my dear sister in many months, and I only wish to have a private word with her. She shall be returned to your custody in a few minutes."

Lady Karmack was baffled by her brother's announcement. "Oh. Then Lady Regan will not be taking up residence in your town house this season?"

Frost shot a silently furious look in Regan's direction. Her dazzling smile was beatific, even while she gripped the blades of her closed fan so tightly, the edge was cutting into her white kid gloves. Without a word, Frost escorted her through the opening in the curtains Dare had provided for them.

Neither Frost nor Regan had invited him to join them. However, Dare had glimpsed the fire in the depths of Frost's eyes. His friend's posture was far from welcoming, and he wagered Regan was about to feel the unpleasant sting of her brother's displeasure.

Frost released his sister the second the curtain closed. "You disobeyed me."

"I did nothing of the kind." Almost eight inches shorter than her brother, Regan did not appear to appreciate her precarious situation. "I wrote you a rather lengthy letter that explained my intention to join Lady Karmack and her family in London."

"And I wrote you a letter that explicitly ordered you to remain in the country," Frost said through clenched teeth.

"Well, that would have been rather lonely since the Karmacks were traveling to town," she said, crossing her arms over the front of her amber bodice.

The angry motion of defiance lowered Dare's gaze to Regan's breasts. The sloped satin neckline displayed a generous amount of flesh. The pressure from her arms plumped her breasts further, inching the enticing globes higher until Dare was concerned that the dear lady might pop out of her scandalous dress.

Not realizing he had been holding his breath until he saw black spots in his dimming vision, Dare dragged a ragged inhale into his empty lungs. It took all his inner fortitude to tear his gaze away from the front of Regan's bodice.

Frost spared him a brief questioning glance before he returned his attention to his sister. "So the Karmacks are unaware of your plans."

"Of course not," Regan said, sounding vaguely insulted by the suggestion. "Lady Karmack prides herself in being very thorough when preparing to travel. I have everything I need to enjoy London befitting my station."

Frost all but snarled at her.

"You have neglected one thing, dear sister. My approval."

To her credit, Regan did not flinch. Darc had witnessed seasoned gents who had crumbled under Frost's intense scrutiny.

Regan sighed. "I thought I had it, Frost. After all, you have paid my bills without protest. Nor did you even question why I would need an entirely new wardrobe—"

"For *school*!" Frost shouted at her, causing her to wince.

For the first time since the trio had entered the small anteroom, Regan shifted her gaze to Dare. His stomach muscles contracted as he felt the impact of her sober blue eyes. Was she asking for his support? Dare could sympathize with Regan's plight. Nonetheless, it was not his place to interfere. Frost would not thank him if he sided with Regan.

Nor was he confident that Regan should remain in Town. Her unexpected arrival was already stirring trouble.

Regan tapped the end of her collapsed fan to her chin. "I am finished with school."

"Finished?" Frost sputtered in disbelief.

"I can produce a letter from Miss Swann extolling my accomplishments. And Lady Karmack concurs," Regan said before her brother could challenge her claim as she slowly circled him. Over Frost's shoulder, she winked at Dare. As he had thought, the outrageous minx was enjoying herself. "She thinks that if you can resist interfering, I might be able to secure a match this season."

Both Frost and Dare scowled at her announcement.

"Marriage," Frost said, curling his upper lip at the word. "I do not recall sanctioning any such notion. Lady Karmack seems to be forgetting that I am your guardian."

"Then behave like it," Regan countered. The hint of impatience in her gentle voice was the first visible sign that she was not as calm as she wanted her brother to believe. "Lady Karmack is under the impression that you sent me away to polish my rough edges so I might make a solid match. Only you and I know that you had other reasons to send me away."

Dare straightened at Regan's accusation. Was she referring to the impulsive kiss they had shared almost five years ago? Whatever game Regan was playing with Frost, mentioning the kiss was not a strategic move Dare would have recommended since from all accounts her brother seemed to have forgotten about it.

"It is unlike you to be coy, little sister," Frost taunted as he stepped in front of the closed curtains to prevent her from leaving the anteroom. "Why do you think I sent you away?"

"Since my banishment has come to an end, the reasons no longer matter, now do they?" Regan inclined head. When Frost did not step aside, she lifted her right brow in a manner that reminded Dare of Frost. "Lady Karmack and my friends are awaiting my return."

Frost moved to the right and pulled the curtain open. "You and I are not finished with this business."

"Oh, I believe we are," Regan said, matching Frost's silky tones. "Whether I reside with the Karmacks or I return to the care of my loving brother, I will remain in London. There is nothing that you can do about it, short of hiring a press gang to cart me off to the other side of the world."

Regan took a step forward and then paused. "I would not recommend the latter. Think of the fuss and scandal."

Dare and Frost watched in silence as Regan rejoined her friends. Vane lowered his head and whispered something into Regan's ear that caused her to laugh. Annoyed, Dare wondered why Vane was courting danger by flirting with Regan. The gent knew Frost's sister was off limits. Frost would happily crack the skull of any gent who touched his sister.

Including him.

As the other Lords of Vice said their farewells to Regan and her friends, Dare murmured to Frost, "I would concede defeat, my friend. With all of us looking after her, Regan will be safe from bounders and fortune hunters."

Frost shot Dare an enigmatic side glance. "Then I am indeed fortunate that you are residing with me this season. I shall sleep the unburdened sleep of an innocent man, knowing that you are on hand to look after our dear girl."

Dare scowled at the growing realization that he would be residing under the same roof with Regan. Granted, Frost was Regan's guardian, and there were certainly enough servants meandering about the town house to ensure nothing untoward occurred. Still, his presence in the Bishops' household could be viewed as improper by the more prudish members of the *ton*.

"Perhaps I should seek other accommodations."

"Come now, Dare," Frost taunted, sensing his friend's concerns. "I thought you were made of sterner stuff than that. Besides, Regan will behave herself or face the consequences."

Unable to form a proper response to Frost's remark, Dare stared sullenly through the parted curtains at Regan. Sensing his regard, she turned her head and smiled at him.

In truth, it was not Regan's conduct that worried Dare. It was his own.

Chapter Five

Seated beside Nina in Lady Karmack's coach, Regan studiously avoided meeting the viscountess's knowing gaze as the coachman drove them to Lord and Lady Quinton's ball. Instead Regan feigned interest in the activity that she glimpsed through the small window.

"Lord Chillingsworth seemed rather surprised by your presence this evening, Lady Regan."

She made a noncommittal sound in her throat and strived not to appear guilty. "It is a pity that the post is not more reliable. As I had feared, my letter has yet to reach Frost, my lady."

"A most regrettable predicament."

At eight and forty, Lady Karmack was a practical, astute woman who had raised five children, three of them daughters. Thea was the youngest of the Bramwell brood. The viscountess had little tolerance for dissembling or lies. Over the years, Regan had not been able to resist testing the older woman's patience.

"It is fortunate that Frost is very accommodating," she assured Lady Karmack with confidence. "By tomorrow afternoon, you will be able to relinquish your duties as my chaperone, and I shall be safely ensconced under my brother's roof once again."

Thea stirred as if she intended to speak. Even Lady Karmack was distracted by her daughter's subtle movements. However, one warning glance from Regan stilled her cousin's tongue. Thankfully, Nina also remained silent.

"Well, then," Lady Karmack said in her brisk, straightforward manner. "It appears that you and your brother have settled the matter during your private discourse."

"As best we could, madam," Regan said lightly.

Before the viscountess could respond to Regan's ambiguous comment, the small trapdoor near the roof of the coach slid open. The coachman announced that they were within walking distance of Lord and Lady Quinton's town house. Even so, the congestion of carriages and coaches had slowed their progress to a snail's pace.

Vane had told Regan and her friends that the Lords of Vice had plans to attend the Quintons' ball after the theater. He naturally extended an invitation for the ladies to join the merriment since Lord and Lady Quinton were unlikely to fuss over a few additional guests in what promised to be a spectacular affair. Without any prompting from Regan, Nina and Thea had begged Lady Karmack to accept Vane's gallant invitation.

With a speculative gleam in her eyes, Lady Karmack's gaze had shifted from her daughter's eager expression to the unmarried earl's handsome face. She had assured Vane that they would find their way to the Quintons' town house later in the evening.

"Perhaps we should consider disembarking and

walking the short distance," Thea suggested, her eyes shining in anticipation.

Regan silently pondered her cousin's excitement with a small amount of concern. Was it Vane or the opportunity to attend a ball that had put those stars in Thea's eyes?

Perhaps it was a tad hypocritical, but Regan refused to examine too closely her own growing eagerness for the ball. This was not about Dare. She had won the first skirmish with Frost. That alone was cause for celebration.

It was a logical explanation.

Regan might even believe it, as long as she could avoid glancing at her reflection in Lady Quinton's gilt mirrors.

Dare nodded to Saint and Hunter as the two gentlemen headed for the Quintons' card room to join Frost. Sin was planning to join them later. For now, he was standing near the open doors with his wife and her two sisters. Vane was nowhere in sight. The second his name was announced, the young earl had been whisked away by his matchmaking mother. Vane was resisting his family's efforts to pair him with a respectable young lady, but Dare wagered his friend would be the next to marry. His love and loyalty to the Courtland family were as deep as Dare's ties to his own. It was a source of strength and weakness.

Dare was intimately acquainted with the latter.

Involuntarily, Dare's gaze searched the ballroom until he found his sister-in-law, Lady Pashley. Adorned in a shimmering light green gown that reminded him of sea foam, Allegra was holding court across the room, while Sin's half sister Lady Gredell had positioned herself in the opposing corner. Dare was not surprised that Allegra had decided to attend Lord and Lady Quinton's ball. He had ignored her at the theater this evening, and his dear sister-in-law did not like to be dismissed so easily.

If she had her way, Allegra would ruin his evening.

Perhaps he should tell the witch the reason for his distraction. Dare smiled faintly at the thought. The truth would likely ruin *her* evening.

"Lord Hugh."

Dare dismissed his sister-in-law from his mind as he bowed to the beautiful dark-haired woman in front of him. "Mrs. Randall. You honor me," he said, releasing her extended hand.

The twenty-eight-year-old widow's beauty over-shadowed many of her younger rivals. Intelligent blue eyes met his as he admired the symmetry of her heart-shaped face. Her unblemished skin gleamed against her lavender ball gown. The wealth of black hair the lady possessed was braided and neatly coiled at the nape of her neck. She was a prize that most of the males of the *ton* had deemed unattainable.

Some accused her of being cold.

Others thought she was aspiring for a titled husband.

Dare wondered if the widow was still in mourning. After three years, loneliness rather than lust might have pushed Mrs. Randall to spend the season in London.

He had never been introduced to her husband. A lieutenant in the Royal Navy, the man had spent most of his marriage at sea. Although Mrs. Randall never spoke of her loss, Dare had made some inquiries and learned that the brig sloop the man was serving on had wrecked on the point of Mount Batten at the entrance of Catwater. Most of the crew had perished.

"Did you think I was merely teasing you, my lord?" she said, her blue eyes twinkling with undisguised amusement.

"Dare," he gently corrected, still not quite believing his good fortune. "You had mentioned that you might attend the Quintons' ball, and hoped that I would make an appearance. To assume anything else would have been presumptuous."

Mrs. Randall brought her gloved finger to her mouth, drawing attention to her full lips. "Such wonderful manners! Is it presumptuous of me to confess that I enjoyed our last discussion? So much so that I hope we may continue it?"

Flattered, Dare nodded. "Of course. Would you prefer to remain here or perhaps retire to the drawing room?"

Mrs. Randall glanced about the ballroom with disdain. "I have spent many years away from Town, and find it too noisy and distracting. In truth, I was contemplating a much quieter setting, that is, if you are agreeable to leaving Lord and Lady Quinton's ball so soon."

So he had not misunderstood the lady's previous invitation, after all.

The lovely widow was asking him to escort her home.

Dare discreetly glanced at Allegra, only to discover that she was openly watching him. Good. She was probably wondering if he intended to bed the lovely widow. With Mrs. Randall's permission, Dare planned to spend the rest of the night exploring that delectable body of hers.

Taking Mrs. Randall's hand, Dare bowed and allowed his lips to lightly brush the top of her hand. "I am agreeable to your"—a flash of amber caught his eye—"Damn!" He straightened and released her hand. So Regan and her friends had not gone straight home after their evening at the theater.

"Is something amiss?" she inquired, frowning in unspoken disapproval at his crudity.

An apology was on the tip of his tongue, but he swallowed it. He had no time to soothe Mrs. Randall's delicate feelings. Dare had bigger problems.

Regan.

He had been too distracted by Allegra and Mrs. Randall to observe her arrival. Unfortunately, her entrance had not gone unnoticed by other gentlemen. Radcliffe, Bolton, and that bounder Fothergill were hovering around her. Frost was going to be issuing challenges if Dare did not interfere.

"Lord Hugh—Dare?"

He could see the unspoken question in Mrs. Randall's eyes.

"My apologies, Mrs. Randall," he said, his concern for Regan washing away the regret he should have been feeling. If his friends learned he was letting a willing widow slip away for Frost's younger sister, he would never hear the end of it. "I must decline your generous invitation. A disaster is imminent, and I am obliged to handle it."

At first, the widow seemed to think that Dare was

jesting. She laughed, but his grim expression swayed her more than his words. "Good heavens. Is there anything that I can do to assist you?"

"Your understanding is enough," Dare said, his voice curt and dismissive. He had to stifle a growl when Radcliffe touched Regan on the elbow to get her attention. "Pray excuse me."

Dare abandoned the beautiful widow without a backward glance.

Regan smiled benignly at Lord Radcliffe. "I confess I know very little of entomology," she said apologetically. Miss Swann had been more concerned with getting rid of insects from one's bed and larder than collecting them. "Do you favor certain specimens above others?"

The twenty-five-year-old earl's brown eyes warmed at her interest. "Indeed. My current studies have led me to concentrate on butterflies."

"Butterflies?" Regan said, privately thinking that there were worse obsessions when it came to collecting insects. "How do you collect them?"

"Do not encourage him, Lady Regan," Lord Fothergill interjected before Lord Radcliffe could reply. "Radcliffe can pontificate for hours on his little hobby."

Annoyed, the young nobleman puffed up his chest as he tugged on his frock coat. "Just because you cannot speak comprehensively on a topic that does not include horses or—"

"French brandy," Lord Bolton cheerfully supplied.

"—or French brandy," Lord Radcliffe echoed, "it does not imply that others possess your limited intelligence, Fothergill." He subtly adjusted his stance, offering the viscount his back. "Now, you were asking about how I go about collecting my specimens."

Regan glanced from Lord Fothergill to Lord Radcliffe, curious if the two gentlemen were about to engage in fisticuffs. It had been ages since she had observed a good fight. "I suppose some sort of netting is used."

"Not always." Lord Radcliffe shrugged off the other man's decisive tap on the shoulder. "I have had remarkable success by making use of a white sheet."

Intrigued, Regan said, "Go on."

"The sheet reflects the sunlight, and naturally a lure must be present to attract the elusive butterfly."

"That is enough, Radcliffe." Lord Bolton glanced at Regan and said, "Such frank discourse is not for the ears of such an enchanting creature."

Regan frowned, feeling both flattered and insulted by the gentleman's protectiveness. She was not so delicate that she would faint at a few earthy words. "Well, I—"

You know Miss Swann was quite clear on the subject of indelicate language, Regan.

She meekly swallowed her protest and smiled at Lord Bolton. "I yield to your good judgment, my lord." Regan even managed to flutter her eyelashes at the gentleman in a beguiling manner. If Nina and Thea had been observing her, they would have burst into a collective fit of giggles at her audacity.

Lord Bolton, on the other hand, interpreted her gesture as an invitation to move closer.

Lord Radcliffe cleared his throat to get her attention. "Ignore Bolton. There is nothing improper about a healthy curiosity regarding science, my lady. Certain butterflies require unique lures, and I have explored several methods. In fact, I hope to write a scientific paper on my experiences with the Purple Emperor."

"Fascinating," Regan murmured.

"Yes, Radcliffe, tell her about the lures," Lord Fothergill said as he silently dared Lord Bolton's protest. "Tell her about the rotten fruit."

Regan's enthusiasm to pursue the conversation waned. "You pelt the poor butterflies with overripe fruit?" It did not sound very sporting.

Lord Radcliffe throat warbled with an uncharacteristically high-pitched chortle. "Goodness, no. I use the fruit as bait. I have also used fish, mirrors, and—"

"His own urine," Lord Fothergill gleefully added before he delivered his verbal blow. "Been pissing on his sheets for years!"

Regan gasped, and quickly slapped her hand over her mouth to smother her laughter. She turned away. There was little she could do to conceal her watering eyes.

Lord Radcliffe's entire face reddened. "Why, you uncouth scoundrel!" he shouted before he launched himself at Lord Fothergill.

It appeared that she was going to see a fight, after all!

A masculine hand seized her by the elbow and tugged her away from the men.

Annoyed by her companion's high-handed manner, she whirled about and said, "See here, Lord Bolt—Dare!"

He did not look pleased. In fact, Dare seemed

positively annoyed at her. "You are too old to be up to such mischief, Regan," he said grimly before he dragged her away from her three companions and out of the ballroom.

Chapter Six

With an uncompromising grip on her upper arm, Dare tugged the protesting Regan through the crowded ballroom and out into the wide hall.

"Unhand me, you brute!" Regan demanded as she glanced behind her.

His jaw tightened at the notion that Regan was seeking assistance from someone to save her from him. "Are you hoping one of your admirers will play the gallant and rescue you from my clutches?" Dare nodded to an elderly gentleman who had stepped aside so they could pass.

"Of course not!" she said crossly, breathless from the brisk pace he had set.

Her vehement denial mollified him. Still, he could not resist adding, "Good. That trio would happily abandon you in order to save their own hides."

Regan did not seem overly concerned by the news. "I was looking for my friends. I was making my way to them, before Lord Fothergill and his friends waylaid me. By the by, where are you taking me? Is this about Frost?"

Dare slowed at her reasonable questions. Where

the devil did could they go when the house was practically filled to the rafters with guests? His gaze narrowed on a small door he could see over his shoulder. Changing directions, he strode purposely toward it with Regan in tow.

"Dare!"

He detected more exasperation than fear in her voice. It was not exactly what he was striving for, but he was not above using a little intimidation to get her to pay attention. Dare opened the door and dragged her inside.

"Where are we—" She glared at his back as he shut the door. "The servant stairs? Do you not think it is a rather odd place for a family meeting?"

He turned to face her. "Still worried about Frost?" he taunted, crossing his arms as he surveyed her from head to toe. "Don't be. You have more pressing concerns."

"Such as?"

Dare brought his thumb to his chest. "Me."

"You? Pooh! I am not afraid of you," she said airily.

Or anyone else, he thought, though he kept his admiration of her defiance from showing on his face.

"You have nothing to fear as long as you behave," he said gruffly, fighting to ignore the invisible tendrils of attraction that he always felt whenever she entered a room. By God, Regan had grown into a beautiful young woman. When he and his friends had returned to their private box at the theater, his attention kept sliding back to Regan. "I would have thought your years at Miss Swann's Academy for Young Ladies would have quelled your penchant for mischief."

"Do not concern yourself with my affairs. I already have a brother. I do not need another."

Dare's eyes flashed dangerously at the word *affairs*.

"It is no trouble at all," he said silkily, moving forward until her back collided with the banister. It confirmed that she was just as aware of the energy crackling between them as he was. "Since I will be residing with you and Frost this season."

Her eyebrows lifted at his announcement. "You are staying with us," she said in a neutral tone.

Dare shrugged. He was not inclined to explain that his brother and sister-in-law had taken over the family's town house this season without any warning. While he could deal with Charles, Dare had no interest in living under the same roof with Allegra. "It is not the first time." Of course, at the time Regan had been a child and he had only seen her as Frost's little sister.

Suspicion tightened Regan's delicate features. "Frost ordered you to watch over me."

She was displeased with the notion.

Good.

Dare was not exactly thrilled with the situation, either. If he had not caught Regan flirting with Fothergill, Bolton, and Radcliffe, Dare would have spent an energetic and delightful evening in Mrs. Randall's bed.

"Frost knows what you are capable of."

Regan rolled her eyes. "Good grief, this is about the fire at Nox, is it not? What happened transpired five years ago and it was an *accident*!" Since Dare had neatly boxed her in physically, she avoided his gaze. "I have been adequately punished for my crimes!"

Intrigued, he tilted his head. "Punished how exactly?"

She exhaled noisily. "Never mind," Regan muttered under her breath. "Now that you have revealed your duties and expressed your lack of enthusiasm for the unpleasant task, may I return to the ballroom? Thea and Nina will be looking for me."

"So you think Frost sent you away because of the fire?"

Of course she didn't. Frost had ordered the servants to pack Regan's belongings the same day he had caught her in a compromising position with Dare. Now that she was facing Dare, though, she could not summon the courage to mention the kiss.

"Maybe Frost did not like the notion of me kissing his younger sister?"

Apparently Dare had no such qualms.

Regan blinked at him, feeling unexpectedly skittish. "I have no desire to speak of the past." She started to slide by him.

Dare reached out and gripped the banister on each side of her so that she could not escape. "You do recall our kiss, *mon coeur*?"

Regan brushed at her sleeve. "Vaguely."

Grinning, Dare could not resist tugging on the curl next to her left ear. "I recall that you were lousy at it."

Her chin snapped up. "I had never been kissed, you cretin!"

"Brute . . . cretin . . . Careful, my lady, your polish is beginning to tarnish," he teased.

"Arse!" Regan hissed as she shoved away his

right arm and walked around him to reach the door. "I cannot fathom why I thought I had missed you."

Her angry admission was a mild blow to Dare's heart. His teasing had hurt her tender feelings, and he felt like a bounder for it. "Regan. Come back here."

"No, thank you," she said, pulling furiously at the latch. With a snarl of disgust, she released the brass latch and whirled around. "I will have you know that your kiss was not what I expected from a Lord of Vice."

"Oh, really?" He stalked toward her, but she was vexed at him enough to meet him halfway. They circled each other like two pugilists. "What did you expect from a Lord of Vice?"

Palms up, Regan opened her arms in a manner that would have made her vulnerable if he were her opponent. "Fireworks!" she spat. "The kind that burn so hot and bright it blinds you. Even at fifteen, I could recognize the difference between a spark and an out-of-control conflagration."

Oh, Dare was tempted to put his hands on her. He wanted to throttle the minx for retaliating for his thoughtless taunt about her inexperience. However, he possessed more control than that.

Until she said, "Since your dismal showing, I have been kissed by dozens of connoisseurs." Her smile was smug.

Dozens. Dare's nostrils flared and his vision dimmed at the notion of Regan practicing the art of kissing on broad-shouldered farmers and country squires. What sort of school was Miss Swann running?

"Dare!"

He had not even been aware that he had seized

her by the shoulders and pulled her against his chest. "Five years is a long time between kisses. Perhaps we should renew our friendship."

"N-n-mmph!" was her wordless reply as Dare covered her mouth with his.

The kiss was hard, demanding, and regrettably brief, he mused as he released her mouth with an audible *smack*. With the taste of her on his lips, Dare belatedly noted that Regan was poised on her tiptoes; all that anchored her was her fists, which were clutching the front of his black frock coat. He caught her by the elbows when she wobbled and steadied her until she could stand on her own.

"Well . . . ," she said, a bemused expression on her face. "I will consider our friendship properly renewed." The softness in her demeanor faded as she found her balance. "Now if you will excuse me. I have tarried long enough."

Tucking his hands behind his back, he permitted her to pass. He did not quite trust himself because he had an irrational urge to reach out and give her a thorough kissing. "Worried that your reputation will suffer if you dally with an improper gent?"

This time the door opened effortlessly. Regan glanced back over her shoulder. "What reputation? With you, Frost, and the others, I have been more or less dallying with improper gents all my life," she said with a rueful smile.

She departed with Dare's laughter echoing in the stairwell.

Dare gave his back to the door and braced his hands on the banister. By God, it was good to have Regan back. Although he had long denied it, he had missed her presence in his life. She had been one of the few people who could make him laugh until it hurt.

She could always slip past the emotional barriers he had erected to protect himself.

It was one of the reasons he should keep his distance from her.

Regan had been dangerous as a fifteen-year-old girl. As a grown woman, she was devastating to his peace of mind.

And how are you planning to keep your distance when you are living under the same roof, my friend? a voice whispered in his mind.

A soft thud drew his attention to the stairwell that was cast in shadows. "Is there anyone there?" he called out, suspecting that one of the Quintons' servants had been eavesdropping on his conversation with Regan.

If anyone was there, he or she was too frightened to reply.

After a few minutes, Dare left the stairwell.

Several hours later, Regan heard a soft knock at the door. Reaching for her shawl, she climbed out of bed and wrapped the garment around her as she headed for the door. She was not surprised to see Nina and Thea on the other side.

"I thought you were asleep," she said to them both.

Thea was the first to enter the bedchamber. "How could we sleep without hearing all the details,"

Nina moved to the bed and sat down. "We were dying to ask, but considering how you had departed the ballroom with Lord Hugh, we dared not ask in front of Lady Karmack."

"Did Lord Hugh escort you to your brother?"

"When Lord Chillingsworth approached you at the theater, he did not seem pleased at all."

"Do not worry about Frost," Regan said, waving away her friends' concerns.

Nina frowned. "Then what of Lord Hugh?"

"Dare?" Regan rubbed her lower lip with her thumb and smiled as she thought of his bruising kiss. "He did not approve of my admirers."

With eyes as wide as an owl, Thea asked in hushed tones, "Where did he take you?"

"The servants' stairs."

"Why on earth would he want to take you—" Thea's mouth fell open. "Good grief, he kissed you!"

Regan clapped her hands together, amused by her friends' identical expressions. "Oh, your faces are priceless! Is it truly so astounding, given that the last time Dare kissed me, Frost banished me to Miss Swann's Academy for Young Ladies for five years?"

"What are you going to do if your brother finds out?" Nina asked, fiddling with one of the tiny ribbons on her nightgown.

"Frost is not going to find out," Regan said, her stern gaze meeting her friends' concerned faces. "You both have to swear not to tell another living soul, and that includes your dear mother, Thea. No one witnessed the kiss. And I highly doubt Dare is in a position to brag about it."

"Oh, we swear not to tell," both ladies vowed in unison.

"After five years of separation, the kiss must have been dreadfully romantic," Nina sighed.

Regan scowled as she thought about Dare's kiss. "Not exactly."

"What do you mean, 'not exactly'?" Thea pressed.

Her arms parted in a gesture to convey her confusion. "He was rather angry with me for kissing dozens of admirers."

Both Nina and Thea seemed baffled by her admission.

Nina was the first to recover. "Miss Swann runs her school like a nunnery. When were you kissed by dozens of admirers?"

"More to the point, where were we?" Thea teased.

Laughing, Regan sat on her bed with a playful bounce. "There were no admirers, silly," she said to Nina. "I was merely taking revenge on Dare's insulting comment that I was a lousy at kissing."

Her friends gasped.

Regan nonchalantly brushed a stray strand of hair from her cheek. "Do not fret. The next time Dare kisses me, it will not be in anger," she assured Thea and Nina.

With Dare residing with her and Frost, Regan predicted that she would have many opportunities to provoke him into kissing her again.

Chapter Seven

"For a gent who spent the night pleasuring the beautiful Mrs. Randall, none of us expected to see you until evening."

Dare winced, forgetting that Vane had disappeared from the Quintons' ball after his friend had been introduced to several ladies who were the product of his mother's latest matchmaking efforts. According to Sin, Vane had been polite, but refused to dance with any of the ladies.

Needless to say, his mother was displeased. However, no amount of tears could sway her son. Before he had made good on his escape, Vane had whispered into Sin's ear, "Bluestockings! Egad, my mother is now presenting them to me in pairs." No one had seen him again until he had wandered into Nox.

Dare closed the ledger he had been studying and calmly entwined his fingers together. "Mrs. Randall was obliged to find her way home without my assistance."

"What?" Vane gaped at Dare. "The widow had picked you out of all of us to be her lover, you lucky ungrateful bastard. How could you be so cruel to her?"

Had he not chastised himself for the same thing? Still, it chafed his pride to be scolded by his irresponsible friend. "While you were fleeing your inevitable fate, I was keeping Fothergill and his friends from chasing after Regan."

Vane sneered. "Fothergill? What the devil was he doing at the Quintons' ball? I thought he and Lord Quinton had once come to blows over a mistress."

"It went as far as a dawn appointment at Battersea Fields," Dare said, trying to recall the details of the event, which had taken place three years earlier. "I believe Quinton fired into the air, while Fothergill used his turn to aim his pistol at his opponent's head. Quinton lost a piece of his left ear that morning."

Vane leaned against the large mahogany desk. "I heard that Quinton conveyed his apologies while the surgeon was attending him. If I had been him, I would have called for my sword." The earl picked up the silver letter opener and tested the sharp edge. He flipped it in the air and caught it by its handle.

Dare smiled. Fothergill had never challenged the Lords of Vice. He preferred to improve his odds by challenging weaker opponents. "If anyone issued Fothergill an invitation to the ball, it was most likely Lady Quinton. Rumor has it that she has not forgiven her husband for the mistress or the duel."

"Another reason why I do not want a wife," Vane said, snatching the rotating letter opener out of the air. "They are vengeful, humorless creatures."

Dare slid the chair back from the desk and stretched

his long legs. "Sin and Reign have fared well in their marriages."

Vane jabbed the point of the letter opener in Dare's direction. "Our friends are too besotted with their wives to stray far from their skirts. Besides, if either one of them seriously considered dallying with a mistress, I wager Juliana would shoot Sin between the eyes, and Sophia would crack Reign's skull open with her walking stick."

Dare grunted his agreement. Both ladies were wholly capable of managing their households and their husbands. "And what of your lady?"

"I do not plan on being leg-shackled," Vane said with resounding confidence. "Why settle for one woman when I can have them all?"

"Your mother seems to have other plans for you, my friend," Dare said, sympathetic to Vane's plight.

Vane set down the letter opener and moved away from the desk. "Eventually, she will grow weary of the hunt"—he shrugged and offered a careless smile—"or run out of marriageable ladies."

Dare and Vane laughed at the outrageous thought. London seemed to have an inexhaustible stable of young, unmarried ladies.

"So was Frost properly appreciative that you had sacrificed your evening with the widow to rescue Regan from Fothergill's clutches?"

"Bolton and Radcliffe, too," Dare said, recalling that Regan had not glanced in his direction for the rest of the evening.

Fortunately, she had possessed enough intelligence to remain close to her friends until they took their leave with Lady Karmack.

"I decided not to mention the incident to Frost."

Vane snorted. "Frost does not need your protection against Fothergill."

"I did it for Regan," Dare said mildly. "Frost is already looking for a reason to stuff her in the first stagecoach out of London. It is not her fault that Fothergill will pursue anything wearing a petticoat."

"How very chivalrous of you, Lord Hugh," Vane mocked. "Tell me, does Regan know that you are quietly protecting her from Frost and unscrupulous admirers?"

"No." It did sound damn noble of him, he thought, the notion ruining his good mood. "If you want to keep your teeth in your head, you will not tell a soul."

"But I have not told you my price."

Dare lunged out of the chair, his fingers missing Vane's coat sleeve by mere inches. *Almost.* The earl feinted to the right and stumbled out the door of the study with Dare on his heels. When he caught up to the grinning fool, Dare would ensure that his friend was more amenable to keeping his mouth shut.

If not for Regan's sake, then for his own.

"Nothing has really changed," Regan murmured as she casually surveyed the drawing room of her family's town house, taking in the veneered walnut wainscot, the marble chimneypiece, and the tapestry of Apollo and the muses that covered the far wall. She walked over the tapestry to admire the scene. When she was a child, Frost had told her that the artisan had used their father's image to represent Apollo. She had believed the lie for years, and used to slip into the drawing room so she could share secrets with her father.

"What did you expect?" Frost said, causing her to turn away from the old tapestry. He had settled in one of the chairs, his turquoise-blue eyes watching her intently.

Regan offered him a faint smile. "I cannot explain it. Perhaps I thought you could get rid of our family history as casually as you did your only sister."

"Regan," Frost drawled in warning. Fascinated, she noticed that his bare hands were gripping the ornate carved wood of the armrests until the veins on the top of his hands were visible. "What else did they teach at that school of yours besides sharpening your tongue?"

"You are responsible for my sharp tongue, brother," Regan countered, amused that she had managed to ruffle his composure so easily. "I fear Miss Swann's lessons were rather mundane in comparison with my education at Nox. Not a single fireworks rocket, sword, or brace of pistols on the property."

Frost's eyes narrowed at her sarcastic inflection, but he refrained from commenting on it. "Did you enjoy yourself last evening?"

"Very much so," Regan said, trailing her finger down the edge of the mantel. She paused to examine the five-inch figure of a white parakeet with a pale yellow beak and bright blue tail. "It was good to see everyone. While we were at Lord and Lady Quinton's, Sin introduced me to his wife, and to the lady's sisters."

"And what was your opinion of Lady Sinclair?"

Regan forgot about the parakeet and walked over to her brother. "I found her delightful. I think she and Sin are a good match."

"Hmm."

"You believe otherwise?" Regan sat down on the settee and smoothed the lines of her skirt. When her brother said nothing more, she brought her fingers to her lips to hide her smile. "Oh, my!"

"What?"

Regan leaned forward, unimpressed with his growled response. "Well, it is apparent to everyone that Sin is smitten with his wife, and you, being one of Sin's closest friends, would naturally want him to be happy. So . . ."

"Quit equivocating, little sister. I have taught you to behave better than that," Frost snapped.

Regan sobered at once, and then spoiled it by bursting into a fit of giggles. "Well, yes, and I must tell you that my forthright manner was quite a bane for Miss Swann." She held up her hand to silence Frost. "It was a matter of simple deduction, really. Lady Sinclair does not approve of you."

Her brother did not even blink. "Define *approve*."

She gave him an exasperated look. "Come now, brother. I have watched you charm legions of females from mere infants to elderly spinsters. What did you do to gain Lady Sinclair's disapproval? Did you steal a kiss from her?"

A tiny muscle under Frost's right eye twitched. With a snarl rumbling in his throat, he pushed out of the chair and began to prowl the room. "I have had quite enough from you, Regan Alice Bishop! Why are you so fascinated by Sin's wife?"

"I am not. I was merely curious about why *you* do not like her," she said, arching her right eyebrow.

Frost stalked toward her. "I am content with Sin's choice of wife. We will leave it at that."

"Very well, brother."

Frost raised his hands in a gesture of surrender and slumped onto the settee next to her. "I am surprised you have not inquired about Dare."

Regan expected a little more subtlety from her brother, but she let the subject of Lady Sinclair drop. "Do you refer to his whereabouts or the fact that he is residing with us this season?"

"So he told you?"

Regan nodded. "He happened to mention it when I encountered him at the Quintons'."

"Oh, I was not aware that you had spoken to Dare at the ball."

She pointedly ignored the question in her brother's tone. "The only thing he was not clear on was the why of it. Has something happened to his family's town house? Was there a fire?"

Frost stifled a yawn with his hand. "Charles and Allegra arrived in town a fortnight past. Dare ordered his possessions packed the same day."

"Good heavens. So Dare and his older brother are still fighting after all these years," Regan murmured.

The animosity between Dare and Charles was scarcely a secret, although few knew the whole story. Regan had overheard bits and pieces of the tale when she was a child. Eleven years ago, Dare, then six and ten, had fallen in love with the Earl of Dyton's daughter, Lady Allegra. Initially the lady had favored Dare with her love, until Charles started to court her. Dare was the son of a duke, but he was the second son. When Dare learned that Lady Allegra had chosen Charles over him, the two brothers had come to blows. With the Duke of Rhode's blessing,

Charles and Allegra were married. The same year, Allegra gave birth to a daughter. According to Frost, the marriage between Charles and Allegra was an unhappy one. In the eleven years that had passed, Allegra had failed to produce an heir for her husband.

Before Regan had been banished from London, she had often heard Vane, Sin, and the others taunting Dare about his dedication to the lady who had chosen the heir over the second son. Some thought he was still in love with Allegra. When Regan was a child, the observation seemed dreadfully romantic.

As a grown woman, she wanted to throttle Lady Pashley for breaking Dare's heart. The marchioness had ruined the man for all other women. Regan started when Frost touched her on the arm. "I beg your pardon. Forgive me, I was not paying attention."

"Did you not sleep well, my dear?" Frost said, his expression softening with sympathy. "I said that Dare's parents, the Duke and Duchess of Rhode, are also in residence, but their presence has done little to alleviate the growing hostility between Charles and Allegra, or quell the marquess's drunken tirades. Allegra has been sending messengers to the town house daily, demanding Dare's assistance."

Regan brought her hand up to her throat and stroked the unexpected tightness. "Has Dare been responding to Lady Pashley's notes?"

Pride flashed across her brother's handsome face. "Dare has ordered them all to be tossed into the fire. Nevertheless, the gent will eventually surrender to Allegra's demands." Frost scowled and glanced at his hands. "The bitch has her tender hooks in Dare, and he cannot seem to break free. I had such high hopes when Dare began to show some interest in the widow."

"The widow," Regan said, her voice cracking. Dare was courting a widow?

"Mrs. Randall." Oblivious to his sister's quiet distress, Frost absently patted her hand and stood. "The lady has set her sights on Dare, and I wager he will stumble into her bed before the season has ended. Even if I have to give him a hard shove."

Very little had changed, indeed. "Maybe Dare prefers not to be shoved into the lady's bed, brother."

Frost gaped at her before he hooted with laughter. "You have grown into such a little prude, sweet sister. The beautiful widow is not fettered with concerns about her reputation. Dare would be a fool to refuse her."

Chapter Eight

Once Regan had arrived, Dare had not lingered at the Bishops' town house. He had thought Frost and his sister deserved some time alone to get reacquainted. There was also the small matter of the kiss he and Regan had shared at the Quintons' ball. Although it had been pleasant, Dare had no intention of encouraging Regan.

Even though he could not stop dwelling on the kiss.

Now Dare glanced across the table at Regan. Her eyes on her plate, she was silently buttering a thick slice of toast. Fifteen minutes earlier, she had joined him and Frost in the morning room and greeted them both with a polite smile. As Regan had walked by Dare, he had found himself tensing. However, she had paused only long enough to give her brother a swift kiss on the cheek before she moved on to the empty chair the footman had pulled out for her.

She seemed too preoccupied with her toast and hot chocolate to look up from her plate.

Despite the silence, Regan seemed to have forgiven Frost for his high-handedness five years ago

when he had sent her away. Dare was happy for
them both. On the surface, Frost did not seem to
love anyone but himself. Still, Dare had caught his
friend staring at his sister. Frost had felt the absence
in his life while Regan was away at school. Both
brother and sister had suffered, though neither one
would have appreciated the observation.

Dare sipped his coffee and thought about his
brother, Charles. He could not think of a single moment when affection played a part in their relationship. For reasons Dare could not fathom, Charles
had always loathed him. Even when they were boys,
they had fought as if they were bitter rivals. It was
only after he had lost Allegra to Charles that Dare
had ceased to care.

"Another summons from Lady Pashley arrived
this morning," Frost said, not glancing up from his
newspaper.

Regan looked askance from Frost to Dare, but said
nothing.

Dare carefully put down his cup before he gave
in to temptation and threw it against the closest
wall. "Did you read it?"

"Naturally," Frost said, unapologetic for his actions. "And then I ordered Landers to burn it as you
had instructed."

For several minutes, nothing could be heard but
Regan's quiet chewing and the occasional clink of
china.

Giving in to his curiosity, Dare said, "And?"

Frost took his time answering the simple question as he folded his paper and placed it on the table. "It appears Charles ran into a little trouble last

evening, and your mother has taken to her bed. Allegra has asked for your assistance."

Dare nodded, unsurprised. Over the years, he had received similar summons. His brother and trouble were entwined. While his father made excuses, his mother took to her bed. Everyone in his family seemed to leave Allegra to him, which he might have found amusing if the lady in question had not betrayed him.

"When you answer your family's imperial summons, you should take Regan with you."

Both Dare and Regan stared at Frost as if he had sprouted horns on his forehead.

Dare was the first to recover. "I am certain Regan has other plans," he said quickly.

Regan glanced down into her cup of hot chocolate as if she could divine answers from its rich depths.

Frost did not seem to be aware of the tension in the morning room. "Regan has always liked a challenge. Besides, it sounds like you may need her help. She might be just the person to coax your mother out of bed, and discourage Allegra from luring you into hers."

Regan struck her silver spoon against the side of her cup of hot chocolate with such force, it bounced off the table and hit the floor with a clatter. "Very clumsy of me," she mumbled, then disappeared behind the table linen.

"Allow me, milady," one of the young footmen said as he rushed to retrieve her spoon.

"My apologies." Regan's face was red from her brief excursion under the table. She cleared her throat. "Ah, what were you saying, Frost?"

"You are escorting Dare to his parents' town

house." The decision made, Frost pushed back from the table and stood. "Make sure Allegra does not try to keep him," he said, winking at his speechless sister.

With the assistance of the maid Frost had procured for her, it had taken Regan thirty minutes to dress and join Dare downstairs. His mischief done, Frost had disappeared to pursue his own interests. What heartened Regan was Dare's reaction as she descended the stairs. She had donned her favorite olive-green zephyrine pelisse with gold rosettes adorning her hips. Her full skirt was made of a lighter hue, and the bottom was a charming blend of zephyrine and satin panels. The bonnet had been created in the capuchin style. It was covered in gold and white gros de Naples, with white rosebuds and greenery tastefully displayed on the low brim. Dare had stared at her, his keen gaze hungrily noting every aspect of her dress, including her gold kid boots. Regan felt her heart pound in response.

What would you do if I brazenly kissed you, my lord?

"I feel as if I should apologize for your brother's behavior," Dare said moments after they had settled in his coach.

His words dispelled the warmth she had been feeling since his ardent perusal.

"Why should you apologize when Frost is rarely repentant for his deeds?" Regan resisted the urge to sigh. "Besides, my brother is correct. You are a dear friend of our family, and if my presence will help to calm your mother and ease the awkwardness between you and Lady Pashley, it would be unkind of me to refuse."

Dare pinched his brow as if in pain. "Unkind? Regan, you are not intimate with the word. Frost has his flaws, but he has sheltered you from most of the cruelty of the world."

Regan did not bother to respond. Lady Karmack had often complained that Regan had been raised in a wild, careless manner that risked both her physical and mental well-being. With Frost as her guardian, she had been exposed to cursing gents, half-naked wenches, and more mischievous pranks than most ladies see in several lifetimes. Oh, Frost had done his best to shield her from much of the debauchery, but she had been too curious for her own good. Nevertheless, Dare was correct when he said that she had been sheltered from cruelty and the unsavory aspects of life. She had always felt safe with the Lords of Vice.

"You have not asked about Lady Pashley."

Regan tilted her head so she could study Dare's austere profile. "She is family. You do not have to speak of it."

Bitter laughter filled the compartment of the coach. "So you are aware of the history between me and Allegra. Who told you? Frost?"

Regan glanced away, deciding that she preferred the activity on the street to Dare's hot, challenging stare. "I was a curious nine-year-old when you and your brother fought over Lady Allegra. Your friends were concerned and spoke freely of the incident."

"Hmm."

Belatedly Regan realized that Dare was likely shamed that she knew pieces of his unpleasant history with Lady Pashley. "Although I had only gleaned bits and pieces of story, I was angry on your behalf. I wanted to pick up Frost's sword and skewer your brother for stealing Lady Allegra from you."

Dare gave her an incredulous look before he tossed his head back and laughed. The bitterness she had detected earlier had vanished as his humor resurfaced. "You have always been a spitfire," he said, shaking his head in amazement. "And what plans did you have for Allegra?"

The nine-year-old Regan had wanted to cut off her long blond tresses and roll her in hot tar. Miss Swann would definitely not approve. Ashamed of the bloodthirsty thoughts of her younger self, she said, "I was planning to rescue her from your brother. Then Lady Allegra could marry you."

She started when Dare unexpectedly took her face with both hands. His right thumb traced her lower lip. "Who knew you possessed such a romantic heart?" He lowered his head and kissed her lightly on the mouth. There was nothing sensual about the kiss. It was almost reverent. Butterfly wings would have exerted more pressure, she thought, as he released her and stretched his legs.

"Do you know why my family calls me Dare?"

Uncertain of his mood, Regan warily shook her head.

Dare removed his hat and combed his hair with his fingers. "The rivalry between Charles and I began almost from my birth. When I was a boy, there was rarely a week when I wasn't sporting a blackened eye or a scrape on my chin. My father encouraged competitiveness. The future Duke of Rhode needed to be battle-ready for his duties, and ruthlessly beat any weakness he glimpsed in his sons. Charles shared our sire's enthusiasm for violence, and often invented reasons to raise his fists against me."

"How dreadful!" she gasped. No matter how much she had aggravated her brother, he had never struck her with his fists.

Dare grinned at what he viewed as a very feminine reaction from her. "I lost most of those early battles with my brother. I was clearly the weaker opponent. Nevertheless, my father continued to encourage my brother because he sensed something that I could not."

"Which was?"

His blue-gray gaze hardened. "That I was getting stronger. Those beatings from Charles were honing my fighting skills and toughening my body. It was during my eleventh year that I knocked my brother to the ground, stepped on his forearm, and broke it."

If Dare was expecting Regan to be sickened by his brutality, he would be disappointed. "Good!"

Amused, he shook his head at her grim satisfaction. "My father was very pleased, too. While the surgeon was setting Charles's arm, my father dubbed me Dare. My courage and unwillingness to surrender to a stronger opponent had filled my sire with pride. *I dare* had become my personal motto."

"After your victory, did the fights with your brother continue?" Unconsciously, Regan reached for his hand, and then realized that Dare might mistake it for pity. When she tried to pull away, Dare captured her hand and placed their clasped hands on his upper right thigh.

"My father's pride in me only deepened Charles's

animosity. Childish pranks gave way to imaginary offenses that led to—"

Lady Allegra.

Of course, Charles would view the lady who held Dare's heart as a delectable prize to be fought over and claimed out of spite.

"Your brother and his wife have caused you much pain," she said, very aware of the heat emanating from Dare's gloved palm. "Why do you bother heeding the summons at all?"

"Duty, honor . . . loyalty to my family." Dare gestured vaguely with his left hand. "I told you the origins of my nickname not to gain your pity, but to help you understand that I earned it. In truth, I am no better than any of them. It is best that you remember that fact."

Dare gently disengaged his hand from hers and stared out the window.

Chapter Nine

With Regan at his side, Dare eschewed the front door of the Moredare residence and entered from one of the side entrances. This was not a formal visit; nor did he want to give Allegra a chance to play lady of the house in front of Regan.

The notion of the two women conversing in the drawing room unsettled him. Frost should not have meddled in Dare's affairs, but he silently admitted that Regan could be useful to him.

A discreet side glance revealed that the pity shimmering in Regan's liquid blue eyes had faded. Good. He preferred the lady who wanted to skewer Charles for his misdeeds.

The Mordares' butler, Maffy, rounded the corner and almost collided with them. "Good heavens, Lord Hugh! You gave me a fright." Since the apron he was wearing seemed inappropriate attire when a guest was in the house, Maffy promptly began to untie the strings.

"Do not bother making a fuss, Maffy. Lady Regan is a friend, and our visit is informal in nature." He rolled his eyes upward to the ceiling. "Is my mother still abed?"

The servant nodded wearily. "Yes, milord. Cook tried to tempt Her Grace with a tray laden with her favorites, but it was returned untouched. Lady Louise is visiting with her now."

"Lady Louise?" Regan inquired politely.

"Louise is my niece," Dare said as they strolled across the marble flooring of the front hall. "Maffy, you may return to your duties. Lady Regan and I shall pay our respects to my mother. Perhaps we can nudge her out of bed." He paused, dreading the answer to his next question. "Where is Lady Pashley?"

"Here."

The Marchioness of Pashley was elegantly poised at the top of the staircase. "You are late, Hugh," she said, her gaze narrowing on Regan. "We were expecting you hours ago."

"I had business that needed my attention," Dare lied.

"Maffy, be so kind as to escort Lady Regan upstairs," Allegra said, confirming that she had been eavesdropping from her lofty perch on the stairs. "I am certain Her Grace will welcome a fresh sympathetic ear while Hugh and I discuss private matters."

It was just the type of imperial summons that usually chafed Dare. On the other hand, he was willing to endure the brief private meeting if his obedience would keep Regan away from Allegra.

The Duchess of Rhode told Maffy she was indeed receiving visitors when she learned that Regan had come to see her.

"Come closer, girl. Let me look at you," Her Grace said, beckoning Regan to approach the tall bed.

It was an impressive throne of seventeen feet of cream-colored Mantua silk and crimson Chinese damask. Maffy had explained that the bed had been built for James II in the late 1660s, and was considered a prized possession in the Mordare family.

Regan reached the side of the bed and curtsied. "Good afternoon, Your Grace. I pray I am not intruding."

"Little Regan," the duchess said, taking both of Regan's hands and giving them an affectionate squeeze before she released them. "Sit down . . . sit down. Oh, my, how you have grown! I believe the last time that I set my eyes on you, you were about our Louise's age." She clapped her hands to gain her granddaughter's attention. "Louise, child, put down the book and greet our guest properly."

Eleven-year-old Louise shut her book with all the enthusiasm of a condemned criminal. If one overlooked the sullen expression, she was a beautiful child. Wearing a white muslin dress with three scalloped flounces at the hem, Dare's niece approached from the other side of the bed, her light blond ringlets bouncing merrily against rosy cheeks.

From her bed, the duchess took care of the introductions. "Louisa, Lady Regan is a friend of your uncle's and Lord Chillingsworth's sister. Lady Regan, this is my granddaughter, Lady Louise."

Both Regan and Louise curtsied. When the girl glanced up, Regan was startled to see Dare's blue-gray eyes set into her finely boned features.

"Why, you have your uncle's eyes!" Regan blurted out.

The last time she had visited the Mordares' town house, Lady Louise had been an infant, and much too sedate for an adventurous young girl.

"I have my father's eyes," Lady Louise corrected, glancing at her grandmother. "Is that not so, Grandmama?"

"Louise has inherited the Mordare eyes. They make an appearance at least once every generation." The duchess sighed. "It is a pity that Allegra has not given us another grandchild. A grandson with my hazel eyes would be lovely."

Lady Louise crossed in front of Regan and retrieved a pillow that had fallen onto the floor. "Papa says that Mama cannot produce his heir because she is barren."

The duchess leaned forward so her granddaughter could add the pillow to the others. "Rubbish. Your mother is young and healthy. She will give Charles his heir." She smiled affectionately at the girl. "There, there . . . you are so good to me, my sweet child. Why do you not take your book and read in the garden?"

Louise embraced the duchess. "Thank you, Grandmama!" The girl met Regan's expectant gaze. She hesitated only long enough to dip into an abbreviated curtsy in Regan's direction, retrieved her book, and dashed out of the bedchamber.

Once the door clicked shut, the duchess placed her palm on the bedding and leaned forward. "I would get my hazel-eyed grandchild if Charles would cease bedding his mistresses and spare some of his mettle for his poor wife. Why, just the other day, another one was pounding at the door demanding payment for the bastard in her belly!"

Slack-jawed, Regan dropped into the chair closest to the bed. She had a feeling that she was about to learn more about Dare's family than he ever wanted anyone to know.

"So that is Lord Chillingsworth's younger sister," Allegra said, inviting Dare to join her on the settee. "I could hardly recognize her with her face freshly scrubbed and wearing a clean dress."

Dare avoided the settee and sat down in one of the chairs. "Put your claws away, Allegra. Lady Regan does not deserve them."

"I recall that she was always chasing after you and your friends." Allegra brought her hand to her lips and softly laughed. "I believe your father told me that when she was a child, she wanted to be a member of your little club."

"Enough. Allegra. Your jealousy is unattractive," he said, trying to leash his temper.

Allegra's lower lip quivered as she stared at him. "Why did you bring *her* with you?"

"Since Charles has the house in an uproar, and my mother has taken to her bed"—*again* was implied, but left unspoken—"I thought Lady Regan might be able to coax the duchess from her bedchamber."

Dare's explanation seemed to placate Allegra. With a breathy sigh, she said, "Your mother is the least of our problems."

"Where is my father?"

Unshed tears filled his sister-in-law's eyes. "Looking for Charles. My husband—he did not return home last evening."

The tale was an old one, and Dare's patience was

being stretched beyond his endurance. "What set my brother off this time?"

Allegra shuddered delicately and rose from the cushion of the settee. "I have been remiss in my manners. Are you hungry? Should I ring Maffy? If you would rather have something to drink, I could have him bring you some brandy."

Dare wondered if Regan was faring better with his mother. "I require nothing from you but answers."

Flinching at his curtness, Allegra nodded. "Very well. A woman came to the house the other day. She demanded to see Charles, and when she was told that he was not at home, the woman asked for your father."

"What did she want?"

"She would not speak to anyone but your father. When he came downstairs, the woman smoothed the fabric over her swollen belly and claimed that Charles was its sire."

It was the one thing guaranteed to upset the entire household. His father had not hidden his concern about Charles and Allegra's inability to produce the future Rhode heir. Allegra had suffered numerous miscarriages since Louise's birth, with each pregnancy shorter than the last. To prove to the world that the fault lay with his barren wife, over the years Charles had impregnated several of his mistresses. Bastards were not heirs, but that did not prevent his brother from spreading his seed throughout England.

Dare rubbed the tight muscles at the back of his neck. "What was my father's response?"

Allegra retrieved the handkerchief she had tucked into the cuff of her sleeve. "Called the woman a liar and a whore." She brought the embroidered linen up to her nose and delicately sniffed. "He sent her away, vowing to toss her in prison for trying to blackmail the family."

Dare sensed that Allegra wanted comforting words from him. Unfortunately he had none to give her. "You and I both know that the poor woman was probably not lying about her relationship with Charles."

"He promised!" Allegra said passionately. "He swore to his father that he was done with mistresses. That he—that he—"

Unable to finish, she collapsed at Dare's feet, her tearstained face buried against his knee.

"Hugh, I do not know what to do," Allegra cried, clutching the fabric of his trousers. "Charles is so furious. I am failing him, and the family."

Dare thought he was impervious to Allegra's tears, but her sobs seemed genuine. He touched her on the shoulder, causing her to cry even harder. As much as Dare hated to admit it, he pitied his sister-in-law. She had married the wrong brother, and both of them knew it.

"Should I apologize?"

Regan finished retying the ribbons of her bonnet and glanced at Dare. "For what exactly?"

When Dare had entered the duchess's bedchamber thirty minutes later, Regan could almost smell the anger that crackled and popped around him as he kissed his mother.

Dare was not inclined to linger and listen to the duchess's numerous complaints. With a curt farewell, he had firmly taken Regan by the arm and hurried her down the stairs. Once they were settled in the coach, he had lapsed into a thoughtful silence. Regan had been almost convinced that he had forgotten about her presence until he had deigned to speak to her.

"You seemed awfully friendly with my mother." He hesitated. "I suppose that she told you about Charles."

Regan was uncertain if Dare would be comfortable with the truth. She considered lying until she saw his expression. He was expecting her to lie to him, and that realization had made him furious.

"I know about Charles's mistress . . . and the babe that she claims is his."

"So my mother is as indiscreet as my brother." Dare removed his hat as he cursed under his breath. "Fantastic!"

Regan glared at him. "I may be many things; however, I am not a gossip," she informed him tartly. "Your family secrets are safe."

Dare groaned and curled the fingers of his right hand around the nape of her neck. Regan stiffened; the brim of her bonnet was knocked askew as he pressed his forehead to hers.

"Forgive me."

Regan would have nodded if she could have moved her head. "Wish you had ignored Lady Pashley's summons?" she asked, his proximity making her light-headed.

He chuckled. "Frost was right to burn that damn note." With a swift kiss to her forehead, he released her. Regan watched him as she straightened her bonnet.

Dare tapped his hat against the side of his knee. "It would not have mattered. My father would have eventually appeared at your brother's door. In my family, all roads lead to Charles."

"Because he is the heir?"

"In part," Dare conceded; his expression was one of contemplation. "My brother has a knack for creating messes. He leaves it to the family to clean up after him."

"What does Allegra expect you to do?"

Dare brushed his nose with his hand. "Everything . . . nothing. It doesn't matter. Charles will not appreciate my interference."

He lapsed into silence. After a few minutes, Dare said, "Allegra is barren."

"I know," she said, her confession drawing his full attention. "Louise told your mother."

She had managed to surprise him. "How the devil does Louise know such a thing?"

Regan shrugged. "Apparently your brother told her. Your mother, on the other hand, vehemently disagrees. She suspects that if your brother would conserve his—uh—mettle, Lady Pashley would be able to produce his heir."

"Oh, for God's sake!" Dare exclaimed, clearly appalled by the conversation Regan had had with his mother. "I should have never involved you."

"Nonsense," Regan protested, annoyed that he thought she could not handle a frank discussion with the Duchess of Rhode. "I got along just fine with your mother."

"Christ."

Louise had not exactly warmed to her, but Regan sympathized. She recalled what it was like to be the only child in the house. "She has your eyes," she mused aloud.

She had managed to startle him. "Who?"

"Louise. The blue-gray color is rather distinct."

Dare's gaze dropped to Regan's hands before it slid away. "Not in my family. Mordare blue. The color surfaces in every generation."

Neither Regan nor Dare spoke the rest of the drive back to the town house.

Chapter Ten

"What happened to our Thursday rule?" Dare asked in lieu of a greeting as he entered Nox's private saloon, which the Lords of Vice used for billiards and other amusements. Frost was standing to the right of the table with one of Madame Venna's girls. His friend had braced his hand and cue on her lovely round backside to position his shot. On the opposite side, Saint had his arm around the waist of a pretty red-headed wench. Hunter had an unknown blonde on his lap and was whispering something naughty in her ear, if her giggles were anything to go by, while her female companion watched.

Frost took his shot and gave Dare a disgruntled look. "When have any of us ever taken that rule seriously? Besides, this is not about our lovely companions, my friend." Everyone was studiously ignoring the now drawn-out sighs coming from the sofa. "*This* is about billiards!"

"And a thousand guineas," Saint added drily.

Dare poured himself a glass of brandy. "With bets like that, Frost will beggar you."

"Oh, there are a few conditions," Saint said, circling the table as he sized up his next maneuver. "First, our hands cannot touch the table."

Which explains Madame V's girls.

Even though Saint and Frost were unable to touch the table, their female companions were under no such restraint. Dare suspected his friends had come up with an amusing way to thwart the first rule.

"And second, the victor must trounce his opponent by more than five." Saint patted his companion on the backside. "Now be a good girl, love, and admire those pretty ankles for me."

The redhead sent a mischievous smile over her shoulder at Saint before she bent over and grabbed the front of her skirt for support. Saint shifted his stance, and placed his palm on the slender plane of her back as he positioned his cue.

"An inventive solution to your quandary, my friend," Dare said, applauding the marquess' ingenuity.

The blonde who had been watching Hunter dally with her friend sidled up to Dare, her gaze as intimate as a caress. "Ooo," she cooed, sliding her hand up and down his arm. "Aren't ye a fine one. It appears my luck 'as improved this evening."

His hands instinctively reached for the woman as she plopped down into his lap. Dare gave Saint an exasperated look when he snickered at his friend's awkward plight. He had not come to Nox for a willing woman, though there were plenty about the premises. After an afternoon of arguing with his father about Charles, he had craved an evening surrounded by his friends.

Dare closed his eyes as the blonde inspected his shoulders and upper arms. Thankfully he had not brought Regan with him this afternoon. He had had his hands full dealing with both his father and, later, his brother. There was no telling what mischief might have occurred if Allegra had pulled Regan aside and whispered in her ear. He had heard the unspoken question in Regan's voice when she commented on the color of Louise's eyes. It was not much of a leap for her to conclude that he had sired the girl. Hell, there was a hellish moment in his life when he had wondered the same thing, when it amused Allegra to torment him with the possibility.

Dare leaned to the right and placed his brandy on the table. Once his hands were free, he gently stopped the woman from sliding her hands lower than his upper chest. "Not this evening, my sweet. You will have to look elsewhere if you want your luck to improve."

"Oh, pooh!" the woman said, exhaling noisily as Dare helped her to her feet. She glared at Frost. "That is two guineas that I owe you."

Frost grinned lecherously at the annoyed blonde. "Don't fret. How I collect on the debt will leave us both satisfied."

The seams of his black frock coat strained as Dare crossed his arms. "You know Madame V frowns on you fleecing her town petticoats, Frost."

Madame Venna was the proprietress of the Golden Pearl. Proximity and mutual respect for the Lords of Vice had resulted in a profitable business arrangement for all of them.

"And you are dreadfully boring when you are inclined to lecture. Trust me, Dare. Hattie will not lose anything that she is willing to give freely," Frost assured him, his gaze returning to the billiards table in front of him.

Dare took a sip of his brandy, noting that they were missing several members this evening. "Where are Sin and Vane?" Although no one would mistaken him for a monk, he usually counted on Vane to amuse the wenches whom Berus sent upstairs to entertain the Lords of Vice. With Sin and Reign now married, Nox's saloon seemed to be overflowing in town petticoats. Even Frost had his limits.

Saint hooted at the satisfying sound of ivory balls colliding. "I suspect we will see Sin later after he has given his marchioness a proper evening on the town."

"Vane is attending the Deightons' ball," Hunter volunteered from the sofa.

Dare sympathized with his absent friend. "His mother appears determined to marry the gent off this season."

"I sent him to the Deightons'," Frost muttered, distracted by his next shot. "He is escorting Regan to the ball. That business with Fothergill and his cronies was troubling."

Dare straightened in his chair, his pity for Vane vanishing. "Why did you choose Vane of all people?" Had Frost not seen how Vane had been fawning over Regan the night they had attended the theater? "Sin would have been a better choice."

Glaring over his poised cue, Frost's turquoise-blue eyes bore into him. "Sin has a pregnant wife to look after. I needed someone to look after my sister properly. As if his very life depended on it."

That man is not Vane.

That man is—

The unfinished thought felt like a mental slap. Dare had troubles with his own family. He did not need to take on the duty of looking after Regan. It was enough that they were residing in the same town house.

As it was, Dare did not know how much intimacy he could bear without breaking. It was difficult enough to face Regan in the morning room.

He thought of Vane smiling at her. Inviting her to dance. Bastard. How many times had the scoundrel touched her without permission?

Worse, still, what if Regan encouraged it?

"Where the devil are you going?" Saint called out.

His legs had crossed the room before his rational intellect had caught up with an impulsive decision that was primitive and bordered on territorial.

Dare wanted to plant his fist into Frost's face for being so reckless with his sister's welfare.

"The Deightons' ball," he said gruffly. "Someone needs to keep an eye on Vane!"

"I absolutely adore your sweet mother," Regan teased, enjoying the way her escort of the evening winced.

"Hush, my dear girl, not so loud," Vane pleaded, dragging her in the opposite direction of his family for good measure. "My mother is not deaf, and she is positively desperate to marry me off to some well-mannered chit."

Regan hid her smile behind her fan. "Well, then you are safe with me, Lord Vanewright, for my brother swears my manners have not improved during my absence."

Vane chuckled. "Giving Frost hell for sending you off to some prissy school for ladies, are you?" He playfully pinched the tip of her nose. "Good for you! All of us thought he was unreasonable when he sent you away. I told him the kitchen fire was my fault, but he refused to listen. He kept muttering that Lady Karmack was right."

Her smile faded as Regan remembered the old pain of that day. "It was more than the fire." She gave him a sheepish smile. "I was not very obedient."

Vane rolled his eyes and gave her hand a friendly pat. "And the decision to travel to London without telling Frost—that is your notion of obedience?"

"I got my way, did I not?" she said, batting her eyelashes at him. "I sensed my brother would accept defeat gracefully."

Vane shook his head. "You should not be telling me such things, my lady. An unscrupulous gentleman could demand blackmail for such honesty."

Regan shut her fan with a snap of her wrist. "Are you claiming to be an unscrupulous gent?"

"My dear Lady Regan, *unscrupulous* is part of the Lords of Vice's motto."

She rapped him on the knuckles. Vane was being outrageously flirtatious. "I distinctly recall that hanging over the front door of Nox there is an unusual rectangular stained-glass panel that has the Latin inscription *Virtus Deseritur*. The translation is 'Virtue is forsaken.'"

Vane lowered his head and whispered in her ear, "Sounds rather unscrupulous in meaning and deed."

Regan's mirth bubbled out like sparkling wine,

comparably light and endearingly sweet. "You are a horrid man," she murmured when she noticed that other guests were watching them. "Frost will put me on a prison hulk if you persist."

"Well, we cannot have that, can we?" Vane said with mock sympathy. She could feel his body vibrating with silent laughter. "I know just the place where no one can accuse us of impropriety."

"Where?"

Vane stepped away from Regan, and bowed. "Will you honor me with a dance, Lady Regan?"

Chapter Eleven

Only vaguely acquainted with Lord Deighton, Dare was unrepentant about using his intimate connection to the Duke and Duchess of Rhode to gain entrance into the viscount's town house. The lord and lady of the house seemed wary as he approached them; however, concern quickly changed to bemusement when he explained that Lord Chillingsworth had asked him to look after his younger sister.

The irony was not lost on the couple that one of the Lords of Vice was guarding an innocent from rakes and fortune hunters. It was an amusing tale that was likely to be retold countless times throughout the evening.

As Dare entered the ballroom, the noise and the heat were stifling. Door and windows had been opened, but did little to stir the air. Dare slowed his stride as he searched the room for Regan and Vane. While anger had driven him since he had learned from Frost that he had delegated his duties to an untrustworthy gent, Dare was uncertain how to proceed now that he was here. He was going to look the fool if Regan preferred Vane's company to his.

"Lord Hugh, is it not?"

Dare halted when he heard his name. He altered his path and bowed to the two young women who seemed to know him. "Good evening, ladies. I believe I have not had the honor of a proper introduction."

"I regret that my mother, Lady Karmack, has been detained by her friends. Otherwise, I would have her make the introductions," the brunette explained, the slight quiver in her voice revealing her nervousness at her boldness. "May I present my good friend, Miss Tyne."

"Miss Tyne," he murmured, reveling in his good fortune that he had encountered Regan's friends.

"Lord Hugh." The soft-spoken blonde curtsied and acknowledged her companion with a nod. "May I present Lord and Lady Karmack's youngest daughter, Miss Bramwell?"

Dare courteously inclined his head to each lady. "It is a pleasure and fortunate that I have encountered you both this evening."

Both ladies preened at his compliment.

"How may we assist you, my lord?" Miss Tyne shyly inquired.

Miss Bramwell was more astute, and got right to the heart of the matter. "Are you looking for Lady Regan?"

"Indeed, I am," he said, gifting both ladies with a dazzling smile. "Her brother, Lord Chillingsworth, is unable to attend the ball this evening, and he sent me to watch over her in his stead."

Miss Tyne appeared puzzled by his declaration. "I thought Lord Vanewright was Lady Regan's escort this evening?"

Dare resisted the urge to grind his teeth at the

reminder. "Naturally Lord Chillingsworth feels very protective toward his sister. If he could, he would hire an entire regiment to guard her."

Understanding flared in Miss Tyne's and Miss Bramwell's eyes like a candle flame newly struck.

"Oh . . . of course." The brunette beamed at him. "Mama will be pleased when she hears that Lord Chillingsworth has embraced his responsibilities for our dear cousin."

Dare quelled the sudden urge to defend his friend. For all his flaws, Frost had done his best raising Regan after their mother had abandoned her children to follow her lover abroad. There was no doubt that her education had been unconventional; however, both brother and sister had been managing just fine until Lady Karmack had interfered.

And Dare had kissed her.

He pushed aside the intrusive thought.

"Do you know where I might find Lady Regan and Lord Vanewright?"

Miss Tyne tipped her head to the left and squinted. "I believe they are . . . there!" She gestured with her collapsed fan toward the section of the ballroom that had been set aside for dancing.

"Lady Regan does not dance," he said flatly.

"Of course she does!" Miss Bramwell tittered. "Once Miss Swann discouraged her from deliberately stepping on the other dancers' toes, Lady Regan emerged as one of Miss Swann's most graceful students."

Regan turned and curtsied to Vane as he bowed. He grinned down at her. She then curtsied to the gentleman to her right.

"You do know how to dance?" her faithless dancing partner murmured under his breath.

"Worried that I will stomp on your toes?" she retorted, smiling at the couple positioned across from them. "Did you think that I would forget that it was you, Sin, and Hunter who taught me the proper way to dance?"

Regan heard Vane choke on his laughter as they walked forward and exchanged positions with the couple opposite.

How could she forget dancing practice with the Lords of Vice? Their lessons included elbowing, the smashing of toes, and outlandish birdcalls. The first time Miss Swann had witnessed Regan's dancing skills, someone had to waft vinegar under her nose to revive the poor woman.

Vane clasped her left hand, positioned his other hand on the small of her back, and spun her about. He was still laughing as they promenaded back to their starting positions.

Regan struggled to keep her mask of disapproval in place. "Behave yourself," she scolded. "No wonder Miss Swann thought that I had learned dancing from a congress of baboons!"

It was too much for Vane. He took two staggering steps away from the other dancers and braced his hands on his knees. His entire body shook with laughter. Regan was apologizing to the other couples when Vane captured her hand and pulled her away from the set.

"Wait!"

Vane led them toward the nearest open door, and they found themselves in a narrow hall.

"You are an atrocious dancer," Regan said,

attempting to catch her breath. She pushed him away, whirled around, and collapsed against the wall. "You made me step on Mr. Osbourne's toes!"

"Everyone steps on Osbourne's toes," Vane said, placing his hand on his stomach as he walked over to her. "Forgive me, Regan. But the notion of you stomping your way through the cotillion was more than I could bear."

"It is your fault, you know," she muttered, reluctant laughter seeping into her blue eyes. "You, Sin, and Hunter. All of you played a terrible prank on me, and made me look like an utter fool."

Vane sobered. "Aw, hell, Regan," he said, bracing his palm on the wall just above her head. "It was a jest. No one wanted to see you hurt."

He touched her cheek.

Regan froze. She held her breath as she noticed that a sudden tension crept into Vane's stance. His eyes darkened as the center blackness swallowed most of the blue-green hue. Vane slowly lowered his head, closing the distance between them until his lips brushed hers.

Regan braced for his kiss.

And then Vane was gone.

Before she could blink, Dare had grabbed her companion by the shoulder, spun him about, and pinned him against the wall.

"Christ, Dare, what is wrong with you?" Vane yelled, annoyed and more than a little embarrassed that his friend had the upper hand.

Regan took a step forward, but one glance from Dare halted her steps. Dare was angry enough to crack the Deightons' plastered wall with Vane's skull.

"You were supposed to protect her from the scoundrels, not behave like one!"

Once again, Regan found herself unceremoniously hauled out of a ballroom. "You are being most unreasonable, Dare."

Vane, on the other hand, might disagree. After all, Dare had only wrinkled his friend's coat, instead of dusting the Deightons' flooring with Vane still wearing it.

"Not another word out of you, Regan Alice," he said sternly as they descended the stairs. "I should paddle your backside for practicing your flirtations on Vane!"

"I did no such thing!" For Vane's sake, it seemed prudent not to mention that he had started the flirting first. "We just got to laughing about my old dance lessons—"

"He was looking down your bodice," Dare said in forbidding tones. "Frost will likely maim Vane for taking such liberties."

"Oh, I wager my brother has stared down a bodice or two," Regan said, deliberately lagging so Dare was forced to shorten his gait. "And knowing Frost, the lady probably enjoyed it."

Dare did not bother responding to her outlandish remark. They both knew Regan had witnessed many things at Nox that were best not discussed at the Deightons' ball.

Instead of taking her out the front door, Dare escorted her to a small antechamber. "You will wait here while I see about the coach."

Regan looked gloomily about the room that was

serving as a cloakroom. "Are you not worried that I might kiss one of the footmen during your absence?"

His harsh expression softened at her sullen tone. "Behave yourself, *mon coeur*," he said lightly. It was the same warning he had offered her when she had written him from school and begged for his assistance. "Talk to no one."

"With whom shall I converse? You have thrust me into a room with cloaks and mantles!" she replied as Dare vanished from the doorway.

Regan sat down on one of the empty chairs that lined the wall.

Oh, this is truly insupportable.

Dare was treating her as if she were an errant child. Miserable, she stared down at the outfit she had selected for the evening. The round dress composed of mulberry crepe and spotted white satin was something a lady wore, not a child. It had taken her maid hours to plait and curl her hair into tiny ringlets, not to mention threading a long string of pearls and white flowers into her hair.

Regan had not worn the evening dress for Dare. Neither he nor Frost had given any indication that they had planned to join her at the Deightons' ball. She had donned the dress to please herself, though she privately confessed that Vane's reaction to her attire had been flattering.

"So, it is you?"

Lady Pashley. Regan could not imagine how this appalling evening could get worse. She rose from the chair and offered the marchioness a tentative smile. "Good evening, my lady. I was not aware that you were acquainted with the Deightons."

Regan could have bitten her tongue off for implying that the woman lacked the connections to move freely in London's polite society. "Forgive me, Lady Pashley. What I meant to say is that after our last meeting, I was left with the impression that you had little time for amusements."

Her apology sounded no better than her greeting. Regan wisely refrained from commenting further.

Lady Pashley wrinkled her nose in displeasure as she entered the small anteroom. "I do not expect you to understand, Lady Regan. However, appearances must be maintained. The Duke and Duchess of Rhode suggested that an evening out might dispel any nasty speculation about the family."

The marchioness was attired in a celestial blue round dress. Her headdress was a turban of striped silver gauze and blue satin with five white ostrich plumes. Around her neck she wore a diamond necklace. The old-fashioned setting hinted that the expensive bauble had likely adorned the necks of generations of Mordare women.

She would make a fine duchess one day, Regan thought sourly.

Lady Pashley gestured to the several piles of cloaks, capes, and mantles around them. "This is an odd place to be resting. Where is your family, my dear?"

The insult was beneath even Lady Pashley. It was hardly a secret that Frost was all Regan had left in the world. "Your concern is appreciated, but unnecessary. I am merely waiting for my coach."

Regan deliberately did not mention that Dare was escorting her home. If the marchioness realized that her brother-in-law was present, she would certainly contrive some excuse to keep him at her side.

"Ah, yes, say no more." Lady Pashley's eyes widened with sympathy. "I would have come to the same conclusion if I had been stuck with Lord Vanewright as dancing partner."

Feeling cornered, Regan studied the tips of her white kid shoes. "Lord Vanewright was an adequate partner. He was simply distracted," she muttered, silently wondering how many guests had noticed their attempt to dance the quadrille.

"Do not fret, Lady Regan." The marchioness pouted her lips. "Most of the people that I was standing next to thought your effort was charming."

Charming.

Regan doubted Lady Pashley was flattering her.

"I will be certain to pass your compliments to Lord Vanewright." Regan moved toward the door, praying her unwelcome companion would follow. "You have been so kind to remain at my side. However, I would not want to keep you from your friends."

"It has been no trouble at all," she said, dismissing her generosity as unimportant. "Hugh would expect nothing less. He would feel it was his duty to look after his good friend's little sister."

Regan would not be surprised if Lady Pashley thought the words *duty* and *burden* were interchangeable.

Unfortunately, the seed of doubt the marchioness had planted began to take root in Regan's brain. Dare had had no intention of attending Lord and Lady Deighton's ball. Had he changed his mind because he felt responsible for her?

Her heart sank at the thought. Not only did he see her as a child, Dare thought her a reckless one, as well.

"I should have known that you would not follow my orders," Dare said, causing both women to start. His blue-gray eyes switched from Regan to his sister-in-law. "What are you doing here?"

Lady Pashley smiled as she subtly nudged Regan aside. "Nothing that you would not approve of, Hugh. I saw you leave the ballroom with your young charge and thought I might be able to assist."

Regan fought back the ridiculous urge to stick her tongue out at the condescending marchioness.

Dare stared enigmatically at Regan. "I believe you have done enough. You might want to find Charles. My coachman said that your husband was out near the horses pissing in one Lady Deighton's ornamental urns."

"Good heavens!" Lady Pashley paled as she clutched Dare's arm. "Once you put the girl in her coach, will you return and help me with Charles?"

Regan braced herself for Dare's apology. He was an honorable man who put his family above all others, even when they did not deserve it. She stifled a sigh as she saw Lady Pashley's triumphant expression.

"My apologies, madam. You will have to look after Charles on your own this evening." Dare stared enigmatically at Regan. "I promised Frost that I would escort his sister home."

Nonplussed by his refusal, the marchioness said, "But what of Charles? You know how difficult he can be and—"

"Charles will eventually find his way home. He always does."

Dare gently guided Regan away from the astonished Lady Pashley.

Chapter Twelve

Regan glared at Dare as he helped her into the dimly lit interior of the coach. "You have the finesse of a press gang leader," she said, sliding across the leather-covered seat to get as far away from him as possible.

The coachman gave him a sympathetic glance. Dare's hand tightened around the edge of the open door. It was becoming abundantly clear that Regan's brief encounter with Allegra had not improved her mood.

After he had issued orders to the coachman, Dare climbed up into the coach. A sane man would have picked the seat opposite his vexed companion. Instead, he settled in beside her.

The coachman shouted to the horses, and the compartment wobbled slightly as their drive home commenced.

"Did Allegra insult you?"

Regan hesitated, and then stiffly replied, "No."

She was lying.

He silently whistled. If he had known that Allegra and Charles had attended the Deightons' ball, Dare would have taken Regan with him as he searched for their coachman. Allegra was upset about Charles, and Dare had not been sympathetic. It was unfortunate, but Allegra had chosen to blame Regan for his indifference.

"Whatever she said, it isn't true."

"I do not give a farthing about Lady Pashley's opinion of me," Regan spat. "She is an unpleasant woman who thinks only of her wants and selfish comforts. It is you and your appalling behavior this evening that is worthy of my ire." She studied him shrewdly. "Did you run into your brother? Is that why you are in such a foul mood?"

"My brother?" Dare said, taken aback. He quickly recovered. The last thing he wanted to discuss was his unfortunate encounter with Charles. Or Allegra. He refused to be made the villain because of his sister-in-law's mischief. In a rush, he recalled how he had discovered Regan in Vane's arms. "This isn't about Charles or Allegra. This is about Vane."

Dare could have sworn the temperature in coach dropped several degrees.

Regan crossed her arms and gave him a withering look. Dare was in a lather about Vane all right, but she was sure something had happened between him and Charles and it had gotten his fire up even before he had found the two of them. He was clearly determined not to talk about it, however. She gave a little huff. Well, that was just fine. "If this is about the kiss—" Regan began.

"Frost asked Vane to escort you to the ball," Dare broke in, his fury rekindling by what he had witnessed in the Deightons' passageway. "Ravishing you was Vane's brilliant idea."

One that was likely to get the gent killed.

"Ravish me?" Her response was a very unlady-like snort. "Oh, do not be so melodramatic! Vane only tried to steal a kiss."

"From my approach, it looked like the gent did more than try!" Dare growled.

"A mere brush of the lips. Nothing more," she carelessly assured him. "As it is, I see no point in telling Frost about our difference of opinion."

"A difference of opinion?" Dare leaned forward. "I caught Vane kissing you!"

"Attempting to is not the same as succeeding. By the by, Vane has you to thank for that. You foiled his best efforts." She tipped her chin up, ignoring Dare's thunderous expression. "Besides, I am not certain that Vane was precisely overcome with passion for me. It felt more like curiosity."

Dare silently contemplated returning to the Deightons' and doing more than just wrinkling his friend's coat. "This will not go well for Vane if you continue to defend him."

Regan shook her head. "I am not defending him at all. It just seems rather hypocritical of you to condemn Vane when you did more than brush your mouth against mine rather recently."

She might as well have slapped him with her reticule. "I do not believe it," Dare muttered under his breath.

Regan shifted until she was facing him. "That is the real reason why you did not punch Vane, when I could tell from your expression that you sorely wanted to spill his blood." Confident that she was correct, she inched forward, causing the hairs on the back of his neck to prickle. "Should I tell you the real question that has been burning like a fever in your mind since you discovered Vane and me together?"

Regan braced her left hand against the wall to keep from falling as the coach rocked and bounced. She was close enough that he could smell the violet water she had rubbed into her skin. If he bent his head, Dare could bury his nose in the softness of her neck and deeply inhale that lovely scent.

His cock stirred within his trousers, reminding him that he had not bedded a woman in months. He had been anticipating that Mrs. Randall would free him from his celibacy. Unfortunately the lovely widow did not seem as enticing as the temptress in front of him.

Dare placed his hand on her right hip to steady her. "Yes. Tell me."

With a slow deliberation, Regan leaned forward until her lips hovered above his. Dare's mouth went dry as she tilted her head to the side and grazed his cheek with her lips until she reached his ear.

"You want to know . . ."

Dare shivered as her breath teased his ear. The thickening flesh between his legs strained beneath the constrictive fabric of his trousers. Dare wondered if Regan would recoil in shock if he took her hand and placed it over his arousal. Despite the game she had decided to play with him this evening, he knew that she was still an innocent. Regan was just discovering her raw elemental power over men.

If she persisted, she would learn the risks of rousing a man's baser appetites.

"Your unspoken question is—Did I *want* Vane to kiss me?" Regan smiled at him as she unhurriedly pulled away from him.

Dare captured her wrist and pulled her closer. "Did you?"

Regan stared down at his hand before she met his fuming gaze unflinchingly. "You asked for the question. I did not promise to tell you my answer."

Regan hid her grin as she entered the town house. Dare followed her in grim silence. After her brief exchange with Lady Pashley, Regan thought Dare deserved to be tormented for his high-handed behavior this evening. Her evening, which included a splendid albeit innocent flirtation with Vane, had been ruined by Dare's arrival.

It seemed only fair to return the favor by not giving him the answer that he craved. And why should she? All her grand plans to impress the stubborn gent were crumbling. Dare seemed determined to treat her like a younger sister rather than a lady who could stir his heart.

The kiss that they had shared had been an aberration.

"Good evening, Lady Regan," Dare said when she reached the stairs.

Regan mentally winced. The formality did not bode well.

"Good evening, Dare," she said softly. "Thank you for escorting me home."

He did not answer. With her head held high, she ascended the staircase. She was not expecting Dare to follow. Like her brother, he preferred a brandy or two before he retired. He would head for the library, or perhaps return to Nox. It remained to be seen whether or not Dare intended to reveal all the details of her evening to her brother.

She paused at the second landing. Hmm . . . Regan supposed she and Dare were even when it came to unanswered questions, after all.

Her only warning came when Dare's hands circled her waist. Regan's cry of surprise came out as a diminutive squeak when he spun her around to face him.

"For a performance worthy of the stage, you should be properly rewarded," Dare said, backing her into the drawing room.

"Rewarded?" she squeaked. His clever ambush had thrown her off balance.

Dare kicked the door shut with his foot. "The kiss that you promised me in the coach."

He was still mildly piqued. The volatile emotion had coalesced with the lust she had deliberately provoked, forming a potent mixture. Although unspoken, Regan had been taunting Dare to kiss her, and for some unfathomable reason the man had decided to accept her silent challenge.

Regan slipped from his loose hold and held up her hands. "I did no such thing," she said, her stomach fluttering at his approach. She did the unthinkable, and wiped her damp palms on the front of her skirt. "What do you want from me? An apology?"

Dare grinned at her and slowly shook his head. "That is not what I have come to claim."

The man was stalking her, and Regan could not decide if she should laugh or flee. All of her womanly instincts screamed that she was playing a high-stakes game with Dare, and she did not know all the rules. She started when her hip bumped against the back of the settee.

As Regan edged away from him, she held out her hand to halt his approach. "Dare!"

"Regan!" He mimicked her exasperated tone. "I promise this will not hurt."

She shrieked in surprise when he lunged for her. Seizing the front of her skirt, Regan circled to the other side of the settee. "You-you . . . stay where you are, sir!"

"I'd rather not," he replied, reversing his direction.

Regan feinted to the left, and then dashed for the doors that led to the small music room. She had managed to open the door several inches before Dare slammed it shut. His other palm connected with the wooden surface, blocking any thought of escape.

Regan spun around so that her back was against the shut door. She was lightly panting, and her heart was pounding in her chest. She looked up at her captor not in fear, but with anticipation. Still, she could not resist adding, "What if my brother returns and catches you kissing me?"

Again.

"Frost can go to the devil," Dare murmured, lowering his mouth to hers.

If this was madness, he willingly embraced it.

Feeling edgy and greedy, Dare moved his lips over Regan's, savoring the taste of her.

After Regan's flirtatious display in the coach, Dare could think of nothing else but putting his hands on the brazen temptress. As he had followed her into the front hall, he had intended to head into the library. Distance and several brandies would certainly quell his desire for Regan, he had thought, and if his efforts had failed, then he could have always sated his unruly body with his hand.

Then Regan had glanced back and bid him "good evening," her voice soft and her dark blue eyes vulnerable. The temptress had vanished. In her stead was the young woman who sometimes came to him in his dreams. The innocent he had vowed to protect, but never claim as his own. The one person he could never resist.

One kiss, Dare thought, and he would let her go.

Regan slid her palms against his chest, but she did not push him away when his lips lightly teased hers. In fact, she angled her head up, encouraging him.

Dare moaned against her mouth. How was he supposed to resist such sweetness? If Regan had an ounce of sense, she should be shoving him away and running for the door.

Instead, she parted those soft lips, silently offering herself up as a virginal sacrifice. Dare wanted to push Regan to the ground and bury himself in the softness between her thighs. His cock felt like a heavy iron bar in his trousers. He cupped Regan's face with his hands and deepened their kiss, penetrating her lips with his tongue. Regan sighed and soon was mimicking the slick, gliding movements of his tongue. Mindlessly, Dare pulled her closer until his arousal was concealed by her skirt. He reached for one of her hands and started to guide it to his aching cock until he realized what he was doing.

The spell broken, Dare was the first to pull away. "Enough!" He gestured at the door. "You should retire to your bedchamber," he said hoarsely.

Dare turned away, attempting to shield Regan from his lust, which was so blatantly defined under his trousers. Even with her unconventional upbringing with Frost as her guardian, Regan could not possibly understand what Dare wanted from her. That knowledge gave him strength to let her leave the room.

Regan did not move. "I would rather continue kissing you," she said shyly.

Without glancing at her, Dare groaned and scrubbed his face with his hand. He had always known that he would succumb to some form of madness if he laid a hand on Regan.

"And I would prefer not to," he lied. "Go to bed."

"No."

Dare glanced up at her refusal. He had not thought it possible, but Regan was even lovelier with her blue eyes glittering with anger and her red lips slightly swollen from his kisses.

"I am not a child, Dare," Regan said, planting her fists into her hips as she swaggered toward him. "Nor are you my brother."

"Thank Christ for that small favor," he muttered, pretending not to hear her gasp of dismay.

He was destined for hell for his wicked intentions toward Regan.

Regan glared at him. "Furthermore—"

Dare could no longer bear it. "Enough, Regan, enough!" He whirled around and seized her wrist. Before she could pull away, he brought it the front of his trousers. "There, you see? I am bloody aware that you are not a child. Now leave me, or I will demonstrate what I do to shameless ladies who tease me."

Chapter Thirteen

Regan stared down at the aspirations that she had written in her diary weeks before she had departed for London.

> *Bedevil Frost.*
> *Fascinate the* ton.
> *Seduce Dare.*

All three laudable ambitions had seemed attainable until she had actually tried to carry them out. Frost was . . . well, Frost, after all. He seemed immune to her mischief, or remorseful about his decision to send her away with Lady Karmack. Regan had yet to fascinate anyone in the *ton*. Beauty and scandal held the *ton*'s fickle attention. It was a pity she did not possess enough of either.

And then there was Dare.

Regan could hardly seduce a man who was so determined to resist her. Nevertheless, he could not disguise his body's response. Dare desired her, though he had made it clear in the drawing room that he had no intention of bedding her. He was too honorable to betray Frost by seducing the man's younger sister.

Nor did she want Dare and Frost to come to blows because of her. Perhaps it would come as a surprise to Frost since her arrogant brother believed the sun would not set without his permission; however, Regan had not considered how Frost might react to her plan to seduce Dare. And why would she? Regan had grown up quietly watching Frost and the other members of the Lords of Vice fulfilling their needs and desires at whim.

Five years of structure and instruction at Miss Swann's academy had not tamed her. Her years away had taught her patience and cunning, but no one could dilute what was in her blood. Regan closed her diary and slipped the small book in the drawer of her desk.

She collected her dark green cashmere shawl from the end of the bed as she headed for the door. Regan was not quite finished with Dare. She had a few more things to say to the stubborn gentleman before she retired for the evening.

Lying on the bed, Dare stirred from his thoughtful repose at the soft knock at the door. He braced himself on his elbows and scowled at the door. Regan would not be so foolhardy as to—

"Dare, are you awake?" she whispered.

He shut his eyes as he considered ignoring her summons. Of course Regan was on the other side. After all, she was Frost's sister. The lady had picked up some of her brother's reckless habits.

Dare glanced down at his half-dressed state. His white linen shirt was unbuttoned and the ends pulled out from his trousers. While he was not appropriately attired to receive guests, his modesty was intact as long as his cock behaved. Barefooted, he crossed the bedchamber and opened the door.

To his relief, Regan was still attired in the mulberry crepe and white satin dress that she had worn to the Deightons' ball. She had even covered her bare shoulders with a green shawl. Like him, she had obviously been preparing for bed. Along with her jewelry, Regan's gloves, shoes, and stockings had been removed. She had also taken the time to remove the pins and adornments from her hair.

Dare had never seen Regan's hair unbound. Even as a child she had worn it in a braid. Her waist-length midnight-colored tresses were a glorious thick bounty that made his fingers itch for a chance to touch it.

"You should not be here, Regan."

It took more than a few chilly words to deter a Bishop.

"Well, yes," Regan said, looking past him. "I thought you might be a bit prudish about conversing in the passageway." She rolled her eyes. "Appearances and all that."

Dare hid his grin as he stepped aside and beckoned her to enter. "Frost will be pleased that you learned a thing or two at that fancy lady's school he paid a small fortune for you to attend."

"My brother does not concern himself with such trifles and you know it," Regan said, walking into the bedchamber. "However, that is not why I have come. I never gave you an answer to your question."

He closed the door and braced his back against it. "And this could not wait until breakfast?"

Curious, Regan went over to the dressing table and picked up the crumbled remains of his discarded cravat. She brought the starched linen to her nose and inhaled. The muscles in his abdomen tightened as Dare watched her set the folded linen aside.

Regan whirled away from his dressing table. "We could wait until morning. Frost will likely be highly amused by the notion that you were prepared to throttle Vane over a rather insignificant kiss."

Regan did not seem to appreciate her importance to Frost. Her brother was not going to be amused by the evening's mischief. Dare met her in the middle of the bedchamber. "I propose that we do not bore Frost with what happened at the Deightons'."

Or in the drawing room.

"Agreed," Regan said, staring at his bare feet. She gave a decisive nod and headed for the door. "Then I shall not keep you from your bed."

The courage that had brought Regan to his bedchamber at this late hour had vanished at the sight of his bare feet. The intimacy of their situation had been her undoing. Bemused, Dare followed her to the door.

"You have yet to deliver your answer, my lady."

Her lips parted in surprise. "Oh! I almost forgot." She grinned up at him. "No."

Dare leaned against the door to prevent Regan from opening it. She made a soft exasperated sound.

"No?" he prompted.

"I will admit that I might have been a bit curious," she said, her blue eyes twinkling as Dare frowned. "Even so, I did not desire Vane's kiss."

"What of mine?" he asked before he could censor his thoughts.

Regan bit her lower lip as she pondered his question. "Perhaps I will give you my reply at breakfast."

Dare caged Regan within his arms. "Tell me now. Your brother can be rather bloodthirsty in the morning."

Especially when he learns that I have put my hands on his sister.

"And encourage you?" She did not try to slip away when he closed the distance between them. "I think not."

"You are standing in my bedchamber after midnight, Regan." Dare teased her lips with his own. "I am utterly encouraged."

Dare laved Regan's lower lip with the tip of his tongue. Regan tentatively parted her lips, and he pulled her closer to deepen the kiss. Warm, wet, and eager, her tongue curled around his, making Dare's head spin. Blindly he picked her up and carried her to the bed.

"Dare."

He could sense her rising panic as he tenderly placed her on his bed. Now that Dare had her attention, he should give her a stern lecture on the dangers of flirting with men and send her back to her chamber.

Instead, he put one knee on the mattress and admired the way Regan's black tresses spread out on the bedcovering. He swept one of the ringlets from her cheek and marveled at its silkiness. "Hush. I have no interest in taking your innocence."

Dare ignored the growing arousal in his trousers that proved he was a liar. He caressed her lower lip with his fingers, and let them trail over her dainty chin to her neck. "There are other ways to pleasure you," he murmured huskily. He splayed his hand across her slender neck, and slowly slid his hand just above the swell of her breasts. "And me."

Regan forced herself to relax as Dare explored the contours of her breasts. With the exception of her shoes and stockings, she was fully dressed. Dare had already vowed he had no desire to bed her, and Regan believed him.

His proximity was making her feel restless. Dare lay down on the mattress beside her. Despite the layers of fabric between them, the heat of his body bled through and caressed her like an eclipsed sun.

"Perhaps I should leave."

Dare had the audacity to laugh at her. "It is too late to be sensible, dear Regan," he chided, delicately nibbling on her collarbone. "Not when I have barely gotten a taste of you."

She shivered in reaction.

Her corset seemed unbearably tight as Regan reclined on Dare's bed. She could barely breathe, and her nipples itched as the tender flesh chafed against her chemise.

Dare's fingers found the edge of her bodice. "Should I play lady's maid for you this evening?" He gave the front of her bodice a firm tug, causing her breast to spill out. "Lovely dairies you have, my lady."

Before Regan could respond, Dare cupped the underside of her right breast and covered her nipple with his wet mouth. She was too shocked to even blush. The throat muscles worked as he suckled at her breast. Regan squeezed her thighs together as pleasure rippled from her breasts to the soft curls between her legs.

"A shame we don't have some cream for such luscious berries," he murmured, his lips leaving a wet trail as he continued his ministrations to her left breast.

Her right nipple was engorged and rosy from his mouth. Regan glanced down at the top of Dare's head, uncertain of her part in this love play. If Dare had hoped to overwhelm her with his brazenness, he had succeeded. Regan threaded her fingers through his dark blond hair, fighting the enthrallment his skillful mouth was weaving. She moaned and guided him to her neglected breast.

"Dare," she pleaded, uncertain what she was demanding from him.

He raised his head from her breast, revealing that he was not unmoved by his efforts. His blue-gray eyes seemed glazed with passion and his lips as red and swollen as her own.

"There is much more," Dare murmured enigmatically, blindly groping for the bottom of her skirt.

Regan's eyes widened as the chill of the room caressed her thighs while Dare slipped his hands through the large slit in her drawers. She pressed her knees together to conceal herself from Dare's hungry gaze. It was a futile attempt at modesty. Regan trembled as his fingers touched her intimately.

"Your nether curls are damp," he said, arrogantly pleased with his discovery. "Do you understand what it means?"

Unable to speak, Regan shook her head. Regan inhaled sharply as Dare traced the wetness with his thumb.

"I thought not," he said, sounding winded. "You are too innocent to understand the temptation that you are offering or the consequences if I accept."

Dare was wrestling with the driving need to claim her maidenhead.

An unexpected surge of panic settled on her chest like a flock of pied wagtails. Regan tried to sit up, but the boning in her corset made her clumsy. "I may be innocent; however, I am not a simpleton."

After all, seducing Dare had been part of her plan all along.

"Pray, cease your mischief, my lord. I cannot *think* when you have your hand on my—my—!"

Regan could not bring herself to dwell on where Dare was stroking her. She tugged on the front of her bodice so she could stuff her breasts back into her dress. Dare was to blame for her current predicament. She was overly warm, agitated, and likely to hit her would-be lover if he laughed at her.

"Regan."

She fell back against the bed and covered her face with her hand. "This is all wrong," Regan said, her voice barely above a whisper.

She was not a worldly courtesan or widow who sought lovers only for pleasure. It was humbling to realize that she wanted more from Dare than a careless tumble on his bed—that she always had. She squeezed her eyelids shut, willing the stinging moisture away.

Regan pulled her hand away and glared at Dare. "You were correct. I should not have come here."

Dare helped her sit up. Without looking at him, she pushed her skirt and petticoat over her legs, not caring if she was wrinkling the fabric. As soon as she was satisfied, she slid off the bed. She might have fallen if Dare had not caught her by the elbow.

"We should discuss this," he said tersely.

"Nonsense." Regan waved away his hand and strode to the door. "For years, I watched my brother and the rest of you dally with whores and mistresses, and until this moment I did not understand what was missing."

"Do tell."

Regan's chin came up at his sarcastic tone. "Affection, respect . . . heart. It is a cold union for a lady."

"That is because most of those women are not ladies, Regan."

Annoyed, Dare threaded his fingers through his hair. His harsh expression softened as understanding washed away his impatience. "I have frightened you."

Yes.

"No," Regan said, opening the door. "It just seemed silly to continue something neither one of us truly wanted."

Dare pounced, caging her body with his own. "Lie to yourself, but not to me. Your desire was not feigned."

"No," Regan said, resisting the urge to turn and bury her face against his chest. "I just want more."

She walked out of Dare's bedchamber, acutely aware that he was not begging her to stay.

Chapter Fourteen

Dare was expecting breakfast with Regan to be a chilly affair.

However, the lady was full of surprises. Instead of sulking, Regan entered the morning room with a friendly greeting to both him and Frost. It was only when she sat down across from him at the table that Dare noted the shadows under her eyes. Her sleep had clearly been no more restful than his after her departure.

"Did you enjoy yourself at the Deightons', Regan?"

Dare tensed at Frost's innocent question. When they had departed from the Deightons' town house, Regan had been content to keep certain details of the evening from her brother. Had she changed her mind? Vengeful women were, by their very nature, unpredictable creatures.

Regan did not look up as she stirred her hot chocolate. "Very much so. Vane was an admirable escort."

Her brother frowned slightly as Regan brought

her hand to her mouth and yawned. "Ah, yes, that would account for your lack of appetite and endless prattling."

Frost was rewarded with a genuine smile from Regan.

"I am unused to the late hours the *ton* keeps, brother." As proof, she put down the silver spoon and took a tentative sip of her chocolate. "Mmm . . . delicious." She sighed.

Frost seemed to be satisfied with his sister's performance. While he regaled him with a humorous anecdote of his own evening, Dare's thoughts and gaze wandered to Regan. Although her sleepless night was visible on her face, the weariness did not detract from her beauty. This morning, she had worn a long-sleeved muslin round dress with enough lace to please the strictest matron. Her long black tresses were tucked into a Parisian mob.

Dare couldn't help recalling how Regan's hair had been spread out like a fan on his bed or the taste of her as he suckled at her breasts. She had taken pleasure in his bold caresses. The wetness he had discovered between her legs had proven that she had desired him.

Thank God, Regan had come to her senses and ended his sensual exploration before he had lost complete control. An innocent like Regan was seeking more than a physical release when she took a lover. Her young heart craved words of love and poetry that filled her soul.

Pretty lies.

Dare had whispered them into other women's ears. Sweet flattery and promises that rarely survived the dawn, but none of his former lovers had cared. The women that he pursued understood that he was only seeking a temporary liaison.

Regan was not the sort of female he could bed and dismiss from his thoughts. Through her connection with Frost, their lives were intertwined. It would not be fair to let her believe that he could offer more than a few nights of passion.

"What say you, Dare?"

Dare blinked, realizing he had been caught staring at Regan. "Forgive me, Frost. The long nights have disturbed my sleep as well."

The delicate pink hue of Regan's cheeks darkened at his obscure reference to his bed. She said to Frost, "It is unnecessary, brother. Your friends are not at my beck and call."

Dare cleared his throat. "How may I be of assistance?"

Regan was slow to respond, but she managed to meet his curious gaze. While her demeanor was not hostile, it lacked the warmth that he always associated with her. "Do not allow my brother to bully you into chaperone duties. I have already sent word to Lady Karmack that I will be joining her, Thea, and Nina this afternoon. Our hostess, Lady Harper, is holding some sort of literary salon, and I believe gentlemen are not invited."

Dare hid his disappointment. If he had spent the afternoon with Regan, it would have given him the opportunity to apologize for his behavior last evening.

"Lady Harper . . . is she not a good friend of Lady Sinclair's mother?" Dare asked, seeking confirmation from his friend.

"Yes." Frost chuckled. "If Lady Duncombe has any influence, you will be playing cards rather than discussing books."

Regan nodded to one of the footmen as he pulled her chair away from the table so she could stand. "Either way, it sounds like a pleasant afternoon. Besides, I honed my gaming skills at an early age."

She leaned over long enough to kiss her brother on the cheek.

Frost captured her wrist before she could move away. "I thought Miss Swann did not approve of gambling."

"Not in the slightest," Regan assured her brother with a guileless smile. "However, her students had a more liberal view when it came to games of chance."

It was annoying when Frost was correct.

After an hour of listening to the recitation of F. D. Hermans's poem "Modern Greece," Regan was beginning to nod off. Thankfully Sin's mother-in-law, Lady Duncombe, announced at the ninety-fourth stanza that her ears had grown too weary to continue. She suggested that the card tables be brought out, and several ladies had seconded the notion. Lady Harper's literary salon had swiftly deteriorated into a genteel version of a gaming hell.

"I have attended two literary salons this month," the dark-haired woman standing to Regan's right said pensively. "On both occasions, whist triumphed over literature. Perhaps my voice is too grating?"

Regan blinked at the anxiety she sensed from the other woman. She belatedly realized that the brunette had been the lady selected to read F. D. Hermans's exceedingly long poem.

"Not at all," Regan protested. "You have a voice worthy of the stage."

The woman gave her a hesitant smile. "You are just being kind."

Regan noticed that Lady Karmack had joined Lady Duncombe's table. She respectfully inclined her head when the older woman noticed her staring. "Anyone who knows me will tell you that I am too plainspoken to be considered kind."

Her companion peered at her with interest. "You are a remarkable woman."

"I have always thought so," Regan said, her eyes twinkling with arrogance and humor. "My brother, on the other hand, views outspoken females as a trial."

"I do not believe we have been properly introduced," the brunette said. "I am Mrs. Randall."

"Lady Regan," she replied, curtsying to prove that she had learned one or two things at Miss Swann's Academy for Young Ladies. "Are you a relative of Lady Harper's?"

Mrs. Randall shook her head. "No, just a friend of the family. After my husband died, Lady Harper was kind enough to invite me to stay with her and her family while I coped with the grief of my loss."

"Forgive me, I did not mean to stir up painful memories."

"Oh, no apology is needed," Mrs. Randall assured her. "Three years have passed since my husband's death. And while a part of me will always love him, I am ready to move on with my life."

Mrs. Randall might have been eight or ten years older than Regan. Beautiful and intelligent, she possessed a quiet grace that would appeal to most gentlemen.

"So you are seeking a husband this season," Regan said shrewdly.

The brunette's lips parted in surprise, and then she began to laugh. "Oh, my goodness. Lady Regan, you are a gem. No one has ever put it so bluntly."

Now it was Mrs. Randall's turn to be kind. Compared with someone like her companion, Regan felt like a chunk of coal rather than a diamond of the first water.

"Nevertheless"—the woman leaned closer so she could not be overheard—"I will admit that there is a certain gentleman this season who has captured my interest."

"Is he handsome?"

"Very much so. On several occasions, he has hinted that he would welcome a closer friendship."

Intrigued, Regan whispered, "Who is it?"

"Oh, I mustn't." Mrs. Randall blushed. "It is too soon to tell if the gentleman returns my affections. If I have exaggerated his interest, I would prefer to keep the gentleman's name to myself."

Regan could not help but think of Dare. Five years ago, he had changed her life with a single kiss, and she suspected that he was not even aware of it until she had taunted him into kissing her last evening. Her breasts tightened as she recalled the sensation of his hands caressing her body and the feel of his mouth suckling her nipples.

All of a sudden the temperature had increased in the drawing room.

She cleared her dry throat. "If you want my

opinion, Mrs. Randall, I would not allow etiquette or pride to prevent you from approaching the gentleman that you desire. You are too beautiful to remain a widow. Be bold!"

Mrs. Randall gave Regan an impulsive embrace. "Excellent advice, Lady Regan. I think I shall follow it!"

Chapter Fifteen

Almost a week had passed since Regan had brazenly knocked on the door to his bedchamber. Dare still could not believe how close he had come to deflowering Frost's sister. As he drifted off to sleep each night, his last thoughts were of Regan, and how she had gazed up at him with a sly feminine awareness that Dare's rigid control had reached his limits. Regan's desire had almost been his undoing.

Although their recent exchanges had been civil, Dare pretended not to notice the challenge he saw in her dark blue eyes.

See me.

Take me.

It was too much for a man to bear.

What he needed was a distraction him from his growing obsession over the lady who deserved someone better than the second son of the Duke of Rhode.

There were plenty of Madame Venna's girls visiting Nox each night. One of those eager ladies could satisfy his needs without demanding anything more than payment for her services. Such carnal unions had been appealing when he was younger. However,

Dare had come to appreciate the exclusivity, albeit temporary, of a mistress. Over the years, he had formed discreet connections that benefited both him and his lovers.

This season, he had had his eye on the elusive Mrs. Randall. If not for Regan, the lovely widow would have been the one who invaded his private thoughts each night.

It is not too late.

Frost and Regan had already departed for Lord and Lady Trussell's ball. Dare had declined their offer to share their coach, preferring the freedom of his own equipage. He had also been acutely aware that Mrs. Randall would be attending the ball.

With Frost watching over his younger sister, Dare saw his chance to pay his respects to Mrs. Randall. If the lady was agreeable, perhaps they could discuss their friendship someplace private, without the prying eyes of the *ton* observing them.

And away from Regan's watchful, hurt gaze.

Dare pressed his fingers to his eyes and groaned. He was a grown man. What he did, and whom he chose as his companion for the evening, was no one's business but his own.

He did not want to hurt Regan. By God, it was the last thing he desired. However, if Dare was leaving her innocence and affection for another gent to claim, then he had every right to drown out his own misery in the arms of someone else.

Banishing the image of Regan from his thoughts, he thought instead of Mrs. Randall. Touching his jaw thoughtfully, he realized that he needed to shave and rang for a servant. He would focus on the lovely possibilities the evening had to offer. Even if he had to lie to himself to do it.

Frost was a tolerable escort. Unlike Dare, who hovered around her most of the evening like a possessive suitor, her brother seemed content to chaperone her from afar. Once he had silently warned off any potential admirer in the ballroom, her brother disappeared for several hours. Regan assumed that he and his friends had adjourned to the library for brandy and cards.

Or he was dallying with his current mistress.

In any event, Frost's private business was not Regan's concern.

Despite her brother's notoriety, several gentlemen asked her to dance. She displayed her dancing skills with pride, and even Lady Pashley nodded, offering her unspoken approval. Regan did not require the marchioness's support. Not when the lady's praise appeared to be more condescending than flattering.

All in all, it was a grand evening at the Trussells'. Hunter, Vane, and Saint had emerged long enough from the card room to dance with her. At her urging, the gentlemen even danced with Thea and Nina. Lady Karmack looked almost apoplectic when she saw her youngest daughter dancing with various members of the Lords of Vice. Her sharp gaze immediately alighted on Regan, for she knew who was responsible for the mischief.

As she waited for latest dance partner to return with a glass of lemonade he had offered to procure for her, Regan saw Dare enter the ballroom from one of the side doors. When had he arrived at the ball? Perhaps, upon his arrival, he had avoided the ballroom, and joined Frost and the others in the card room.

Regan brightened when she saw Dare look about the room. Was he searching for her? Smiling, she contemplated how to politely dismiss her dance partner when she saw his gaze fix on someone. A grin stretched across his face as he started to cross the room.

Regan's heart constricted, and she gasped in pain as Dare bowed gallantly in front of Mrs. Randall.

Good grief! Was Dare really the gentleman with whom Mrs. Randall had expressed a desire to form an intimate connection?

And she had told the beautiful widow to be bold!

Regan pressed her hand against her abdomen and tried to fight down the nausea churning in her stomach.

"I think they make a charming couple. Do you not agree?" Lady Pashley literally purred in Regan's ear.

Regan started. She hadn't heard the marchioness come up beside her. It was difficult to conceal her displeasure as Lady Pashley's sleeve brushed Regan's arm. Dare's sister-in-law was the last person that she wanted to confide in. "To whom are you referring?"

Lady Pashley was too intelligent not to see past Regan's feigned ignorance. "Hugh and Mrs. Randall. Rumor has it that half the gentlemen of the *ton* have been sniffing around the lady's skirts since last season when she came out of mourning. She had refused all respectable and not-so-respectable offers until she was introduced to our Hugh."

Regan internally cringed at the notion that she had anything in common with the marchioness. "I was not aware that Dare was acquainted with Mrs. Randall."

Lady Pashley's smile reminded Regan of a very hungry cat. "Oh, I have been watching their awkward courtship since long before your unexpected arrival in London, my dear. As a married woman, it is rather sweet to watch others fumble about as they work up the courage to take what they want."

"So you believe Dare plans to marry Mrs. Randall?"

The marchioness chuckled softly. "Heavens, no. Even the second son of a duke can do better than marry the widow of a lieutenant, nor would His Grace approve of such a marriage." Lady Pashley placed her hand on Regan's arm and guided her to the right so they had an unobstructed view of the couple. "Hugh's interest in the charming Mrs. Randall will only last a few months. If they are not already lovers, they will be soon."

"How can you tell?" She was beginning to feel sick again.

The marchioness gestured at the couple. "Little things, I suppose. Note how he has positioned himself so that no one can approach her without his permission. Hugh is clearly staking a claim. Oh, look, see how Mrs. Randall gazes shyly up at him? A clever lady appeals to a gentleman's protective nature."

Regan's eyes were beginning to sting. Lady Pashley was not exaggerating. There was an intensity to Dare's stance. He was staring at Mrs. Randall as if she were the only lady in the room.

"How did you become such an expert on courtship?" Regan asked numbly.

"I am an expert on Hugh." Lady Pashley smiled

at Regan's startled expression. "Do not look so surprised. Hugh is family. I do not expect you to know this since you were nothing more than a child; however, there was a time when I was forced to choose between Hugh and Charles."

And Dare had never quite forgiven her. His love for Lady Pashley had been grand and all-consuming; her decision to marry his brother had left Dare so bereft that he'd never since looked beyond sating his carnal needs with a legion of mistresses.

Regan swallowed the lump forming in her throat.

"You have a beautiful daughter, Lady Pashley, and someday you will be the Duchess of Rhode," Regan murmured as she watched Mrs. Randall laugh at something Dare said to her. "You made the right choice."

"Hmm . . . one would think."

Regan did not respond. She supposed that in hindsight, a titled adulterous husband dimmed the lady's appreciation for her good fortune. Regan gritted her teeth as Dare offered the crook of his arm to Mrs. Randall. Together, they strolled out of the ballroom.

Dare had every intention of bedding Mrs. Randall this evening.

Lady Pashley gave Regan a triumphant look. "I predict that Hugh will not be joining you and your brother at breakfast."

"Dare is a gentleman," Regan lied as she struggled not to give in to her disbelief and rage. "He is probably escorting Mrs. Randall to her coach."

"What a charmingly naive explanation for Dare's absence!" The marchioness clapped her gloved hands together in delight. "Do you honestly believe it?"

No.

"Yes," Regan said fiercely. If she believed the worst of Dare, she would never be able to maintain her composure in front of Lady Pashley. "What right do you have to judge your brother-in-law so harshly? To accuse him as being a ruthless seducer without grounds?"

The humor fled from Lady Pashley's expression as she gave Regan something close to a pitying glance. "My dear girl, where do you think Louisa got the Mordare eyes?"

Chapter Sixteen

Home.

Regan had never been so grateful to see an evening come to an end. With her eyes closed, she remained seated on the stone bench on the terrace and listened to the sounds within the library that heralded Dare's return. Her younger, impulsive self might have rushed to his side the moment Dare had opened the door.

Her years away from London had taught her patience.

How long had she been sitting there on the terrace? Long enough, she thought, for the cold stone to chill her. Regan had returned from the Trussells' ball hours earlier with only a silent house to greet her. Not that she minded overmuch. Frost rarely returned home until dawn, or at all. It was Dare who watched over her, deliberately allowing his evenings to intersect with hers.

Until this evening.

Oh, how she loathed Lady Pashley. Men were too easily fooled by a comely face. The marchioness knew exactly what she was doing when she revealed

Dare's interest in the attractive Mrs. Randall. Regan had not needed Frost and Vane to confirm Lady Pashley's revelation. She had discreetly observed the widow as she and Dare exchanged pleasantries before they had left the Trussells' ballroom together. Was it apparent only to another woman that Mrs. Randall was half in love with Dare?

Unlike Regan, the widow was not bound by polite society's dictates. She could take as many lovers as she desired as long as she was discreet.

Was that why Dare had vanished from the ball as Lady Pashley had hinted? Had he spent the last few hours in Mrs. Randall's bed?

Just then, Dare stepped out onto the terrace, startling Regan from her bleak musings.

He seemed equally surprised to see her. "Why are you not in bed?" he demanded gruffly.

Regan picked up the glass of brandy that she had set on the seat of the bench. "I thought a brandy would help me sleep." She brought the glass to her lips and sipped. It was strong, but she was silently proud of the fact that she did not wince.

"Did Frost see you home?"

Regan took another sip of her brandy. "I am perfectly capable of summoning the coachman without Frost's assistance." *Or yours.*

"Damn it, Regan! If your brother was unavailable, then you should have sought out Saint or Hunter . . . hell, even Vane would have sufficed."

"Do not be so tedious!" she snapped.

The knowledge that he had just left the widow's warm bed to lecture *her* on what he viewed as her reckless conduct was unbearable. Regan braced her hand on the wall and rose to her feet. She sucked in her breath as she staggered to catch her balance.

Dare tried to snatch the glass of brandy from her hand, and missed when she jerked it away from him. "You are foxed."

Regan smirked at him. "A condition that I am certain you and the other Lords of Vice must be intimately acquainted with." She strolled by him and into the library to prove that she was in control of her limbs. "Nevertheless, your opinion, as usual, is abysmally incorrect."

Before he could stop her, she downed the rest of her brandy. She set the empty glass on Frost's desk with more exuberance than was needed. "The only overindulgence that I am guilty of is sitting in the night air too long."

Regan slipped into a low curtsy to prove that she had regained her graceful balance. "Now that I have had my brandy, I shall bid you good night."

Dare grabbed her arm before she could move away from him. "For God's sake, Regan, what maggot has gotten into your brain this evening?"

"Why do you care?" she said, the pain in her heart bleeding into her voice. "More to the point, why do you pretend to care?"

"Pretend?" he echoed, puzzlement darkening his blue-gray eyes. "No pretense is necessary, Regan. I do care about you."

Not enough, she thought.

Regan shrugged off his hand. "Why are you here? What happened? Did your widow kick you out of her bed?"

Dare became unnaturally still at her question. "Who told you?" he asked tonelessly.

"No one had to tell me anything," she said, over her shoulder as she made her way to the door. "I saw you slip out of the ballroom with Mrs. Randall. When you did not return, it was apparent to everyone that seduction was your intention."

She had managed to open the door several inches before Dare slammed it shut.

"Everyone?" he said, his brows lifting. "That many. And here I thought I was discreet."

"Perhaps you were careless in your eagerness," she said waspishly. Regan tried to shove Dare's arm away. "Step aside. You will not enjoy the consequences if you provoke me."

Regan sputtered in outrage when she found herself captured in Dare's uncompromising embrace. "Never threaten a man with such a tempting offer," he said lazily. "He just might be of the mind-set to accept your challenge."

Very conscious that her backside was molded against his front, Regan struggled for her freedom. Dare was not hurting her, but he did not seem inclined to release her.

"Blast you, Dare!" she seethed, hating how her breasts tingled and tightened at his nearness. No man had ever created such a need within her. *And he just came from Mrs. Randall's bed.* Oh, it simply wasn't fair!

Dare chuckled in her ear. "Such language, Lady Regan," he scolded. "And here I thought you liked my hands on you." One of his hands slipped to her waist.

Regan responded by ramming her elbow into his stomach.

She heard a satisfying "oomph," and Dare immediately released her. Regan whirled around to face him, her fists clenched at her sides. "You conceited scoundrel! Touch me again, and I will—I will—"

The humor faded from his face, and his eyes became hooded. "Summon your brother?" Dare supplied when she could not come up with a suitable threat.

"I do not need Frost," Regan said fiercely, her eyes bright with tears. "I am furious enough to tear you limb from limb!"

"I can see that." His demeanor was amazingly calm as he faced her. "You're jealous."

The tears that had been threatening to fall receded as her temper switched from seething to a brittle cold. "Your vanity is endless." With her head held high, she marched away from him. "And you, Lord Hugh, can go to the devil!"

What happened next was more reflex than fury.

When Dare grabbed her shoulder and whirled her about, Regan's fist came up and bashed him in the nose.

"Christ!" Dare bellowed, stumbling back. He stared at Regan wide-eyed. "A bloody facer . . . by a *female*!"

Horrified by her violent display, Regan rushed to Dare and touched him on the arm. "My God, I did not mean to hit you. I—"

Dare pounced. There was no other word to describe the man who one minute was hunched over in pain, and the next had seized Regan by the shoulders and sent them both tumbling to the floor. Regan gasped at the feel of him pressed on top of her.

"Not jealous, eh?" Dare grinned down at her, pleased by his own cleverness. "Such shameful behavior, Regan Alice." He made a disapproving noise in his throat. "Spilling my blood over another female."

Relief gave way to exasperation. "Need I remind you that you are not bleeding?" The slight pink on his cheek proved that her fist must have given his face a glancing blow and missed his nose entirely. "What is shameful is pretending that I hurt you!"

"Well, it worked, didn't it? It put you exactly where I wanted you," he said without a scrap of remorse. He shifted his legs against hers, making sure he had her effectively pinned. Regan's breath caught at the intimacy of the position. "Now tell me more about your jealousy and this penchant for violence."

Regan grimaced as she brought her fingers up to cover her eyes. Despite his flirtatious teasing, her spirits plummeted. "I feel like such a fool."

Angling his body so the floor supported most of his weight, Dare peeled her hand away from her eyes. "On the contrary, you feel soft and rather lovely; though not all of you," he said, rapping his knuckles on the boning of her corset.

Regan laughed. "Let me up before Frost finds us."

"Impossible. I locked the door and took the key."

She glanced back at the closed door. Baffled, Regan met his clear blue-gray eyes. "When did— You did what?"

"Despite the rumors you heard this evening, I had no intention of bedding Mrs. Randall," Dare told her. He stared down at her. "How could I, when all I could think about is you?"

And then he sealed his confession with a kiss.

Dare tensed, half expecting Regan to punch him again. He was learning that she had become quite unpredictable, and possessed a fierce temperament when provoked. A sane man would have scrambled off her and counted his blessings that she had not buried her sharp knuckles into his nutmegs.

But he wasn't sane. At least not when it came to this woman.

He found her fascinating. Regan was a wild, spirited creature who not only challenged him, but also stirred a tenderness within him that he thought long dead. She was fully capable of arousing him, even when she was doing her best to kill him.

Dare deepened the kiss, his tongue sweeping hers. She made a soft, kittenish sound of pleasure that made him even hotter and harder. Although beautiful, he wanted to rend the dress that she was wearing with his bare hands. He loathed the barriers that kept him from exploring her body with his fingers and mouth.

By God, he wanted to do more to Regan than just touch. Just as Dare had said, it was the reason he had not accepted Mrs. Randall's soft-spoken invitation to join her in her private sitting room. On the drive to her town house, Dare realized that he wanted more than a willing woman who offered nothing more than a single night of pleasure.

He craved a complicated, outrageous female whose innocence and notorious, protective older brother stood between him and his desires.

But now he no longer cared about the risks.

Dare was tired of fighting it. He wanted Regan.

"I need to see all of you," he said. He lifted her and immediately began to undo the glass buttons at the back of her dress.

"Here?" Regan crossed her arms over the front

of her bodice. Soon he had the laces of her corset loosened.

"I cannot wait," he said, his tone intense. The short sleeves slipped down her arms until the bodice of the dress collected at her slender waist. Her corset and chemise still covered her breasts, but not for much longer. "Lift your hips."

Regan's dark blue eyes seemed fathomless as she stared up at him. "Are you undressing, too?"

"Soon." Dare tossed her dress and petticoat aside. Her stiff corset quickly followed, until she was wearing only her thin chemise and drawers.

Perhaps in an effort to distract him, Regan boldly reached for his frock coat. With a determined expression on her face, she sat up on her knees and pushed and divested him of his coat and waistcoat. Dare swallowed his grin when Regan gazed at his chest as if in a daze. He loved that the sight of his body affected her this way. He became harder just at the thought.

Dare tossed aside his cravat and grabbed the bottom of his shirt. "Help me," he said hoarsely, and lust coiled like heavy smoke in his gut as Regan complied. He felt her fingernails scrape against his back as she pulled his shirt over his head.

"Your turn," he said, gently easing Regan onto her back. "No, no . . . do not cover yourself." Dare cupped her breasts through the thin linen of her chemise. Her plump nipples stabbed his palms at his interest.

Unwilling to wait a second longer, Dare seized the front of the undergarment and tore the delicate fabric in two, leaving her bare and open to him.

"Dare!" she exclaimed as he nibbled his way

down from her tempting breasts to her navel. His hand groped for the drawstrings of her drawers, and tugged until the knotted bow unraveled.

He groaned as her hipbone was uncovered. "You are so lovely," he murmured, kissing the hollow next to the bone. "I plan to taste every inch of you."

"Every inch?" Regan echoed, bemused.

Dare shot her a heated glance before he moved lower. Ignoring her weak protests, he parted the intimate folds between her thighs and laved the tender moist flesh within.

"Dear heavens!" she gasped. Regan tried to wiggle away from his bold carnal kiss, but Dare held her hips and pulled her closer.

He teased the delicate nubbin with the tip of his tongue. Regan trembled and writhed under his sensual ministrations. He throbbed painfully within his trousers, but Dare ignored the demands of his body. He was too enthralled with the notion of giving Regan her first taste of pleasure.

Dare grazed her hipbone with his teeth. "Has anyone kissed you thusly?" he asked, already knowing her answer.

"N-nooo!"

Emboldened by the wetness coating her womanly folds, he rubbed the swollen nubbin with his fingers. Regan moaned, her hips moving restlessly.

"It almost hurts," she said, shaking her head from side to side.

Dare groaned as his fingers stroked the entrance of her sheath. Her answering arousal deepened his penetration. The pain that Regan was feeling had nothing to do with her virginity. "Let me ease you," he said, his throat tight from his self-denial.

Rolling off her, Dare unfastened the two buttons near his left hip and quickly freed himself, his cock springing free. The air did little to cool his ardor. He shoved his trousers down until he could kick the garment free from his legs.

Seeing Regan's wide-eyed expression, Dare decided haste was kinder than letting her fret over the size of him. He crawled up her body and fitted himself between her legs. With his hand, Dare guided his rigid length until the swollen head began to push inside her tight sheath.

"Do you feel how your body is responding to mine?" he asked, pushing into her with slow abbreviated strokes that he was certain were likely to kill him.

"Yes," she replied, releasing the breath that she had been holding as she took him into her body.

As he pushed farther into her welcoming heat, sweat beaded on his brow when the head of his cock met the resistance of her maidenhead. Regan bit her lower lip and arched her spine against the growing discomfort. Her movements unintentionally pushed him deeper.

"Regan," he said, begging her to understand that he was fighting instinct and was at the mercy of his own needs. Withdrawing slightly, he surged inside her, claiming her completely.

Regan gasped at his invasion. Her fingernails were digging into his shoulders, but he barely felt it. Their gazes met in a lengthy silence.

"You will damn me if you demand that I stop."

A ghost of smile teased Regan's lips. "And here I thought we were already damned."

Dare groaned and buried his face against her

breast. "This is not the moment to make me laugh, Regan."

Then he began to move and Regan ceased to think. The pace he set was languid and tortuous. The liquid glide of his cock within her tight sheath was almost his undoing. He nuzzled her breast, then laved the swollen peak with his tongue.

Regan threaded her fingers through his hair and moaned. Dare drew hard on the nipple before he released it. He stretched and claimed her lips. Her tongue teased his. In a nimble move, she curled her tongue around his and coaxed him to deepen their kiss. Dare cupped her buttocks, driving his strokes deeper at her boldness.

She exhaled sharply as his mouth moved to her neck. Dare gave her a not-so-gentle bite. Regan was trembling and panting with the need Dare had created within her that only he could assuage.

He would not fail her.

Lost in the feeling of Regan's body beneath his, and her heady scent in his nostrils, Dare's measured strokes soon became more intense and powerful. Clutching him tightly, Regan cried out and stiffened as each thrust brought her closer and closer to the edge. And then Dare flung her right over it. Her cries of pleasure rang in his ears. He drove into the heart of her, and clenched his teeth against the roar of his own release as his hot seed filled her.

With a final shudder, he collapsed on top of Regan. He felt a deep satisfaction seep through him when he felt her soft embrace pull him even closer.

Regan loved the feel of Dare's weight on top of her and fullness of his thick manhood still inside her.

"Dare?" She stroked his back. "Did I hurt you?" she asked when he did not respond.

Dare groaned and used his arms to lift himself from her. "I should be asking you that question." He carefully withdrew from her body and reached for his trousers. Rolling over onto his back, he used the garment to cover himself.

"I am very well." Regan told herself that she was not disappointed that she had not gotten a proper look at him.

He reached over and stroked her cheek. "You do not have to lie," he said gently. "Although I tried to ease your pain, there must have been some discomfort."

"Some," she admitted. "Though there were certain parts of our lovemaking that were very nice." It seemed too wanton to lie on her brother's rug naked, so she sat up and reached for her discarded dress.

Dare smiled, his earlier humor resurfacing. "When I have recovered, I would be honored to discuss your favorite parts at length." His gaze traveled down the length of her body before returning to her eyes. His smile widened. "Or mayhap later. The hour is late, and you are too sore for what I have in mind."

Regan frowned. "I do not believe I am sore."

"Indeed?"

Dare settled the matter by rolling onto his side and slipping his hand under her makeshift covering. She flinched as his fingers touched her intimately, tenderly.

Regan sighed and accepted her defeat gracefully. "I am a little sore."

"Hmm . . ." He sat up. "We should get dressed."

It was such a mundane task after everything she

had experienced this evening. Regan watched, admiring Dare's body as he pulled on his trousers. She sighed, staring at her own clothing. Her chemise was ruined. Since she was going straight to her bedchamber, Regan eschewed her undergarments and donned her dress.

Dare pulled his shirt down over his abdomen. He glanced down at the pile of Regan's undergarments on the floor. He quirked his right eyebrow but refrained from commenting. "Allow me to help you," Dare said quietly.

Regan offered him her back. "Only fasten a few so I can remove it on my own."

He kissed the nape of her neck. "A sensible notion. However, if I had my way—"

"I believe you already have, my lord," she quipped, and was rewarded with a low chuckle.

"I wish I could join you in your bedchamber." Dare turned her until they were facing each other. "I was too rough the first time. You deserve a soft bed so I can make love to you properly."

"Nonsense. Everything was perfect."

He gave her an endearing lopsided grin that always seemed to melt her heart. "You are not much of a judge, fair Regan, being that this is your first time."

Regan leaned forward as Dare lowered his mouth to hers. His kiss was sweet and reverent; an unspoken apology for his frenzied lovemaking.

She moaned against his lips. "Come up to my bedchamber."

Dare rested his forehead against hers. Then he shook his head and stepped away from her. "I need you to be sensible." He gathered up her undergarments and pushed them into her hands. "Clearly, I am not capable of the task where you are concerned."

The small admission from Dare cheered Regan immeasurably. "We could tarry longer in the library! I have become quite found of this room."

"Behave!" Dare delivered a playful swat on her backside and nudged her toward the door. "We cannot linger. If Frost finds us together, he will probably castrate me, and send you to a nunnery until you are eighty."

Chapter Seventeen

The next morning, Regan was certain that nothing could ruin her buoyant mood. Dressed in a gray bombazine round dress with a white-and-yellow twisted band of satin fabric adorning the bodice, she felt very much the lady of the house.

Seated across from Dare in the morning room, she glanced at her brother's empty chair and wondered at Frost's tardiness. Despite the late hours that her brother kept, he was usually the first to come downstairs.

Dare gave her a not-so-subtle nudge under the table. "Stop it."

Regan swallowed the small portion of poached egg she had been savoring. "Stop what exactly?" she politely inquired.

Although she had been tempted to kiss Dare when she entered the morning room, Regan had resisted such a display in front of the staff. But that didn't mean she wasn't thinking about it . . . and about last night.

Dare waited until the footman stepped out of the room before he replied. He gestured vaguely in her direction. "You look like a lady who was thoroughly ravished by her lover."

Regan looked down at the dress she had selected this morning and frowned. "There is nothing wrong with my attire."

She quietly conceded that the gray bombazine dress did not suit her coloring or her temperament. However, she had chosen it after much deliberation. It was staid, practical, and respectable. No one, including Frost, would ever guess the wicked things she and Dare had done in the library.

Dare leaned forward so his voice would not carry beyond the table. "I don't mean your clothes. I am referring to your expression. You look too damn happy, Regan."

Regan brought her hand up to her mouth in an attempt to smother her laughter. "Too happy," she reiterated. "Honestly, Dare, that is hardly a criminal offense."

"Frost is not a fool," he said sternly. "Your skin gleams like pearls from the Orient, the gold flecks in your blue eyes glimmer like stars, and you move like a lady aware of her body."

Regan privately acknowledged that she was very aware of certain parts of her body. Dare was a large man, and he left a most delicious impression on a lady.

"Why, that is almost poetic. Have you ever immortalized your passion for a lady with a verse or two?" Regan asked, brightening at the prospect of Dare composing poetry on her behalf.

Dare put down his coffee. "Christ," he muttered, rubbing his neck as if it pained him.

Regan suspected Dare would snarl at her if she

tried to comfort him, so she picked up her fork and resumed eating her breakfast. "Forget about the poetry," she said magnanimously. "I have the works of Byron, Bowles, and Coleridge to flatter my romantic heart."

"Stay away from poets, my dear sister," Frost said as he entered the room with his butler following in his wake. The wrinkled condition of his coat revealed that he was just returning from his evening. "Clever bounders, the lot of them."

Regan glanced at Dare. With his gaze on the morning paper, he did not seem inclined to offer an opinion on the subject. "Now you are teasing me."

"On the contrary." Frost kissed her cheek as he passed, and sat down in the chair beside her. "You would not believe the number of foolish chits who succumb upon hearing that romantic drivel."

Although her brother's insult was not directed at her, Regan felt her cheeks grow warm. She had just been teasing Dare about immortalizing their passionate encounter in a few lines of verse.

"So you do not whisper sweet flattery in your lover's ear, brother?"

"Regan."

The warning came from Dare.

Frost was amused by her question. "No words are needed when I am with a lady." He raised his hands and wiggled his fingers. "I have other uses for my hands and nimble tongue."

Dare glared at his friend. "Show some respect, Frost. Regan is your sister, not one of Madame Venna's girls."

Regan almost choked on the piece of poached egg in her mouth as she recalled how Dare had used his mouth and hands on her. He had tumbled her with the ease and skill that her brother was boasting about.

Untroubled by his friend's scolding, Frost picked up his buttered toast and slathered it with blackberry jam. "You surprise me, Dare. I thought a certain lady would have taken the starch out of your—"

"Pray excuse me." Regan abruptly rose from her chair, cracking her knee against the leg of the table.

Although she was well aware that nothing had happened between Dare and Mrs. Randall, she was in no mood to listen to the lies he would utter to satisfy her brother's curiosity. The reminder that Dare had been attracted to the widow made her angry enough to clench her teeth.

Regan forced her mouth to relax into a pleasant smile. "I will leave you and Dare to continue your enlightening discussion in private."

Her brother sighed with feigned remorse. "A pity. I hope you are not leaving on my account."

It was apparent to her that Frost wanted her to leave the room. The questions he was bound to ask Dare about his evening were not meant for a lady's ears. What was left of her buoyant spirits evaporated as her thoughts drifted back to the beautiful widow.

"Not at all," Regan said coolly. "Gentlemen."

Frost's turquoise-blue eyes narrowed on Dare as soon as Regan departed from the morning room. "Where, or more to the point, who did you spend your evening with?"

Dare did not even blink as he lied. "No one."

"And what of Mrs. Randall?"

Dare picked up his cup of coffee and sipped. It

had grown cold, but he drank it anyway. "It is unlike you to pry, Frost."

"I have my reasons."

Dare shrugged, deciding that it was safer to stick as close to the truth as possible. "I escorted Mrs. Randall home, but declined her invitation to share a brandy with her."

Something akin to relief flashed across his friend's face. "Then what did you do?"

"Why do you ask?"

"Just answer the question, Dare."

"I returned to the town house, and retired early." In his mind, he saw himself lowering Regan to the floor of the library. The frantic fumbling with buttons and tapes, and the desperate need to bury himself inside her. "Why all the questions?"

"I just came from the Golden Stag."

The Golden Stag was a particularly dangerous gaming hell that attracted the criminal class. Anyone with a hefty purse was welcome, and there were many ways of losing a fortune that had nothing to do with the cards or dice. The unsavory hell was a favorite among daring young noblemen who thought that they were invincible.

Or Frost.

Dare pushed away his cup of coffee. "Tell me that you did not enter that place alone."

Frost grinned at him and picked up a knife. Dare silently conceded that his friend was fully capable of defending himself against cutthroats. "No lectures. I hear enough of them from Sin and Reign. Besides, the hell or the reasons why I was there are not important. I heard some distressing news that may interest you."

Perplexed, Dare braced his hands on his knees and leaned forward. For Frost, rumors and gossip could be as useful as gold. Last year, it was while patronizing the Golden Stag that his friend learned Lord Ravenshaw had planned to marry off his sister to Lord Mackney. The dowry from the marriage would have gone to settle the man's debts.

Reign had not taken the news very well, since he had had his eye on Lady Sophia for some time. Instead of throttling Ravenshaw, their friend stole the lady from under the earl's nose and promptly married her by special license.

"What news?"

"Mrs. Randall is dead."

Chapter Eighteen

The news of Mrs. Randall's death spread through London like a wildfire. Regan had learned of the widow's death when she, Thea, and Nina had called on Sin's wife, Juliana. The marchioness had not been alone in the drawing room. Reign's wife, Sophia, was present with her infant daughter, Lily Grace. The Rainecourts had recently arrived in town to join their friends.

From the window, Regan watched Sin and Reign fence in the Sinclairs' back gardens. Stripped down to their white shirts, both gentlemen were fine specimens of masculinity. Regan would have called Thea and Nina to the window if the gentlemen's wives had not been present. To do so would have been rude.

"I cannot fathom it," Regan said, shaking her head. Like everyone else in town, the women had been discussing the murder. "I saw Mrs. Randall last evening at Lord and Lady Trussell's ball."

Although she carefully omitted that the widow had quit the ballroom with Dare, there had been too many witnesses for that fact to be overlooked for long.

Dare. Was he aware of Mrs. Randall's death?

Regan stilled as she recalled her exchange with her brother that morning. Of course, Frost had known that Mrs. Randall had been murdered. It explained why he had been eager for her to leave the morning room. He had wanted to be the one to break the news to Dare.

"This is a tragedy, indeed," Thea said, her voice quivering with emotion. "No lady is safe in her bed while a murderer prowls London's streets."

"Thea, I do not believe Mrs. Randall was slain in her bed," Nina interjected. "I heard one of the servants say that she was found dead on the floor of the drawing room."

Flustered and annoyed by Nina's correction, Thea shifted on the cushion so she did not have to look at her friend. "Mama said at breakfast that some villain broke into Mrs. Randall's residence in the middle of the night, and throttled the poor woman as she slept."

Nina frowned. "But—"

Sensing that a quarrel was imminent, Juliana tried to ease the tension by saying, "Ladies, please. There is so much idle speculation flying about London that it is difficult to discern rumor from truth. There is no reason to contribute to it by scaring one another."

"You know something about the murder," Sophia said in such a matter-of-fact manner that everyone, including Regan, stared at her.

Juliana grimaced. Cradled in her arms was Reign and Sophia's daughter. The marchioness seemed quite at ease with the babe. It boded well for the future since she herself would be delivering Sin's heir in September. "No more than you, and we can thank our husbands for our ignorance. Sin has already threatened to send me to the country. He is worried about my nerves."

"What nonsense," Regan murmured as she turned back to glare at the overprotective male through the glass. She winced as Reign planted his boot in Sin's stomach.

In deference to Juliana's delicate condition, Regan refrained from mentioning the violence just beyond the terrace.

"I wager, at this point, he is thinking more about his own fragile nerves" was Sophia's dry retort. "Reign was so protective of me during my confinement that I think he would have delivered Lily Grace to spare me the agony."

Regan walked away from the window and joined the women. Since Thea and Nina were seated on the settee opposite Juliana and Sophia, Regan sat down in one of the empty chairs.

"Was Mrs. Randall a close acquaintance, Regan?" Juliana asked, happy to direct the conversation away from the agonies of childbirth.

Regan tugged at the edge of one of her limerick gloves. "No. Our first introduction took place at Lady Harper's literary salon." She delicately cleared her throat. "Was she a good friend of yours?"

Juliana carefully handed Lily Grace back to Sophia when the infant began to fuss. It was then that Regan was struck by the physical similarities of the two women. Side by side, Juliana and Sophia could have passed for cousins. "No. Mrs. Randall was an acquaintance of Lady Harper's."

"Forgive me," Sophia said, signaling for her maid to take the child. "I believe my daughter is hungry."

Once Lily Grace was in the arms of the maid, the countess reached for her walking stick and climbed to her feet. A childhood accident had damaged the countess's eyes, and she needed the walking stick to move about unfamiliar rooms. Her visual limitations were not overtly obvious to the casual observer, and the lady was content to keep it that way. Still, Sophia took no chances when it came to her daughter. With the maid at her side, she left the drawing room.

With the countess's departure, Thea and Nina resumed their speculation on how the murderer had entered the widow's residence undetected. Regan allowed her thoughts to wander back to Dare.

As much as she loathed admitting it, he had an intimate connection to Mrs. Randall. He had escorted Mrs. Randall home the night she had died. Had the lady invited Dare inside? Regan scowled. Of course she had. Worse still, Regan was not the only one who had noticed Dare's interest in the lovely widow. Had it not been Lady Pashley who had predicted at the Trussells' that Mrs. Randall and Dare would become lovers this season if they had not already done so?

Regan bit her lower lip as jealousy rose like bile in her throat. It was ridiculous, she thought. Here she was, resenting the poor woman for catching Dare's eye. She was a horrid, horrid person.

Feeling guilty, she glanced up and started when she noticed Juliana's sympathetic gaze. Was the marchioness aware of Dare and Mrs. Randall's friendship? And if so, what else did she know?

Before Regan could inquire, the woman looked away.

"I have not heard any cursing, so I believe it is

safe," Juliana said cheerfully, rising from the settee. "Shall we check on the gentlemen, ladies?"

Regan, Nina, and Thea stood. Regan deliberately lagged behind the others as she realized that Dare was likely the last person to see Mrs. Randall alive.

Well, Dare, she silently amended, *and the villain who murdered her.*

In another part of town, Dare's brooding thoughts mirrored Regan's. Frost's startling news could not have been any more shocking than Dare's midnight mischief with Regan on the library rug. Thankfully, Frost had not believed that Dare had anything to do with Mrs. Randall's untimely demise. After all, Frost had explained bluntly, if Dare was likely to murder anyone, he would have started with certain members of his irksome family.

Dare could not fault the gent's uncanny logic.

Unfortunately, he was not feeling as confident about his conversation with the magistrate. When two Bow Street Runners arrived at Frost's door, Dare realized that his departure from the Trussells' ball had probably been observed by half of London. The magistrate had informed him when he entered the office that their private interview was merely a formality. It was entirely possible that Dare had been the last person to see Mrs. Randall alive.

Dare snorted. He was not oblivious to the fact that he was a suspect. Oh, the magistrate had been respectful, but his questions had been blunt. Was it not true that Dare left the ball with Mrs. Randall? Did the widow invite Dare inside? Had he entered her residence? Could he explain the intimate nature of his friendship with Mrs. Randall in detail?

He had kept his temper in check. After all, the magistrate and his Runners were only doing their job. They were trying to catch a murderer before he struck again.

Mrs. Randall was dead.

His heart constricted with grief and pity at the thought. Dare still could not grasp that the vibrant, beautiful lady had been murdered.

Perhaps if I had accepted her invitation and had stayed the night . . . ?

No. Regrets were pointless. Dare had made his choice. Although he had not been aware of it at the time, his desire for Mrs. Randall had started to wane the night his gaze had settled on Regan in Lady Karmack's private box.

Mrs. Randall's murder was tragic, and he would do everything in his power to assist the Runners as they hunted for her killer. Everything, that is, but blame himself for the poor woman's death.

The magistrate had thanked him for his cooperation and let him walk out of the office. If the man believed Dare was responsible, he wisely did not voice his suspicions aloud. His father had considerable influence. Charles was proof that officials were willing to look the other way if properly compensated for their blindness.

Dare did not return to the Bishop residence. Unwilling to share his dark thunderous mood with anyone, he had ridden his bay to Hyde Park. The brisk ride should have helped him clear his head and heavy heart, but the unease only increased.

He was not certain why he ended up at his family's town house. He rarely found comfort within these walls. The Mordare family had its own troubles.

When he visited, he faced his brother's animosity, his father's overbearing defense of Charles, his mother's fragile nerves, and Allegra's neediness. It was an exhausting family.

"Uncle Hugh!"

Dare caught his niece in his arms and spun her about. Laughter filled his father's library. Their greeting complete, he stepped back and admired the eleven-year-old girl. "Louise, you look so pretty." He playfully tugged on one of her blond curls. "What do you do with your day when you tire of breaking young noblemen's hearts?"

On a surface, it was difficult not to see the resemblance between Louise and her mother. His niece had inherited Allegra's delicate features and bountiful blond curls. Her blue-gray eyes confirmed her Mordare blood. For a time, he had been tormented by the possibility that Louise was his. Allegra had done nothing to allay his concerns. However, Dare, for once, had taken comfort in his brother's selfishness. Charles would have never married Allegra if he had suspected the unborn child had not been his.

Louise rolled her eyes in exasperation. "Lessons. Why must I study so hard? Botany, geography, Latin and French." She counted off her subjects on her fingers. "Then later, there are dance and music lessons."

He grinned, recalling that Regan had also chafed under the strict decrees of her tutors. "And what does the duchess say when you complain?"

The girl sighed. "Grandmère insists that gentlemen loathe empty-headed chits. She fears I will become a penniless spinster if I do not pay attention to my lessons."

As the granddaughter of the Duke and Duchess

of Rhode, Louise's dowry was secure as long as her father could not gain control of it. "Poor little mouse," Dare murmured sympathetically. He pulled her to his side and kissed the top of her head. "Do not let the duchess frighten you. Between you and me, I think that you are smarter than all of us."

"Inciting mutiny in our household, Dare?" his father said, his low raspy voice laced with amusement.

Dare stiffened subtly at his father's approach. His hand dropped to Louise's slender shoulder. "Not at all. Merely speaking the truth."

The duke beamed at his granddaughter. "Maffy told me that your tutor is searching the upstairs for you, Louise. A clever girl would be discovered with a book in her hand. Eh?" He tapped his cheek.

"Yes, Grandpapa." Louise walked over to his father and dutifully kissed his cheek. She glanced back at Dare and raised her hand. "Farewell, Uncle. Mama will be disappointed that she missed your visit."

Dare just smiled in response and watched until the girl had closed the door before he addressed his father.

"I thought you were watching Charles," Dare said, the warmth fading from his voice.

His father's indignation was not feigned. "What are you spouting about? I have. After this business with his latest mistress, I have expressly ordered him to curtail his night mischief."

"Then Charles is ignoring your dictates. He has been prowling the streets unfettered, Father."

The duke's weathered face reddened in anger. "Not unfettered, damn you," the duke said, walking over to his desk. His pace was measured as if each step caused him pain.

"He visits his clubs daily."

"Nothing wrong with that. A man has a right to his pleasures."

"I am certain that it was not Charles's notion to attend several society balls with Allegra at his side?"

The duke hesitated. "It was your mother's suggestion. She thought the *ton* might forget about your brother's troubles if he appeared content with his wife."

"When has Charles ever been content in his marriage?" Dare countered. "If you recall, you and Allegra's father, Lord Dyton, encouraged the alliance when it was becoming blatantly apparent that your heir cannot keep his bloody cock in his trousers."

"Funny, the same can be said about you, little brother," Charles said from the open doorway.

"It is frightfully exciting!" Nina whispered in Regan's ear as the ladies watched Reign and Sin fence. With only their impressive skills to protect them, both men displayed their lethal grace as they parried and riposted. "What if one of them misjudges his opponent? Blood could be spilled."

Amused, Regan glanced at her friend. She had grown up in the shadow of men and the danger they seemed to crave. "Why, Nina, I had no idea that you were such a bloodthirsty creature."

"Oh, I do not want either one of them to be injured!" the blonde hastily protested. "I just do not understand how Lady Sinclair and Lady Rainecourt can bear it. Their husbands are taking such horrible risks—"

"The risks are part of the appeal," Regan replied, her gaze returning to the two gentlemen. Perhaps it would have been more sensible for the men to have worn plastrons and wire mesh masks. The quilted padding would have at least spared their shirts, she thought, as she studied them with a critical eye.

Reign and Sin bore the marks of their bout. Sin's shirt had been sliced open on his left sleeve and Reign had a bloody graze across his ribs. Their shirts were drenched in perspiration but neither seemed inclined to yield. "Do not fret, Nina. Sin and Reign are evenly matched."

"Besides, both men are aware that they will have to face unhappy wives if they maim each other," Juliana said, not taking her gaze off her husband.

"The foils have been buttoned," Regan explained to Nina and Thea. "It will not spare them from injury, but neither one will perish from their bout."

Sin feinted and delivered the coupé before Reign could parry. In a dastardly move, the marquess swept his leg under his friend. Sophia cried out as Reign landed on his backside. His concentration broken, the earl glanced at his wife. The tip of Sin's foil pressed into Reign's cravat.

"Do you yield?"

Reign cursed under his breath and raised his hands. "Aye."

As the ladies applauded the gentlemen's efforts, Regan stepped forward. "I challenge the victor," she announced, ignoring her friends' stunned expressions.

It seemed unfair for the men to have all the fun.

Chapter Nineteen

Dare felt Charles's casually delivered insult like a blow to his chest, and then he relaxed. For a moment, he thought his brother was referring to Regan. But that was impossible. No one knew about his night with Regan, and Dare intended to keep it that way.

He crossed his arms and leaned against his father's desk. "You speak of ancient history, Charles," Dare said mildly, his gaze following his brother's movements.

Dare refrained from reminding Charles that he was responsible for what had transpired eleven years ago. Allegra would have never come to his bed if his brother had not demanded that she seduce Dare in an attempt to conceal the fact that she was carrying Charles's unborn child in her womb.

"I was not speaking of Allegra, Hugh," his brother said, circling closer as he paced the room.

"Charles . . . Dare . . ." The duke's voice deepened as he foresaw where their discourse would lead them. "What is done, is done."

"Yes, and I believe I have you to thank for that

part, Father," Charles said caustically. "Every day, I get down on my knees and thank God for your staunch principles."

The duke slammed his fist down on the surface of his desk. "Dyton was prepared to put a bullet in your brain for your damn carelessness!" he roared back.

"Bah, I could have done better," Charles sneered. "Everyone knows you fumbled the entire affair. Dyton would have settled if you had offered him more money."

Unimpressed with his brother's posturing, Dare watched their father as his face turned a fascinating purple. He stepped to the right, blocking Charles's course toward the duke. "I think everyone agrees that you emerged relatively unscathed. Dyton was appeased and you were rewarded with a faithful wife and intelligent daughter."

Not to mention numerous bastards throughout the kingdom.

Charles punched Dare in the jaw. He staggered backward several steps before he found his balance. It was so typical of his brother to express his displeasure with his fists. Unlike Regan's, this one stung. "Do not presume to lecture me about my own life!" his brother shouted at him. "I know what I have, and what I have not!"

Dare would have smiled, but the bastard's knuckles had grazed the corner of his mouth. "Oh, yes, I heard about your pregnant mistress. Are you hoping for another son?"

This time when his brother tried to land a punch, Dare went low and knocked Charles off balance with a well-placed kick. Anyone who sparred with Sin or Frost learned a few nasty tricks. Charles stumbled forward and grasped the edge of the desk.

Their father had stepped back, his blue-gray eyes gleaming in anticipation. The duke had always liked to see his sons pummel each other until they were senseless. It was a pity Dare was not in the mood to accommodate him.

"It appears that we will have to continue our discussion another time, Father," Dare said, bowing to his sire. "Do yourself a favor, and muzzle your feral dog before he angers the wrong gent. Or better still, castrate him so he does not go out and humiliate the family again. At this rate, the duchess will be spending the rest of her days in bed."

"Bastard!"

Dare smirked. "No, that is what they call the sons you have managed to produce with every silly maid and whore in England."

Charles roared and threw himself at Dare. They crashed into several chairs, toppling them over as the brothers struggled for the upper hand.

It was just typical day at the Mordare residence.

"Sin, you cannot be serious," Juliana said, her worried gaze switching from her husband to Regan.

When she saw that she could not sway Regan or Sin, she appealed to Reign. Vane and Hunter had arrived minutes earlier, but the marchioness was intelligent enough not waste her breath on them. After all, it was Hunter who had suggested that protective clothing. "Reign, talk some sense into them."

"Regan can wield a foil," Reign said as he positioned the wire mesh mask over her face. "Who do you think taught her?" He glanced pointedly at the marquess.

Juliana gaped in amazement at her husband. "Sin!"

Sin shrugged, giving his wife a sheepish look. "It seemed sensible at the time."

Reign tapped on her mask. "Though I'll wager that you haven't been practicing."

Regan sneered at the earl. "Ha! You would lose that bet." She peered at her cousin through the mask. "Thea, tell Reign about the parasols."

Sin laughed as he secured the canvas bib at her throat. "Tell me that you did not—?"

"Oh, she did," Thea assured him, which caused everyone to laugh.

Regan did not mind. The bit of mischief had been an attempt to provoke Miss Swann into dismissing her from the school. She often wondered if Frost had bribed the woman with a small fortune to compensate for Regan's disobedience.

Nina wiped the tears from her eyes. "Miss Swann could not understand how a dozen parasols were damaged in a single day."

"I thought she would break one over Regan's backside for sure when she figured out who was responsible," Thea added.

Hunter's brow furrowed. "Were you ever mistreated?"

Regan appreciated his concern. "No. Miss Swann tried to hide it, but I think she came to admire my daring."

"I doubt anyone could remain mad at you for long." Vane handed her the foil. The small bell guard fit into her hand as if it had been fashioned for her. "We certainly couldn't."

Sophia leaned heavily against her walking stick. "Sin, you will remember that she is hampered by her skirt, will you not?"

Regan grimaced behind her mask as Sin assured the worried countess that they were merely playing. Irritated by the marquess's assurances, she lunged and would have hit her target if Sin had not twisted his body to avoid contact.

Hunter, Vane, and Reign cheered her aggressive attack. Her skirt and petticoat were indeed a hindrance, so Regan pulled the hem of her dress high enough to reveal her drawers. Although her legs were covered, she was certain her friends were speechless. Thea and Nina did not understand that the Lords of Vice, and now Juliana and Sophia, were family. Besides, the gents had seen more of her during the occasions she had gone swimming with them.

Regan danced backward to avoid Sin's foil. The thirty-six-inch blade was light, but the effort it took to counter her opponent's attacks was tiring. It galled her that Sin was being lenient, and the knowledge spurred her to be relentless.

She was the first to score a point.

Everyone applauded, including Juliana and Sophia.

"You are weakening," Sin taunted, raising his foil to salute her.

She returned his salute. "And you, my friend, smell worse than the docks" was her cool retort.

Vane, in particular, found her insult amusing.

Moving forward and backward along the narrow strip Sin and Reign had defined with stones, Regan was breathing heavily when Sin's buttoned foil struck the middle of her bodice.

"Enough?"

Regan was pleased that Sin was panting, too. Once more to determine the victor.

"Agreed."

They began anew. Blinking away the perspiration that was stinging her eyes, Regan cursed the mask that they had insisted she wear. She clenched her teeth in frustration as Sin struck her blade downward with enough force that the blow rippled up her arm.

She was not strong enough to resist Sin's earnest attacks. When their blades crossed, the marquess pressed. He assumed that he had the upper hand so he was unprepared when she used a small circular motion to disengage. She took advantage of his surprise and aimed for his flank.

"What the devil are you doing?"

Momentarily distracted by Dare's appearance, she turned and Sin's blade struck her on the arm. Though her long sleeves offered a certain amount of protection, the fabric could not spare her from the pain. Regan covered the injury with her hand as her foil tumbled onto the grass.

Somehow Dare was the first to reach her.

"You have the common sense of a flea!" Dare growled at Sin. He removed her wire mesh mask and pulled the strings that tethered the canvas bib to her neck. To Regan, he asked, "How badly hurt are you?"

Sin extended his hand in a helpless gesture. "My apologies, Regan. I had not expected you to suddenly turn—"

"It was an accident," Regan said, feeling rattled and smothered by all the attention. Everyone had crowded around her and was talking at once. "I was careless."

"I could not agree more," Dare said harshly. With his arm protectively around Regan, he glared at his friends. "Whose asinine notion was it to have Regan fence with Sin?" He pointed at Vane. "This sounds like something you would suggest."

Vane had not quite forgiven Dare for tossing him against the wall for kissing Regan. "Oh, really? And how did you deduce that I was the guilty one, Dare?"

Regan heard Reign quietly order his wife and the other women to return to the drawing room. Dare and Vane were going to come to blows if they continued to pound their chests. She grabbed Dare's wrist to get his attention.

"It is not Vane's fault, or anyone else's for that matter." She sagged wearily against his chest. "I was the one who suggested the bout."

Hunter crouched down and retrieved Regan's foil from the grass. "A reasonable request," the duke spoke in her defense. "I recall numerous occasions when Regan honed her fencing skills with Sin."

Dare ignored Hunter. "You?"

Regan tipped her chin up so she could glare at Dare. "Yes, it was my asinine notion, and I might have won if you had not distracted me."

"Me?" His mouth thinned at the realization that he had been responsible for her being hurt.

"She almost had me, Dare," Sin conceded. "As she said, it was just an accident."

Regan nodded. "Besides, it is nothing more than a scratch," she said, praying that she spoke the truth. She peeled away her fingers so she could inspect her injury. "See? It barely cut into the meat."

Dare held her a little tighter. "Christ!"

Hunter squinted at her bloody sleeve. "I will summon the surgeon."

"Yes."

"No," Regan said, countering Dare's assent. "While I appreciate the gesture, none of you would fuss over such a insignificant scratch. It just needs to be cleaned and bound. I doubt it will even leave a scar when it heals."

Dare's body was literally vibrating with bridled fury. Regan was not even aware that she was holding her breath until he announced to everyone, "I will take care of her."

Hunter, Sin, Reign, and Vane all froze and stared at their friend.

Even to Regan, Dare's words sounded terribly like a promise.

Chapter Twenty

Rolling onto his side, Dare pulled the sheet around his waist. Alone in his bed, he conceded that there had been worse days in his life. He thought of the years of beatings Charles had given him when he was a boy. For days, he had hobbled about like a man with the weight of eighty years on his bowed shoulders as he waited for his young body to heal.

Allegra's face also surfaced in the darkness of his bedchamber. He could still recall how she looked at sixteen, achingly beautiful and tragic, as her father, Lord Dyton, dragged her into the front hall of Rooks House, the Duke of Rhode's county seat.

As Allegra sobbed at her father's feet, Lord Dyton had demanded to know which of the Duke of Rhode's sons had impregnated his daughter. Charles immediately accused Dare of the dastardly deed. It was then that he learned that Allegra had given herself to Charles, Dare's rival and lifelong tormenter. Instead of denying the accusation, Dare had foolishly offered to marry Allegra.

His generosity was Allegra's undoing. Inconsolable and almost unintelligible from her broken sobs, she pointed a trembling finger at Charles and claimed that he was the sire of her babe.

Dyton was suspicious, but he was a pragmatic man. Better that his daughter marry the heir of the dukedom than the second son. While his brother howled in outrage at Allegra's duplicity, Dare had stared at the young woman he had loved and saw the ambition in her heart.

Since that awful day, he could tally a thousand more unpleasant days to his life, but nothing compared to standing there helplessly as Sin's blade struck Regan's arm. Dare had wanted to pick up Regan's foil from the grass, snap off the buttoned tip, and stab one of his dearest friends' heart for hurting her.

Christ, I am going mad.

"Dare?"

Hearing Regan's voice only confirmed his suspicions. Dare's eyes snapped open, and he peered at the open doors that led to a small balcony. Unless she had sprouted wings, there was no possible way Regan could be standing on the balcony.

Dare sat up in his bed when Regan stealthily entered the room. "Are you awake?"

"How the devil did you manage this latest mischief?" he demanded, noting that she wore only a flimsy nightgown. The white linen gleamed and fluttered like a flag as she approached the bed.

"I have not done it in a few years, but I climbed up on the railing and jumped to the other balcony."

"You did what?"

"Hush. I am not certain if Frost has returned."

"You must not have been too concerned. May I remind you that your brother's balcony separates us?"

"I knew of no other way to reach yours."

Dare groaned and fell back against his pillows. "A sensible chit would have used the door!"

"Calm down," she whispered. "I heard strange noises and thought Frost had returned. Knocking on your door would have been too brazen, even for me."

His heart twisted in his chest as she grinned down at him.

"Regan . . . Regan, you will be the death of me if you persist." Dare took her hand and pulled her closer until her thighs bumped against the mattress. "What was so important that you risked your foolish neck on this nocturnal adventure?"

"I came to see you," she said simply.

Regan leaned over and kissed him on the mouth. Dare wondered if she was aware that he was naked under the sheet and hard as marble. His cock was poking up like a foot soldier's pike.

She straightened and Dare almost whimpered at the loss of her mouth against his. Wordlessly, Regan reached down and grabbed the bottom of her nightgown.

"Regan," he said helplessly. How was he supposed to resist her?

She pulled the garment over her head and let it drop to the floor.

Without asking, she lifted the sheet that covered him from the waist down. Dare did not stop her. He was curious to see how far Regan would go with her exploration.

His cock jutted from the hair that covered his genitals. Dare moaned as her fingers circled its blunt head. There was no way he could conceal his desire for her.

"I wish I could light a lamp," she murmured almost to herself. "You seem so much larger than the paintings and sculptures that I have admired."

He lightly pinched her nipple. "Are you teasing me, you shameful minx?" Dare raised his hips off the mattress when her hand slid down the shaft of his cock and squeezed. "Or trying to stop my heart?"

"The night we were in the library, everything happened so fast."

Instantly contrite, he felt like a callow youth for his haste. "I know. I rushed things. You deserve better than a quick tupping on the rug."

There had been a fever in his blood that night. A madness that could not be sated with a mere kiss.

"Oh, I was not complaining."

Dare noticed that she had removed the narrow linen bandage he had secured to her upper arm after he had cleaned her bloodied furrow with some of Sin's brandy.

"You should have left the bandage on."

"Do not scold," she said, climbing onto the bed. "My arm is fine, and Frost might have noticed."

On all fours, she dipped her head lower and flicked the tip of her tongue experimentally down the length of his straining cock.

Dare jolted as if a lightning bolt had struck him in the testicles.

Christ!

"Mmm . . . salty," she murmured as her dark hair tickled his stomach.

With each moist stroke, the lady grew bolder. Dare's fingers clawed the sheets as she gently suckled the head of his cock. Her untutored exploration was almost his undoing. He wanted to guide her, push the throbbing flesh deeper and show her how to tease him with her lips and clever tongue until his seed burst out of him.

"No," he said, banishing the erotic vision of his cock plunging rapidly in and out of her mouth from his thoughts. She was a novice to such carnal games. He did not want Regan to be repulsed by his lust. "Ride me."

Her head came up at his husky command. "How?"

Dare slid his hands to her waist and coaxed her to straddle him until the tip of his arousal prodded the curls between her legs. "Take my cock into your body. That's right, sit on me," he said, grinding his teeth as she slowly covered him inch by agonizing inch.

"It is difficult to view you as a chair," she said so prudishly, Dare had to grin.

"Think of me as your faithful horse."

Regan's bravado returned. "Will I have to reward you with carrots?"

"We will reward each other." He cupped her firm buttocks and pulled her down against him. "Now ride, my lady."

At first, Dare's sensual command seemed silly. His manhood was stretching her almost uncomfortably. Locked together as they were, Regan could have happily covered Dare with her body and allowed sleep to claim her. Dare, on the other hand, had something more energetic in mind.

It took Regan several attempts, but she quickly found her rhythm as she moved up and down the length of his arousal. Dare was her anchor in this storm of carnal pleasure. Bracing her palms against his chest, she approached lovemaking like she did most tasks in her life—with joy and vigor.

Dare moaned at the fierce pace she had set.

"Am I hurting you?" she whispered.

"In the most delightful way," he said, his restless hands stroking her everywhere. She arched her back as one of his hands slid down her flat stomach and his thumb found a sensitive spot between her legs. "Do your worst, *mon coeur.*"

Mon coeur. My heart.

Regan loved that endearment best.

Thea was always telling her and Nina that men were rather thickheaded when it came to understanding a lady's heart. Was Dare aware that Regan had offered him her heart long before he had claimed her maidenhead?

Had he tasted that love when he had kissed her five years ago?

The pleasure that had been building suddenly exploded, its fiery trails spinning wildly as they spread out over her body like a shimmering net of starlight. With her heart hammering in her chest, her arms bowed and her head dropped to his damp shoulder.

The feeling was so exquisite, she felt like crying.

Dare murmured something to her but she was too dazed to pay attention. Whatever he said was meant to comfort her, and that was enough.

Regan wearily turned her head and Dare's hard mouth sought hers. His kiss was possessive, an unspoken claim that she willingly embraced.

Blindly, Dare's hands seized her hips, encouraging her to continue the maddening pace that had left her limp and sated. His tongue speared her mouth, mimicking the actions of his manhood. Regan found the comparison strangely arousing.

"Fill me, Dare," she said, and bit his earlobe. "As deep as you can go. Over and over."

Dare seemed to take her words to heart. With a throaty growl that could have been laughter, he managed to flip Regan onto her back with his manhood still buried deep inside her.

He wrapped her legs around his plunging hips. Her thighs were trembling as she squeezed him. Dare rewarded her by biting her right breast. Regan's eyes flared open at the stinging pain.

"You have marked me!" she exclaimed.

Dare gave her another hard kiss. "Lest you forget that you are *mine*."

His declaration pushed her over the pinnacle that she had not been aware existed. Regan threw her head back against the pillows and cried out. Dare clamped his hand over her mouth to muffle her sounds of pleasure. It took only a few bone-jarring strokes, and he collapsed on top of her, his considerable weight burying her into the mattress and bedding. As Regan stroked his back, she felt the subtle pulls of his manhood and the viscous warmth of his seed filling her womb.

Too sated to fight the weariness in her limbs, Regan closed her eyes and drifted off to sleep.

Regan fell asleep.

Dare could not decide if he was flattered or insulted. He took pride in his skills as a lover, but he had never left a woman so depleted that she fell asleep with his cock buried deeply inside her snug sheath.

He was still hard.

Dare wondered if his body would ever be sated. Regan's proximity was hell on his hard-won control over his carnal appetites.

Her eyelids fluttered open when he tried to withdraw from her. "No, not yet," she mumbled sleepily. "I like the feel of you inside me."

Dare caressed her cheek. "How can you sleep when I am smothering you?"

"Not sleeping . . . just resting with my eyes closed," Regan assured him as she snuggled up to his hand. She reminded him of a well-fed kitten.

Ignoring her faint protests, he compromised by rolling them both on their sides, leaving his cock nestled inside her. Regan inched closer as her left leg lazily slid up and down his leg.

His breath caught in his throat as he stared into her face. Lying in bed with a lover after the lust had receded was a new experience for him. He had shied away from tenderness, because it was a path that led to love and commitment. The only person he had given tenderness was the woman in his arms. The risk had appeared minimal because Regan had been a child. Dare had never dwelled on the fact that one day, the child would grow into a woman.

He smoothed the damp strands of hair from her face. "You are so beautiful." In the shadowed interior of the bedchamber, her pale skin gleamed.

"Did you hit your head on one of the bedposts,"

she teased, her hand automatically touching her mussed tresses. "No lady is beautiful when she feels this damp and sticky."

Dare flexed deep inside her to get Regan's attention. He claimed her swollen mouth, drinking in her gasp. Dare did not release her until they were both breathless. "She is to the gent who is responsible for her disheveled condition."

"Oh."

She blinked rapidly, and Dare tensed, bracing for her tears. Regan quickly recovered and smiled at him. "Before I return to my bedchamber, do you want to dishevel me again?"

Regan giggled as Dare grabbed the sheet and pulled it over their heads. He had a few hours to demonstrate how wicked he could be with her between the sheets.

Chapter Twenty-one

With Dare watching for any sign of life coming from Frost's bedchamber, Regan slipped into hers and swiftly dressed. When she emerged, they stealthily made their way down to the kitchen hand in hand.

Both of them were ravenous. This time for food.

Sitting on the kitchen floorboards with a lighted candle between them, Regan and Dare supped on cold lobster pie, thick buttered slices of bread, Cheshire cheese, and apple compote.

When they spoke, it was rarely above a whisper because they did not want to rouse any of the servants. Dare presented Regan with a fork laden with lobster pie. It was a novel experience to have a gentleman feed her. Leaning forward, her lips parted so she could accept his offering.

"You are not climbing the balconies again," Dare said, stabbing a lobster morsel for himself. "I will not tolerate it."

Regan's eyes narrowed as she was chewed and swallowed the food in her mouth. "Very clever of you to stuff my mouth before you lectured me on my conduct."

"Be reasonable, Regan. You could have slipped and broken your neck." He waved the fork to emphasize his point. "What if Frost had opened the doors to his balcony and caught you leaping about like an acrobat?"

Regan brushed the crumbs from her fingers. "My brother did not discover me, so what I would have said or done is moot." She selected a slice of cheese, broke it, and offered him half. "Stop worrying about Frost."

His fingers covered hers. "I still have not gained your oath that you will never traverse the balconies in that manner again."

She tilted her head to the side, mildly curious to see how far she could push him. "And what will you do if I do not give it?"

Dare's blue-gray eyes gleamed with something akin to anticipation. "I will drag you into my bed and fuck you until you are so weak, you will be incapable of denying me anything."

Regan shivered at the thought of his hands and mouth on her body again. "You are supposed to be discouraging me, my lord."

He took the cheese from her hand and popped it in his mouth. "Your promise, Regan."

She shrugged. "Very well. You have it. No more acrobatics."

Dare nodded, apparently satisfied that she would keep her promise. "How is your arm?"

Regan glanced down at her bare arm. "Fine. I had forgotten about it till now." When he reached over for one of the buttered slices of bread, she noticed the shadow of a bruise along his jaw. "Earlier, at Sin's house, you looked like you had been brawling with someone."

"Charles."

Had Lady Pashley summoned her brother-in-law once again? "Why did your brother punch you?"

"Who said he needed a reason," he replied, rubbing his jaw. "He also tried to break a chair over my head."

Regan was infuriated on his behalf. "And what did you do?"

"Return the favor," he said nonchalantly.

She crossed her arms. "I do not believe this. Where were your mother and father while your brother did his best to murder you?"

And where was Lady Pashley? Regan silently asked. Had she been the one to provoke the fight?

"I do not know where my mother was. I had come to speak to my father about Charles and—" He glanced down at his hands, reluctant to continue.

"And?"

He picked up the glass of wine that they had been sharing. "I suppose you have heard the news about Mrs. Randall."

It was Regan's turn to glance away. "Yes. I heard the tragic news when I called on Juliana and Sin." She stared sadly at the dishes about them, realizing that her appetite had fled. "Is your connection to Mrs. Randall causing some concern?"

Dare put down the glass of wine. "My connection?"

"You were seen speaking to her at the Trussells' ball."

"Not exactly a crime."

"You told me that you had escorted Mrs. Randall home that evening. There was some speculation that you and the widow were lovers."

"Damn. I had wondered why you were so upset about Mrs. Randall. Who told you that we were lovers?"

"Well, Mrs. Randall told me—"

Dare was taken aback by her admission. "You spoke to the widow about me?"

Regan wrinkled her nose. "At Lady Harper's literary salon, Mrs. Randall confided that a certain gentleman had caught her interest. I did not know that she was referring to you until I saw you approach her at Lord and Lady Trussell's ball. Lady Pashley seemed to think that if you were not already Mrs. Randall's lover, you planned to be soon."

Dare muttered something unintelligible under his breath. He bent his knee and casually braced his arms against it. "I told you the truth that night in the library. I escorted Mrs. Randall home. Nothing more. Allegra lied. Mrs. Randall and I were never lovers."

But you desired her, Regan wanted to say, but she held her tongue. Her jealousy seemed petty since the poor woman was dead.

Dare pushed aside the various dishes that separated them, so he could crawl to her side. Sitting on his knees, he pulled her into his arms. "Listen to me, Regan Alice. Before your arrival, I will admit that I had contemplated an intimate liaison with the widow."

He tipped her chin up with his fingers when she

lowered her head. "Then I saw you at the theater, and suddenly all my thoughts wended their way back to you. I told myself a dozen times that it was wrong. Still, I thought I might go mad if I could not have you in my bed."

Desire flared to life between them. Her body responded to the intent that she read the intent in his eyes. Regan's eyelashes fluttered downward as she leaned in for a kiss.

"Not here," she whispered. "Anyone might stumble across us."

"Indeed," Frost said, his palms planted firmly on the long wooden table behind them.

Regan and Dare sprang apart, but the damage was done.

Frost stared down at his friend with cold amusement. "If you wish to deflower my sister, Dare, might I suggest something more discreet like the library or better still, your bedchamber. Then again, a clever gent like you has already figured out how to take what you want."

"Dear sister, now that you have enjoyed your repast, I would suggest that you return to your bedchamber," Frost said mildly.

Dare helped Regan to her feet. "No."

"Utterly charming," Frost said to Dare. "You seduce my sister, and I am the villain for wanting to protect her."

On the surface, his friend did not seem particularly violent. Still dressed in his evening clothes, Frost had been home long enough to remove his frock coat and untie his cravat. His hands were empty, but that did not mean that the earl was not fully capable of using his fists to express his displeasure.

"This is not what is seems," Regan began.

Dare winced. Frost was an expert at seduction. There was no lie she could utter that he would believe. "Yes, it is."

Regan gaped at him as if he were crazy.

"How did you know?"

"About the library?" Frost pushed off from the table and approached them. "There were two glasses of unfinished brandy on the desk. One of the servants reported that he heard odd noises coming from within. It was not difficult to deduce what might have occurred in my absence."

"And my bedchamber?"

Frost tapped his earlobe. "I have excellent hearing, and, oh, by the by, your bed squeaks."

Both gentlemen ignored the soft choking sound coming from Regan.

"A few weeks ago, I had assumed that the charming Mrs. Randall had coaxed you away from your self-imposed celibacy." He glanced down at Regan, who had begun picking up the dishes and candlestick that littered the floor. "One might have thought our Dare had the makings of a monk until the widow began flirting with him."

If his friend persisted, Regan was likely to think that Dare had lied about his connection to Mrs. Randall. "Can we not leave your sister out of this?"

Regan screamed and scrambled backward as Frost lunged for Dare and seized him by the front of his shirt. "You involved my sister the second you took her maidenhead."

"It wasn't his fault, Frost," Regan said, her voice laced with desperation.

Her brother glanced over his shoulder at her. Regan looked very much as if she had been thoroughly ravished. Her long black hair was tousled, her lips red from Dare's kisses, and she had not bothered with a corset. "Was it not? I asked Dare to look after you on my behalf. Not fuck you senseless."

Regan cringed at her brother's crudeness.

"Do you want an apology, Frost?" Dare demanded. "You have it. I should have never touched her. If you wanted to issue a formal challenge, I will accept. I deserve a bullet for what I have done."

Frost bared his clenched teeth at Dare. "Why could you not keep your bloody cock in your trousers?"

"I seduced him," Regan said quietly.

Dare and Frost glanced at her.

She brought her hand to her heart. "I am the one who is responsible. I planned to seduce Dare even before I had returned to London."

"Regan." Dare realized that she was willing to toss aside her pride if it would keep Frost from harming him.

Regan wrapped her arms across her breasts. "I wrote my goals in my diary. I can show you, if you like."

Frost released Dare. "Childish games. All girls play them."

Regan lifted her shoulder. "Perhaps. It still does not negate that I did everything I could to tempt him."

"Do not listen to her," Dare murmured. "She will say anything to keep us from fighting." He did not need to hide behind Regan's skirts. Her lack of faith in him was starting to annoy him.

"I see. So when is the wedding?" Frost asked.

Regan shot Dare a wary glance. "Well, I-I . . ."

Frost grinned evilly at Dare. "And what say you, my friend? Now that you have sampled marital bliss in the arms of my sister, are you prepared to give her your name?"

Knowing where this was heading, Dare's face hardened.

"Dare?" Regan asked, confusion and hurt creeping into her voice.

"His silence should make his intentions clear enough for you, dear sister." Frost placed his hands on Regan's shoulders. His expression was not unkind when he explained, "Dare will never marry you."

Her gaze sought out and locked onto his. "Is this true?"

He could not shake the feeling of being hunted. "You have met my family," Dare said harshly, cursing Frost for putting him into the position of hurting Regan. "I have nothing to offer you, or any woman."

Regan's dark blue eyes had a glassy cast as she fought back her tears. "I see."

Dare was half tempted to knock out Frost just so he would have a few minutes of privacy to speak with Regan. He was certain that he could make her understand why marriage was not something he contemplated.

Regan stepped away from her brother's embrace. Knowing her, she was probably unhappy with both of them. "Thank you for your honesty, Dare," she said, her face expressionless and pale. "Now, if you will excuse me, I believe I will retire."

Dare knew he was in the wrong. His hands clenched impotently at his sides as he watched Regan leave the room. "You son of a bitch. Was that necessary?"

Frost picked up Regan's untouched wine and brought it to his lips. "Yes. My sister fancies herself in love with you, Dare. A clean, sharp thrust is kinder all around since we both know you would never allow yourself to yield again to the maddening sentiment." He sipped the wine.

"How can you be so certain?" Dare demanded belligerently.

His friend glanced away from the empty doorway, and Dare felt uncomfortable scrutiny of those knowing turquoise-blue eyes. "You and I are more alike than we care to admit."

Dare brushed by his friend. "Go to hell, Frost."

"Oh, one more thing," Frost said, halting Dare's departure. "You might find the limited accommodations at Nox more to your liking."

Dare nodded brusquely. "I will leave immediately."

"Trust me, it is for the best. I would regret putting a bullet in you, Dare, really I would. However, if you touch my sister again, I will overcome my distaste for the task."

Regan lifted her tearstained face when she heard the soft knock at the door. She knew the man on the other side was not Dare. From the window, she had observed his departure from the residence. If he had sensed her presence, he had resisted the urge to glance up and offer a silent farewell.

The door to her bedchamber opened and closed. Regan counted her brother's confident footfalls as he strode toward her bed.

"I thought you might be awake."

He crouched down at her feet so she was forced to look at him. Regan stared, unmoved by the regret she saw in his eyes. Frost possessed the almost otherworldly masculine beauty of a fallen angel. This evening was proof that he had the devil in him.

"Have you come to gloat?" Regan brought the handkerchief to her damp cheek. "Congratulate me for making a fool of myself over Dare?"

Frost took her hand. "Dare sends his apologies, but he thought it best that he take up residence at Nox until he can find better accommodations."

"No, *you* thought it best." Regan sniffed. "Please, do not bother lying. Besides, it no longer matters. Dare is gone."

Her brother sighed. "Your pain matters to me."

Regan flinched when Frost unexpectedly seized her elbow and scowled at her upper arm. "You have been wounded. Why did you not tell me? How did this happen?"

It was uncharacteristic for her brother to fuss over an inconsequential scratch. Regan sighed. "Are you terribly disappointed in me?"

"Am I—?" Comprehension bled into his handsome face. Frost shook his head. "No, love, one youthful indiscretion has not turned you into our mother. I just wish that I had trusted Dare less, and paid closer attention. I thought his brief infatuation for you had faded when he started sniffing after the pretty widow."

Mrs. Randall.

"So you did send me away because Dare kissed me!" she said, sounding indignant. "I *knew* I had been banished for that blasted kiss."

"In part," Frost admitted. "The day I had discovered you in Dare's arms, Lady Karmack had been blistering my ears over my negligence with regard to you. She was concerned that you would end up a—"

"A courtesan," Regan finished. "Lady Karmack voiced her concerns on numerous occasions. She feared that I would succumb to my wicked nature."

The viscountess had been correct, after all.

"Or marry one of the Lords of Vice." Frost retrieved a clean handkerchief from his waistcoat. Her brother despised a lady's tears. He had often claimed that they were a cunning weapon to manipulate hapless fools. Regan remained motionless as Frost tenderly wiped away the evidence of her grief.

A surge of frustration washed through her at the outrageous suggestion that she had been nudging Dare toward marriage. She pounded her fist against her upper thigh. "I was not trying to trick Dare into marrying me."

"Of course not."

"I do not see you proposing marriage to every lady you tumble." Regan jabbed her finger in her brother's face. "And do not presume to tell me that different rules apply to gentlemen."

Frost chuckled at her displeasure. He reached out, pulled her into his lap, and cuddled her as if she were a child. "But darling, they do, and you are too intelligent to dally with a gent who will only break your heart."

"Are you telling me that Dare is incapable of love? Of marriage?"

"No," Frost said in measured tones. "I am telling you that his heart belongs to the one woman who will never be his. Marrying Dare would be disastrous."

Chapter Twenty-two

A less optimistic man might have declared the night a complete disaster. The fact that he had exited Frost's town house unscathed warranted a small amount of rejoicing.

He supposed he had Regan to thank for his good health. If the lady had demanded his head, Frost would have gladly fetched his sword.

Dare braced his boot against the empty bench and tried to get comfortable as the coachman drove him to Nox. Despite the late hour, the lower club rooms would be filled and perhaps the private rooms as well. He was not concerned about finding a bed. Berus would prepare a room for him. If Dare desired, the steward could procure one of Madame Venna's girls to soothe his bruised pride, and to provide a distraction for the remaining hours of the night.

Dare intended to climb into bed alone. He did not want another woman, not when his body still ached from the hours he had dallied with Regan in his bed. The intoxicating musk of their lovemaking lingered on his skin and in his nostrils. Just as he had marked her delicate flesh, she had returned the favor. His left shoulder bore evidence of her sharp teeth, and his back was crisscrossed with long scratches made by her fingernails, the result of several powerful releases Dare had managed to wring from her body.

No, another female would not do. Nor did he want to sully the memory of his time with Regan. This evening, she had come to his bedchamber needing him as much as he needed her.

Not enough to marry her, his mind whispered, adding to his guilt.

Frost was within his rights to toss his arse out of the town house.

Had Regan been willing to risk her reputation to get him to come up to scratch? She had told Frost that she had intended to seduce Dare, and had written her goals in a damn diary. Had she been telling the truth, or had she lied to protect him from her brother's wrath?

Dare ordered the coachman to halt as he recognized his surroundings. Nox was not far, and there was enough activity on the streets that he was not worried about footpads. He left his belongings in the coach. Berus would send someone to collect them later. The coachman gave him a wave of farewell, and Dare continued down the dimly lit street toward the club.

He had almost reached the property when someone tackled him from behind. Dare's gloved palms took the brunt of the impact as he fell on all fours. An unseen boot stomped his lower back, forcing him flat on the dirt and gravel.

"Watch him!"

The gruff warning came too late. Dare rolled over

and kicked out at his unknown assailants. He grunted with satisfaction as the bottom of his boot connected with the soft belly of one of his attackers. The man staggered backward and gagged. There were three of them, Dare counted as his leg swept under the tallest member of the trio. He reached down to pull the man up.

These ruffians had chosen the wrong gentleman to rob. Dare punched the man in the face. He pulled his elbow back to deliver another punishing blow.

" 'It 'im, Willy," the stout gent with the soft belly shouted.

Dare turned to address the third man, but he was not quick enough. He saw stars as the blunt wooden club struck him just behind his left ear. Dare dropped his quarry and fell to his knees. He shook his head to fight off a wave of dizziness. If he lost consciousness, his attackers might slit his throat and leave him for the watch to find.

He was roughly grabbed from behind, his arms pinned at his back. Dare used the back of his head to connect with his captor's chin. The man howled in pain but did not release him.

"Quit dawdling and get down to business," the one holding Dare hissed. "Ye 'ave friends who want to send ye a message."

The shadowy stout figure approached him with something in his hand. "Hold him tight, Briggs," the man said, swinging his wooden club forcefully into Dare's gut three times in rapid succession.

A low sound of pain burst from his lips along with most of the air in his lungs. He would have collapsed if the man behind him had not held him up.

"Again. Just in case our man's ears are stuffed

with dirt." The man holding Dare gave his pinned arms a vicious twist.

Dare bared his teeth and braced for the pain. He groaned as the wooden club struck him in the groin, and again in the thigh. His eyes watered as the pain shot up and down his spine.

The tall brute grabbed Dare by his hair and yanked hard to get his attention. "And this one is from me." The man's fist felt like a hammer as it smashed into Dare's jaw.

He felt as if his eyeballs were bouncing within his skull like dice. Dare struggled as he watched the stout man pull out a knife. With a sudden burst of strength, he threw himself backward, using his captor as a fulcrum, and kicked both men hard enough to send them sprawling. The man holding him could not manage the extra weight. Dare landed hard on his arse. Crawling forward, he seized the wooden club and brought the weapon down on the stout man's kneecap.

The footman screamed and clutched his wounded leg.

"Not so tough are you . . . when the odds aren't in your favor," Dare said, his breath coming out in short puffs. He spat the blood from his mouth. "I usually try to refrain . . . from violence. For you gents, I'll make an exception."

"Run!" the man at his back shouted before he disappeared into the night.

The other two scrambled to their feet and ran off in opposite directions. The need to avenge himself clawed at his chest. However, Dare was in no condition to fight anyone. With his hand splayed over his stomach, he limped toward Nox.

* * *

"I refuse to believe Frost sent those ruffians after you."

Dare opened one eye and looked at Vane. He was pacing at the end of the bed. His unexpected arrival and battered appearance had caused quite a stir at the club. Shouting orders, Berus and a footman half carried Dare up the stairs and placed him in a bed. Hunter had dashed off to wake up a surgeon while Vane and Saint had searched the area for the three men who had attacked him.

"I did not say that Frost was responsible," Dare mumbled, almost too weary to speak. "Just that he was furious enough to do it."

No one had asked him why Frost was furious with him, which made him wonder if his friends had noticed his growing fascination with Regan.

The surgeon had inspected his injuries and proclaimed to the relief of everyone that nothing had been broken. Dare was going to be sporting some very colorful bruises for a few weeks, which was nothing unusual as far as he was concerned. The surgeon had given him some laudanum for the discomfort, and ordered several days of bed rest.

"Nah," Hunter drawled from one of the chairs in the bedchamber. "If Frost wanted to see you hurt, he would have delivered the message himself."

"I agree." Dare glanced up at the steward, who was hovering nearby. "Berus . . . my apologies for keeping you from your duties."

The steward leaned over and tucked the sheet into the bed. "No need to apologize, Lord Hugh. It has always been my pleasure to look after the Lords of Vice. I just wish we could have caught those ruffians."

Dare silently concurred. Trouble at Nox usually started in the gaming hell, not outside it. "This was not a random robbery. Someone ordered them to watch the club."

Saint stirred from his slouched stance against the wall. "Perhaps it was a message to any member of Nox? Someone angry with the Lords of Vice?"

Vane snorted. "The list would be endless."

"Did one of the ruffians call you by name?"

"No." Dare winced as he tried to sit high on the small mountain of pillows Berus had provided. "They just delivered their message."

"You might not have been their intended quarry," Hunter mused aloud. "Saint, I heard that you and Lord Turley almost came to blows the other night."

"It wasn't Turley," Saint said flatly.

Vane's brows lifted as his curiosity got the better of him. "How can you be so certain? After all, you and Lord Turley share a mutual interest in—"

"Do not bore us with your ignorance, Vane," Saint said, talking over the earl. "I may not like the man, but I can assure you that Turley had nothing to do with this ambush."

"How do you know?" Vane persisted.

Saint sighed. "Because Turley is quite aware that we would retaliate, and it would not end well for him. It isn't Turley."

"There is another possibility," Dare interjected before Vane could ask another question. "I was the man those hired ruffians were waiting to ambush."

Hunter leaned forward in the chair. "Who else have you annoyed lately?"

"My brother."

Chapter Twenty-three

"This is some sort of jest, is it not?"

It had taken Regan four days to summon the courage to visit Dare while he resided at Nox. Four agonizing days. Now that she was standing at the front door of the club, Berus was telling her that she was not permitted to enter.

"Berus, I have spent half of my life playing in the rooms within the club. How can you stand there and tell me that I am not welcome?" Her lips quivered with hurt, which was a nice touch to gain pity. Unfortunately, her disappointment was not feigned. She was hurt.

"Pray forgive me, Lady Regan," the steward said, his gaze sympathetic. "I have my orders."

Regan's chin came up as outrage coursed through her body. "Did Frost tell you to keep me out?"

"Lord Chillingsworth felt these steps were necessary for your protection. You are no longer a child, and if word gets out that you are a regular visitor at a notorious gentlemen's club, your reputation may suffer for it."

She had seen Frost at breakfast. He had not

seemed overly concerned when she had told him of her plans to go shopping in the afternoon. Probably because he already knew that she would not be able to sneak away to see Dare.

The cunning fiend!

"Lord Chillingsworth was not thinking of my reputation when he issued his imperial order," Regan said, seething that her brother had been one step ahead of her all along. "What of the other members? Did they agree with my brother's decree?"

"I do not know, Lady Regan." Berus had positioned himself so that Regan could not see into the front hall. "He was alone when he gave me his instructions."

Blast, there had to be a way around her clever brother. "Is my brother inside?"

"No, milady," Berus replied so swiftly, Regan knew he spoke the truth. "Pardon me for saying so, but I do not think you will persuade Lord Chillingsworth to rescind his order."

Well, he was not the only founding member of Nox. "What of the others? Are any of them upstairs?"

Loyal to his employers, Berus's expression grew less genial. "I see where you are going with this, Lady Regan, and I would not recommend pitting your brother against the other members."

Regan tried to appear contrite. "Forgive me, Berus. You must think I am a terrible person."

The suspicion in his visage did not fade. "Not at all, milady."

Regan glanced back at the coach waiting for her. "If you want to know the truth, it is Lord Hugh that I wish to see. The last time that I saw him, harsh words were exchanged and he was asked to leave our town house. I feel so badly about the discord between him and Frost, so I have come to apologize."

There. She had spoken the truth. How could Berus refuse such a heartfelt plea?

"Lord Hugh is not in residence at this time."

"Where is he?" When the steward hesitated, Regan pressed on. "My brother instructed you not to allow me entry into Nox. He did not order you not to discuss the other members' whereabouts."

"I see your point," Berus said, nodding thoughtfully. "Lord Hugh can be found at the Duke of Rhode's town house."

Regan was astounded by the news. "I cannot believe Dare would take up residence in that household."

"Forgive me for not being clearer." The steward glanced over to his shoulder to make certain no one was behind him. When he was satisfied that they were alone, he said, "Lord Hugh was summoned to the town house early this morning. From what I could gather, there was some sort of family crisis. He has yet to return."

There always seemed to be some sort of crisis in that family. Small wonder that Dare shunned the notion of marriage. His honor kept him shackled to his demanding family.

"Thank you, Berus," she said, turning away. She paused midstep. "Oh, one more thing. Who sent the messenger?"

"I believe it was Lady Pashley."

Regan recalled her brother's words the night he had asked Dare to leave.

His heart belongs to the one woman who will never be his.

She nodded to Berus and headed back to her waiting coach. Perhaps it was not honor and duty that tied Dare to his difficult family, but rather the undying love that burned in his heart for the woman who had married his brother.

"I will wait in the drawing room."

Maffy hurried after Dare. "Lord Hugh, Lady Pashley was quite insistent that you join her in her private sitting room."

Dare slowed once he reached the staircase. After four days, his body was healing nicely, but his abdomen was still tender. If not for the colorful bruise on his jaw, no one would know that he had been in a fight. "I am certain that she was, Maffy. However, you may tell my sister-in-law that I am not in the mood for her games."

"It isn't a game, milord."

Dare halted and stared at the butler.

Maffy leaned closer and whispered. "It is not my place to speak on Lady Pashley's behalf. Nevertheless, there are reasons for her unusual request. Even the family is not aware of her circumstances. When the maid tried to bring her a tray this morning, the marchioness refused to unlock her door. I tried to coax her to open the door, and that was when she begged me to get a message to you. Lady Pashley would not ask this of you if it were not important."

The hell she wouldn't, Dare thought.

"Fine," he said brusquely. "Lead the way."

Dare was mildly perspiring by the time he reached Allegra's bedchamber, but he had climbed the stairs without assistance so he considered it a triumph of sorts.

Maffy knocked softly on Lady Pashley's door. "Madam, Lord Hugh has arrived."

There was a muffled noise on the other side of the door. "Only Hugh can enter," she instructed before she unlocked the door.

"If you need me, I will be downstairs, milord."

Dare waited until the butler had disappeared around the corner before he opened the door to his sister-in-law's bedchamber.

"Allegra?"

No one had opened the curtains. The air seemed stale, and the dim interior was far from welcoming.

"I am in the sitting room," Allegra announced from the other room. "Pray, close and lock the door before you approach."

Dare obeyed her request and tucked the key in his waistcoat. If Allegra was playing games with him, he wanted the means to his escape close at hand.

"Maffy said that you refused your breakfast tray." Dare glanced at the bed, noting that the bedcovering appeared undisturbed. He could not imagine that Allegra had straightened the bedding herself. "Why are you sitting in the dark?"

Allegra was seated at her dressing table. Instead of her nightgown or morning dress, she was wearing an evening dress.

"Open the curtains if you must," she said wearily.

Dare strode to the nearest window and flung the draperies aside. He turned around at a soft sound of protest. "Dear God," he exclaimed as saw Allegra's face.

Allegra brought a hand up to her cheek. "Now you understand why I do not want anyone to see me like this."

Dare abandoned the window and walked over to the dressing table. Not quite healthy himself, he used the edge of the table to get down on his knees. "Let me see," he said, gentling his voice. He peeled back the hand that concealed her swollen right eye. There were marks at her neck and down her arms. "What happened?"

He thought of the widow, Mrs. Randall. Someone had entered her house and throttled the poor woman to death. Had a stranger slipped unnoticed into the house?

Tears flowed freely from the corner of her eyes. "It was Charles. Last evening, he came to me, and we had a dreadful row. He blames me for not bearing him an heir, and I foolishly suggested that his mistress might give him the son that he craves." She retrieved her crumpled handkerchief from the table and dabbed her eyes. "That is when he struck me. I fell to the floor, and suddenly he was on top of me. His hands were around my neck, and I was certain— Oh, Hugh, I think he meant kill me."

Coldness washed over Dare. "What happened next?"

"Your father. He heard the commotion and came downstairs to investigate. The library door was locked, but he could hear Charles shouting at me so he started pounding on the door. It is what frightened him off."

Dare stood. His father had defended Charles's violent behavior for years. His friends were convinced that his brother had hired those ruffians to attack him, and now Allegra was a victim of his abuse. Was the duke prepared to accept that his heir needed to be locked up before he actually succeeded in murdering someone?

"Where is Charles?"

Allegra rose from her seat. "He ran off. No one has seen him."

"And my father?"

"His Grace ordered a coach, and has been searching for Charles ever since."

Allegra threw her arms around his waist and laid her cheek against his chest. Dare hesitated, and then he wrapped his arms around her. The woman in his arms had been through a hellish ordeal. All she wanted was some comfort.

"Despite everything, you have always been a good friend to me," she murmured against his chest. "I do not know what I would do if you had not come."

"You're family," he said gruffly. "I will always be there for you and Louise."

Allegra pulled away and stared up at him. His jaw tightened at the sight of her swollen eye. "Does Mother or Louise know what happened?"

She grimaced. "No. Before he left, your father told me to go to my room and not speak of it."

His father's orders enraged Dare as much as his brother's attack on Allegra. He would wager that the duke was attempting to fix the damage Charles had wreaked.

Dare placed his hands on Allegra's shoulders. "Let me speak with Maffy. He can tell the family that you have taken ill, and will be receiving all your meals in your room."

"Thank you, Hugh."

Allegra slowly rolled onto her tiptoes and kissed him on the mouth. Dare did not pull away. He had expected the feel of her lips against his to summon memories of the past when they had been sixteen, and he believed that she was the only woman for him.

The sweetness of what they had shared had turned to bitter ash long ago. There was a question in Allegra's lopsided gaze when she stepped away.

"Do you ever wonder?" she said wistfully.

Dare shook his head. "Never." He dug into his waistcoat pocket and pulled out the key. "I will send Maffy to you, and then I plan on tracking down my father."

"Hugh?"

He glanced over his shoulder when he had reached the door.

"I do . . . wonder, that is." She wrapped her arms around herself. "Maybe it is because I live with the regret that eleven years ago, when my father demanded to know the name of my unborn child's sire, I did not surrender *your* name."

Chapter Twenty-four

Regan did not return to the town house. She had told her brother that she was spending the afternoon shopping, and it would have looked suspicious if she had returned without making a few purchases.

What's more, she was vexed enough to beggar Frost for his latest high-handedness.

She had stopped by Lady Karmack's town house in the hope that Nina and Thea might join her, but her groom was informed that the ladies of the house were not at home. Regan did not fare any better at Sin's residence. Lady Sinclair was not receiving callers. Undeterred, Regan ordered the coachman to take her to Bond Street. It was an excellent place to begin her shopping

Four hours later, Regan was rather pleased with her efforts. A visit to one of the local milliners yielded half a dozen caps, three straw hats, and four bonnets. She found parasols and reticules in Widegate Street, shoes and dancing slippers in Lower Holborn, and hosiery and gloves in Birmingham. The delightful French dressmaker in Upper King Street assured Regan that the seven dresses she had ordered would be ready in a week.

While her groom and coachman tied down her purchases, Regan perused the nearby bookseller that also ran a circulating library. She hoped to find a romantic tale or two that might lift her flagging spirits. Throughout the entire afternoon, it had been very difficult not to imagine Dare and Lady Pashley together. Had there been a family crisis, or was that merely an excuse to conduct their secret tryst?

The afternoon Regan had joined Dare at his family's town house, he had seemed reluctant to engage his sister-in-law even on the most civil level. Later, he had warned Regan to stay away from the marchioness.

Perhaps his animosity toward Lady Pashley had been feigned. After all, the lady was married to his older brother. Discretion, patience, and cunning were crucial when conducting an illicit affair. Regan knew personally that Dare was extremely resourceful when properly motivated.

Was that why Dare had been looking for a mistress this season?

With another lady in his bed, no one would suspect that Dare and his precious Allegra were still lovers. "Ugh," Regan muttered under her breath. What had she ever seen in such a scoundrel?

Disgusted with the entire affair, Regan paid for her books and exited the bookseller's shop. She nodded to a gentleman who tipped his hat to her and allowed her to cross in front of him onto the sidewalk. In the late afternoon, the streets were heavily congested with pedestrians, costers peddling their wares in wheelbarrows, barrel-laden wagons, gentlemen on horseback, and fashionable coaches.

Regan tried to stop to get her bearings, but the steady flow of pedestrians moving in both directions could not be stemmed. She clutched her books to her breast and continued forward, her gaze sweeping the street for her coach. *Was the coachman obliged to drive on?* she wondered, ignoring the tiny frisson of panic in her spine.

She moved to the outer edge of the sidewalk and peered ahead. A sigh of relief escaped her lips as she recognized the Chillingsworth crest. The coachman saw her and waved.

As Regan shifted the books in her arms so she could return the man's wave, something struck her in the back and she went flying into the busy street.

The air was filled with masculine exclamations, curses, and ladies' cries of dismay as she landed inelegantly face-first into the filthy street. Regan grimaced, then used her palms to push herself onto her hands and knees and glanced behind her. All she saw was a sea of concerned faces. Who the devil had shoved her? Belatedly she recalled her books. They were scattered several feet in front of her. She reached for the closest one, but hastily snatched her hand back as horses and the wheels of a coal cart trampled over it. The bearded driver of the cart scolded her as he drove past. Another carriage severed the spine of another book. Regan shivered and scrambled backward toward the sidewalk.

An unfamiliar gentleman grabbed her upper arm and helped Regan to her feet. "That was quite a tumble that you took, miss," he said, escorting her back to the sidewalk. "Are you hurt?"

Regan shook her head.

While Regan assured several bystanders that she was fine, another helpful gentleman rescued her books and the shoe that she had not been aware that she had lost. As she slipped her foot into the shoe, she glanced down at the front of her dress and groaned. Oh, her beautiful walking dress was ruined!

Her brother's large coachman swaggered up to her, using his hands and size to make a path to his mistress. "Are ye injured, milady? I saw the whole thing from my perch and have never felt so helpless in my life." He tucked her books under one arm and led Regan back to the waiting coach.

The fresh-faced groom accepted the books from the coachman, giving Regan a worried look. "Are ye really all right, milady?"

"I am fine," she assured the boy, though she was not certain that she was telling the truth. Hesitantly she asked, "Did either one of you see the person who pushed me?"

The groom and the coachman exchanged a long glance.

"Are ye telling us that some ruffian shoved you into the street?" the coachman said, his caterpillar eyebrows coming together. "Pardon me for saying so, but yer brother won't be liking this. No, not at all."

"Then perhaps we should not tell him," she said, but the coachman had already shut the door in her face.

It was seven o'clock when Dare entered Nox. He was tired and hungry, and would have paid a small fortune for a glass of brandy. Upstairs, as Dare entered the large private room, he noticed that Vane, Saint, and Hunter were seated, their bodies vibrating with unreleased tension.

"What has happened?"

Dare belatedly noticed Frost leaning against the billiards table. He had not spoken to his friend since his departure. It explained why the others were so grim-faced. They probably thought he and Frost would come to blows over Regan.

"Good evening, Frost." Dare genially inclined his head. "I trust you haven't come to put a bullet in my head?"

The corners of Frost's mouth curved upward. "And risk putting a hole in my fine coat? It seems a shame to ruin my tailor's efforts. Besides, the gents have been telling me that you have a few acquaintances who do not like you very much."

"Did you hire them?"

Dare tensed when Frost shifted his stance and crossed his arms.

"What do you believe?"

Dare slowly exhaled. "I believe, if you truly wanted a man dead, Frost, your face would be the last thing he sees."

Frost snorted softly, and then his head tipped back as silent laughter shook his body. "A damn scary fellow, I am. A man would have to be touched in the head or in love to annoy me, would you not agree?"

Dare glanced down at his black boots and remained silent.

"You may not have been the gentleman those ruffians were after," Vane said, the first willing to break the resounding silence in the room.

"How do you know?"

Hunter stirred and gave Frost a wary look. "There was another attack this afternoon."

Dare immediately thought of Sin and Reign. Both gentlemen had families to look after and protect. "Who?" The hairs prickled on the nape of his neck when Frost walked over and placed his hand on Dare's shoulder.

The earl's turquoise-blue eyes cut Dare to the quick with a single glance. "My sister."

Across town, Regan was sitting in Lady Karmack's drawing room. The viscountess had invited a few of her closest friends for an evening of intelligent conversation and musical appreciation. Regan counted close to sixty guests in attendance.

Thea leaned over and whispered, "Not the crush that Lord and Lady Trussell's ball was, but I commend Mama on her guest list." Her cousin looked incredibly lovely in a pink dress with an antique scalloped lace flounce at the hem. The Karmack diamonds glittered from Thea's ears and neck.

"I daresay the gentlemen outnumber the ladies," Regan murmured back. "Not counting your father, I do not see a single gentleman older than the age of forty in this house."

Although it might not have been apparent to the other guests, Lady Karmack had created her own version of Tattersall's. Instead of horses, she offered her female guests some of the *ton*'s most eligible bachelors from the wealthiest families to admire.

"Oh, look, could Mama be any more obvious." Thea gestured toward their friend. Nina sent them a pleading glance as Lady Karmack presented yet another nobleman for the young woman's inspection. "If we do not stop her, Mama will be inviting Nina to check the gentleman's teeth."

Regan snapped open her fan and used it to conceal her mirth. "Or to see if his feet have been adequately shod."

Both women collapsed in giggles, earning a warning glance from the viscountess.

"Oh, we must stop. Else, Mama, will seat me next to Lord Charlton at supper."

Regan frowned, unfamiliar with the gentleman. "Why would that be so bad?"

"You would not be asking if you had had the pleasure of his acquaintance. One of Lord Charlton's favorite tricks is to spit liquids through his broken front tooth."

"You jest!"

"No, I am completely serious!" Thea stood and extended her gloved hand to Regan. "And you will be, too, unless you want Mama to seat *you* next to him. Now come, let us rescue poor Nina."

"How could you have allowed Regan to go out for the evening?" Dare demanded as they traveled in Frost's coach to Lord and Lady Karmack's town house. He was still furious at his friend's carelessness with Regan.

If Dare had been there, he would have locked Regan in her bedchamber and stood guard outside her door. Better yet, he would have joined her in the locked room and made love to her until they both collapsed, sated and exhausted.

Dare could sense that his friend was amused by the question.

"You should know better than most that my sister is headstrong and does whatever suits her," Frost said with a hint of unfathomable pride in his voice. "I might have reconsidered if I had learned of the attack on you. However, no one saw fit to tell me of the incident."

"My apologies, Frost. I was in no condition to pay you a visit," Dare said drily. *Or pick up a quill pen for that matter.* "I suppose Vane, Saint, and Hunter thought they were protecting me—"

"So all of you did wonder if I had a hand in that bit of mischief," he mused aloud, though he did not sound upset about the unspoken accusation.

"The suggestion was raised and swiftly discarded," Dare replied. "I did not summon you because of—" He searched for the proper words. "—this awkward business with Regan. I have ruined our friendship and I am sorry for it."

Frost did not respond immediately. When he did, he said, "I have a feeling that you, Regan, and I will muddle through this 'awkward business,' as you call it, and our friendship will be put to rights again."

Dare silently marveled at his friend's optimistic outlook. Until Berus had told him that Regan had come to Nox and asked to see him, Dare had assumed that Regan despised him. "What are you not telling me?"

"Do not fret, my friend," Frost said easily, his eyes gleaming in the shadowed interior of the coach. "I have no intention of forcing you to marry my sister."

The coach slowed as it reached their destination.

Wary, Dare asked, "What of Regan?"

Frost shrugged. "She has come to the conclusion that you would make a dreadful husband."

For some reason, her conclusion annoyed him.

The door to the coach opened. "This is your stop," his friend said congenially.

"Are you not joining me?" His instincts were warning Dare that Frost was up to something. He disembarked from the coach and turned around to glare at his friend.

Frost leaned forward. "I told you earlier that I have other plans. Once you are satisfied that Regan is safe at the Karmacks', then you may see to your own pleasures."

Gaining entry into Lord and Lady Karmack's residence without an invitation was simple enough. According to the butler, if a gentleman was in his prime, unmarried, and possessed a respectable fortune, he was more than welcome to join the gathering.

It was not until he entered the drawing room that Dare realized how unbalanced the Karmacks' supper table would be. Apparently the viscountess had gone to great lengths to improve her youngest daughter's marriage prospects.

Dare's blue-gray gaze narrowed as he saw Regan standing near the pianoforte with six admirers surrounding her.

Lady Karmack was parading London's blooded stock in front of Regan as well.

Dare's breath came out in short puffs. Frost knew precisely what Lady Karmack was planning, and he must have heartily approved. Now he understood why Frost was confident that their friendship would recover. Any discord between them would end once Regan married.

Frost was correct. There was nothing to worry about. Regan was safe at the Karmacks'.

Dare turned to leave, but his knees locked at the sound of Regan's distinctive laughter.

The hell she was.

Dare rolled back his shoulders. He snapped his head to the right and the bones in his neck crackled. Then with grim determination in his gaze, he marched toward Regan and her admirers.

Chapter Twenty-five

"Good evening, Lady Regan . . . gentlemen."

Regan returned Dare's greeting with a curtsy, speechless that he was attending Lady Karmack's little gathering. Before she could form a proper response in front of their audience, Dare took matters into his own hands.

"Lady Regan, if I may, I need to speak with you privately. I have a message from your brother," he said, taking her firmly by the elbow.

"You have *spoken* to Frost?"

"See here, Mordare," a slender blond gentleman protested. "You cannot just drag off the lady whenever it suits you."

"It's Bailey, is it not?" Dare said silkily, causing the gentleman to take a step out of striking range. "Do not interfere. This is family business."

"Family business," she muttered. "Do you not have enough of your own to keep you occupied?"

Dare escorted her upstairs until they reached the family's private quarters. He gently nudged her into the nearest bedchamber.

"We cannot go in here," she weakly protested. "It is unseemly."

And she was still vexed with him.

"I will not detain you for long."

She gasped at Dare's embrace. It was the last thing she had expected after their parting. Regan buried her nose against his coat and inhaled. His unique masculine scent had always felt like home to her.

Dare pulled back and touched her face. "Frost told me what happened while you were out shopping. Are you hurt?"

So his strong sense of duty had lured him back to her side. Regan stifled her sigh as she shook her head. "My limbs have stiffened in the passing hours since the incident, and I have a few bruises. Otherwise, I am fine."

"Are you certain someone pushed you?"

The urgency in his voice surprised her. "Someone struck me from behind. I know you do not believe me—"

"I do." His chin dropped to his chest as he seemed to struggle to offer her some kind of explanation. "I want you to be more vigilant in your outings. Take a groom with you, and always keep your friends close to you."

Concerned, she unthinkingly reached for his arm. "Dare, what is it?"

Dare scrubbed his face with his hand. "It could be nothing. A coincidence, nothing more," he said, unwilling to explain further. "This town is full of dangers, and, of late, there has been too much violence."

Regan thought of Mrs. Randall, and then of the strong anonymous hands that had shoved her into the busy street.

"Dare, why have you come?" she said, her eyes clear and steady as she committed his face to memory. "Tell me the truth; Frost did not send you."

His mouth tightened at her soft accusation. "Frost is aware that I needed to see for myself that you were unharmed."

She stepped back and opened her arms. "As you can see, I have recovered from my ordeal. Although your concern is appreciated, I do not want you to ruin your evening on my behalf."

Dare gestured at the door. "So with Lady Karmack's assistance, you think one of those gents downstairs will want to be your next protector?"

Regan glanced away, lifting one of her shoulders in a careless fashion. She had come to support Thea this evening, though Dare did not deserve such reassurances. Especially, since he could offer none to ease the pain in her heart.

"Lady Karmack frowns on the word *protector*. In her opinion, it does not sound very respectable. The viscountess refers to the gentlemen downstairs as potential *husbands*," Regan said, taking satisfaction when she noted fury in his blue-gray eyes.

"So, like your friends, you did come to town in order to secure a husband," he said emotionlessly.

"I came to London for *you*!" she said, bringing her fingers to her lips. "I was willing to settle for a relationship on your terms . . . your rules. God, I was such a fool, because now I understand that you will always let *her* stand between us."

From Dare's expression, he knew that she was referring to Lady Pashley. "Regan."

She held up her hand. "Do not touch me. I do not want to be appeased. I want—I want—"

"What?" He walked up to her extended palm. "What do you want, Regan?"

She squeezed her eyes shut, and then blinked the tears away. "I want you to escort me back to Lady Karmack's drawing room."

Regan brought her chin up and silently goaded him to give her a counteroffer.

They stared at each other in silence.

Finally Dare said, "I have kept you from the drawing room too long, and I have business to attend to. With your permission, I will escort you back to your new friends."

Without his private coach, Dare had to use a hackney coach to drive him to several of his father's clubs. Now that he knew that Regan was unharmed and protected at the Karmacks', he could continue his search for his father and brother. Charles, in many ways, had always been unpredictable, but his father had become conventional as he aged.

Dare located the duke on his third stop.

He was not a member of this staid, respectable club. Not anymore. When he was seventeen, Dare and the other members of the Lords of Vice had been kicked out for some outrageous prank the seven of them had concocted one night when they had been too foxed to consider the outcome of their actions. Their families could not stave off the inevitable outcome; nor had Dare and his friends cared.

Even so, when he invoked his father's name, he was admitted into the club. Dare could not understand his good fortune until he saw his father. He was sitting alone at a table and appeared to be quite drunk.

"Father." Without waiting for an invitation, Dare sat down at the table. "How long have you been here? I have searched all of London for you today."

"Not all, my dear boy . . . not all." He raised his hand and signaled for one of the waiters. "A glass for my son. And another bottle of brandy."

Dare waited until the glass and bottle were produced, and the waiter left them alone. "Allegra summoned me to the house."

The duke blinked. Christ, were those tears in his father's bloodshot eyes? "Allegra . . . oh, my dear poor Allegra," he said, shaking his head. "How does she fare?"

"I have not seen her since this morning. Needless to say, she was battered and frightened." Dare kept his voice low, but he wanted to shout at his sire. "What in the hell happened last night? Where is Charles?"

"Charles." His father rubbed his eyes. "I do not know. I lost him in the darkness. I searched, and searched . . . finally, I ended up here."

Dare leaned forward. "Father, we have to find him. Hire a Runner if necessary."

The duke's gaze widened as panic chased away his exhaustion. "This is Charles whom we are discussing. Not some lowborn criminal. No, no Runners. We will find him ourselves."

Dare gripped the edge of the table. "Need I remind you that Charles almost murdered his wife? Neither one of us can vouch for his mental state, though we both know that he has gotten worse."

"Charles has always been spirited. No more than you." His father poured more brandy into his glass. Most of it missed the glass and formed a large puddle on the table. "We should have remained at Rooks House. Charles never does well in London. Too many distractions."

Dare brought his hand to his lips and pinched his lower lip as if he could prevent himself from speaking the words that needed to be said. It did not help. He pointed a finger at his father. "Charles isn't spirited, Father. He is angry, violent, and often cruel to the people who love him. He hurt Allegra last night, and there is a chance that he has attacked other women," Dare said, not wondering for the first time if Mrs. Randall had been the victim of a random robbery. Then there was the incident with Regan.

His thought drifted back to the afternoon in the library when Charles had overheard Dare arguing with their father about him. Dare had said that Charles could not keep his bloody cock in his trousers. His brother had entered the library and replied, *Funny, the same can be said about you, little brother.*

At the time, Dare had thought his brother was referring to Allegra. What if he had been wrong? What if Charles had known about Dare's pursuit of Mrs. Randall . . . and Regan. Dear God, what if Charles had been the one to push Regan into the busy street.

"What are you talking about?" his father demanded harshly, drawing attention from a few of his fellow members.

Dare seized the older man's wrist when he reached for the bottle of brandy. "Sober up. Mother, Allegra, and Louise need you. If Charles returns to the house, you might want to think about locking him up in the cellar and summoning your physician."

The duke yanked his arm free and stood. "You

have no right to speak to me in such a manner. I—"
He thumped on his chest. "I, alone, know what's best
for Charles. I don't need your help. Go home. Leave
me in peace."

As Dare exited the club and headed for the hackney coach, he pondered his father's angry words.
Go home, the duke had said.

It stung a little to silently admit that Dare didn't
have one. Of course, the choice had been his, a
symbol of his pleasure-seeking way of life and freedom from his family's demands and needs. Hooked
into his soul like ballast, he had been dragged down
into the unexplored depths of debauchery and in-
dulgence.

Not that he had fought his downfall very hard.

Until recently, Dare had not understood how
empty his life had been. He stared up at the blackness overhead, allowing the cool night air to wash
over him. Slipping his hand into his frock coat, his
gloved fingers brushed the edge of the paper he had
tucked away in the inner pocket.

Perhaps it was time to lay claim to what truly belonged to him.

Chapter Twenty-six

Something stirred Regan from her slumber. She opened her eyes and saw a shadowy figure leaning over her. Before she could take a deep breath to scream, a hand was clamped over her mouth.

"It's me." He peered at her. "Why are you in bed?"

When she realized that it was Dare, she moaned in relief.

"Whatever you do, don't scream."

Regan sank her teeth into the fleshy part of his palm.

Dare softly yelped and staggered backward. "Bloodthirsty woman," he said, his voice a hoarse whisper. "Are you trying to wake the entire house?"

Regan climbed out of bed and walked over to her dressing table. She was wearing her nightgown, but Dare had seen her in less. "What are you doing here, Dare?" She lit the small oil lamp.

"I had to see you," he said, reaching for her.

She evaded him and went to the doors that opened to the balcony. She opened them and peered over the iron railing. "How did you get into the room?"

Dare kissed her on the neck. "The balcony."

Her forehead furrowed as she thought of the risk he had taken to reach her. Regan glanced over her shoulder. "You could have broken your foolish neck."

He spun her around and pulled her against his chest. "You are not the only one who can climb a balcony."

Dare kissed her before she could ask him how he had opened a locked door. The kiss was demanding, all-consuming. The bruising pressure of his mouth expressed his residual anger over their earlier parting as clearly as if he had spoken. In retaliation, she bit his lower lip and then eased the sting with her tongue.

"Christ, I've missed you," Dare murmured after he dragged some much-needed air into his lungs. His chin dropped to his chest as he began to work the bottom of her nightgown up her body. He groaned. "No, I should not be doing this."

Regan grabbed his wrists to prevent him from pulling her nightgown over her head. "Why are you? I thought you were staying away from me."

"You're right," he said abruptly, breaking her hold as he released the hem of her nightgown and smoothed the fabric over her hips.

"I am?" Insulted, Regan tried to shove Dare away, but he was as solid as a marble column. "If I had the strength, I would toss you over the balcony. How dare you sneak into my bedchamber like a thief and—"

Dare placed his hand over her mouth. "Hush, love. Do you want to bring the entire household down on my head?"

Regan nodded vehemently. Although she was certain it was too early for Frost to find his bed, she longed for her brother to give Dare the beating he deserved for trifling with her heart. Her words came out muffled, but Dare seemed to comprehend the direction of her thoughts.

Giving her an exasperated look, Dare leaned forward until they were almost nose-to-nose. "You are a perplexing creature, Regan Alice. I'm doing my best to keep my hands off you, and you want to see me castrated for it." He removed his hand from her mouth and spun her around. "Now get dressed. We haven't much time to tarry."

Dare gave her backside a firm smack to emphasize their need for haste.

Regan whirled back around and seized him by the front of his dark evening coat. "And what gives you any right to order me about in my brother's house?"

She expelled a high-pitched squeak when Dare tugged her closer so that she was standing up on her toes. "What gives me the right? Arrogance. I'm stronger than you, and am willing to fight dirty to get what I want."

Regan sputtered at his outrageous boast. "That is not a reasonable answer!"

"Give me an hour, and I will have one for you."

"Oh, really," she said, angling her head so she could stare down her nose at him. It was difficult but she was angry enough to manage the small feat. "You do not need an hour to convince me. I already know you have the manners of a cross-eyed donkey."

Instead of an angry retort, Dare merely grinned at

her. "Arguing with you would be a waste of breath. I intend to marry you, Regan."

His declaration managed to render Regan speechless.

At any other time, Dare might have savored the quiet. Now it was beginning to irk him.

Regan's soft kissable lips parted in mute surprise as her fierce grip on the front of his evening coat went boneless. If Dare didn't have his fingers wrapped around her upper arms, she might have landed on her delectable backside.

"Say something," he demanded, giving her a little shake.

Regan blinked. Wariness crept into her stunned expression. "You do not want to marry me."

"Care to wager on it? You'd lose."

Things were not going well. Instead of being happy, Regan looked confused and a little sad. His ribs felt like they were going to rupture if the pressure continued to build in his chest.

She smoothed away the wrinkles from the front of his evening coat. "No . . . Even if I agreed, it cannot be done."

"Have some faith in me. I do not make promises that I cannot keep." The arrogance and determination that had driven him since he had left his father's club evaporated when Regan started to tremble. "Ho! There, there . . . Christ, don't cry. I thought you would be overjoyed that I finally came to my senses."

"You call this coming to your senses?" Regan laughed even as she wiped away the wetness clinging to her eyelashes. "You sneered when I told you that Lady Karmack was interested in finding me a husband."

"I sneered because you do not have to look for one. You have me."

Regan was not particularly overwhelmed by his declaration. "Why?"

"Why?" He frowned at the question. "Because I am tired of fighting the attraction between us. Although I tried to deny it, that need was there, just beneath the surface when we kissed at Nox five years ago. Time has not caused it to wither. Denial has not smothered it. My feelings for you continue to flourish despite my futile attempts to resist—"

"Of all the insulting things to say!"

His throat burned as bile and panic rose. With all the ways he had imagined revealing his plans to Regan, Dare had not considered that she might reject him. "Do not try to lie and tell me that you do not feel it. We belong together."

Her lowered gaze did not bode well.

"Is it not true that you defied your brother and came to London for me? Earlier this evening at Lady Karmack's, you claimed that you were willing to accept a relationship on *my* terms."

Her chin snapped up. Anger blazed in her blue eyes. Dare preferred it to sorrow and defeat. "You are twisting my words."

"You want to hear my terms? Fine. I want to marry you. Tonight." He caressed the silky strands of her hair, wondering if he could convince her to not pin it up for their wedding. "I will settle for nothing less."

"You told Frost that you had no intention of marrying me. Now you come to me and claim otherwise. Why? This is about Lady Karmack's small gathering, is it not? You fear that you might lose me to another," she said solemnly, her watchful gaze studying his face.

"You are wrong."

"Be honest, Dare. If I had not arrived in London, you would be happily bedding Mrs. Randall or some other lady who had caught your eye this season."

One of the tiny muscles under his left eye twitched. The unpleasant realization that Regan had struck closer to the truth than Dare cared to acknowledge did not mean that she was correct. "It is unfair to hold me accountable for something that never happened. You did come to London, and seeing you again gave me a chance to come to my senses. There is no other woman for me but you."

Dare had grown weary of talking. He captured her lips with his and tried to explain without words his feelings for her. As his mouth moved reverently over her lips, he could taste the salt of her tears. Threading his fingers into her dark tresses, he silently coaxed her to open her mouth. His confidence grew as Regan tentatively returned his kiss.

They were both breathless when he pulled away.

"Oh," she said as another tear slid down her cheek. "I believe you."

Relief swept over Dare. Still, he would not be satisfied until he heard the words from her lips. "And what about you? Has another man caught your fancy? Perhaps one of those preening peacocks hovering over you at Lady Karmack's?"

Regan gave him a watery smile. "No. There is no one else."

The pain in his ribs lessened at her confession.

"Good. Then it is settled. Get dressed. We're getting married."

"Now?" She made an exasperated sound when Dare opened her large mahogany wardrobe and retrieved a dress from the clothes press. "It is impossible. We cannot marry without a special license—"

"The license is in my coat pocket."

The whites of her eyes widened as luminous as moonlight. "You have a *license*?"

"I purchased it shortly after Frost ordered me from the house." He held up a dress. "What about this one?"

"But why?"

Dare glanced at the dress and scowled. "Do I have to have a reason? It seems fine enough for a—"

"I am not talking about the dress!" She marched over and plucked it from his hands. "Although it certainly will not do. I was referring to the special license."

He stepped aside and watched as she searched for a dress. "After what was said, I assumed I would need more than an apology."

Regan straightened and shook out the dress in her hands. Her right brow lifted as she peered over the fabric in her outstretched arms. "Hmm . . . I do not recall receiving an apology or an offer of marriage from you at Lady Karmack's."

"That was because you were too busy flirting with those gents!" he snapped. He immediately regretted his outburst. A man did not coax a skittish lady into marriage by slapping at her with his sour temper.

She brought her hand up to her opened mouth. Dare braced himself for tears or a severe scolding because he deserved both for being so clumsy with his words.

After a moment of silence, Regan surprised him by laughing. Soft melodious sniggers began in her chest until they frothed and bubbled through her fingers and she had to let her hand fall away so she could catch her breath. Staggering backward, her back bumped against the door of the wardrobe as she hugged the dress tightly to her chest. "Good grief, you were jealous. How perfectly splendid!"

Dare stalked toward her. "You sound rather pleased with yourself."

"Oh, I am." She bit the tip of her first finger and stared at him artfully. "Lord Hugh Mordare, worried about a few—what did you call them?—Ah, yes . . . peacocks!"

Regan Alice was enjoying herself at his expense, but his pride could take the licks and scrapes. He grabbed the edge of the door of the wardrobe with one hand and braced the other on the wood above Regan's head, caging her with his body.

"Keep your bloody peacocks. I won't begrudge a few wishful glances from lovelorn gents if you end my torment and marry me." His lips brushed her right temple. "Marry me, Regan."

Dare moved closer, letting his hips brush against hers. He was aroused, and had been since he had entered her bedchamber. If he could not gain her consent with reason, then perhaps he should try seduction.

"You need more than a special license," Regan argued, forcing Dare to concentrate on the task at hand. "You will need Frost's approval."

"Do not worry about Frost." Regan was one year

under the age of consent, and that had slightly complicated matters. While Dare had secured the necessary papers, he doubted Regan would approve of his methods. So he refrained from mentioning them.

Dare cupped Regan's face with both hands. "All I need is your consent. What say you? Will you marry me?"

Chapter Twenty-seven

At the stroke of midnight, Lady Regan Alice Bishop married Lord Hugh Mordare in the Marchioness of Netherley's drawing room. At Dare's insistence, Regan had worn the same amber dress she had donned for her first night in London. Bearing witness to their union, the marchioness stood beside Regan, quietly weeping into her handkerchief. Next to Dare, Vane stood like a silent sentinel.

It was not until Regan had entered Lady Netherley's drawing room that she realized Frost and the rest of their friends would not be joining them.

Her new husband had neglected to inform her that they were essentially eloping. Always a practical man, Dare had managed to marry her without bundling her into a traveling coach and heading for Gretna Green. Before she could work up any ire over Dare's high-handedness, Lady Netherley rushed up to them and proclaimed their nuptials the most romantic she had ever witnessed.

With a watery glance at Vane, who was studiously ignoring her, the marchioness told the couple that their love match had given her renewed hope that she would find the perfect lady for her wayward son.

Vane snarled at his sweet mother and sent Dare a glare that promised retribution before he excused himself. Satisfied that their paperwork was in order, and his duty fulfilled, the vicar was the next to depart. Dare had not told her how much he had offered the vicar to marry them at such a late hour; however, both men seemed content with their private arrangement.

Soon, Dare was announcing their departure to Lady Netherley. As he once again expressed his gratitude to the marchioness, Regan took a moment to admire the ring Dare had placed on her finger. The five-carat pale honey–colored topaz gleamed like captured firelight within its silver-cream circle of natural pearls. It should not have surprised her, but the rose-gold ring fit her finger perfectly. Regan cast a sly glance at her husband. A gentleman who carried a ring and a special license in his coat pocket had not been exaggerating when he expressed his earnest desire to be leg-shackled to her.

"Are you ready to depart, my lovely bride?" Dare asked, his eyes silently pleading for assistance. Sentimental and slightly tipsy from the wine she had imbibed to toast the bride and groom, Lady Netherley appeared reluctant to release Dare from her clutches.

Regan hid her smile as she casually walked over to Dare and the marchioness. "Yes, my lord. I confess, I have not yet grown accustomed to these late evenings." She placed her gloved hand on Dare's arm and smiled at their hostess. "Lady Netherley, we cannot thank you enough for everything that you have done for us. Bless you and your romantic heart."

Lady Netherley released Dare and opened her arms to give Regan a wobbly embrace. "Think nothing of it, my dear girl." Regan winced at the marchioness's fierce hug. "There is no shame, now that you and Dare have done the right thing. And you can trust me to keep your secret."

"Come, love," Dare said curtly, deftly separating the two woman. "We have kept this good woman from her bed long enough."

Regan glanced back at Lady Netherley as Dare dragged her out the open front door. "But—" She barely had enough time to raise her hand in farewell before the woman was out of sight. "I am going to lose one of my evening slippers if you do not slow down."

Dare immediately adjusted his pace. "My apologies. I feared if we tarried further, Lady Netherley would insist that we spend the night under her roof."

"And would that be so awful? She is a delightful woman. Vane is very fortunate to have such a loving mother."

Regan nodded to the coachman as she ascended the narrow steps and climbed into the coach. She listened as Dare ordered the coachman to return them to her brother's town house. Regan looked up and caught him watching her while she adjusted her skirts to make room for her husband's long legs.

"Lady Netherley is a resourceful and generous lady. Nevertheless, I have no desire to spend my wedding night comforting her," he said, sliding onto the bench beside her.

A soft thud halted their conversation. The door of the coach opened, and Vane's muscular frame filled the doorway. He was hatless, and his cheeks were flushed as if he had run to catch their coach before it had departed.

"I had not realized the hour. Forgive me for not being there when you said your farewells to my mother."

Regan gave Vane a tender smile. "We understand. It must have been difficult. Everyone is well aware that your mother has such high hopes that you will soon make a good match."

Vane snorted. "Well, that will be impossible since Dare has stolen the prettiest lady in London from me."

Dare scowled at the playful reminder that Vane had flirted with Regan on several occasions. "Count your blessings, my friend. I spared your pretty face, did I not?"

Regan rolled her eyes, ignoring the sudden heat rising in her cheeks. She was dreadfully fond of Vane, but he was not the man she had longed for during her absence from London.

"I wish . . ." Vane lowered his gaze as he sought the proper words. ". . . I wish you both a happy and loving marriage." The corners of his mouth quirked into something akin to devilish as his gaze alighted on Dare. "A little luck wouldn't hurt, too. Especially when Frost—"

"There is still time for me to bloody your nose, you silly jackanapes." Dare leaned forward and pounded on the small trapdoor. "Let us be off."

Vane seemed untroubled by Dare's casually delivered threat. "Save your fists for Frost." He closed the door as the coach moved forward. "You'll need them!"

Regan tilted her head and stared at Vane's diminishing figure until he was swallowed by the darkness. "What did Vane mean when he said that you needed to save your fists for my brother?" She gasped as the answer struck her like a carriage whip. "Frost does not know about the wedding."

"Your brother is resourceful. He will learn about it soon enough."

Regan gaped at him. How could Dare be so nonchalant? Frost was likely to murder them both when he learned that they had married without his consent. "Wait! How is this so? You needed my brother's permission to marry."

Dare brought her hand to his lips, kissing the knuckle above the ring he had placed on her finger. "And I had it. An excellent forgery of the man's handwriting, if I do not say so myself. The vicar never even questioned it."

"Oh, my God." Feeling a little dizzy, Regan gave him a bemused stare. "Is that even legal?"

"No one will challenge the authenticity of the letter," he assured her. "Not even your brother. Frost adores you. He would be the last one to drag you into a messy scandal."

No wonder Vane was certain that Dare would need his fists. While Frost may permit the marriage to stand, his pride would demand a blood price.

"Good grief, is Lady Netherley part of this deception? Is that the secret she was referring to as we were leaving the house?"

Dare hesitated, and shot her a wary sideways glance. "Well, I might have embellished our unfortunate predicament when I approached the vicar."

Regan swallowed. "Unfortunate predicament?"

"I may have confessed to the good man that you were enciente."

She slapped his hand away when he tried to reach for her. "Of all the outrageous things! How could you tell everyone that I was—" Regan stopped in midsentence as her gaze locked on the trapdoor. She lowered her voice to a mere whisper. "In a delicate condition."

Flustered and embarrassed by his lie, Regan was mad enough to kick him in the shin. Forgetting about the coachman, she shouted, "You had absolutely no right!"

"How do you know it is a lie?" he quietly countered.

The question took the wind out of her high dudgeon. Indeed, how did she know? Her blue gaze narrowed on her new husband. "A woman knows such things. I am definitely not—not *that*!"

"Of course you're not," Dare said soothingly. Ignoring her feeble attempts to avoid touching him, he pulled her close so her body molded against his side. He smoothed back the strands of hair that had come undone during their brief struggle. "I only meant to sway the vicar to our side. However, since the lie has distressed you—"

"It has."

"Then I can only think of one thing that will satisfy us both." Dare lightly kissed her pouting lips. "I will dedicate myself to the task of making certain that I spoke the truth."

"Wait!"

Uninterested in continuing their conversation, Dare crushed Regan against the leather-cushioned bench as his mouth plundered hers. Her arms curled around his neck, Regan sighed and pulled him closer.

For once, she was willing to let Dare have the final word.

Chapter Twenty-eight

Life with Dare would never be boring, Regan mused. With Dare's hand on her backside, he managed to help her climb up the ivy-covered trellis and onto the balcony.

Regan collapsed into the nearest chair. "Sneaking back into my bedchamber is more laborious than I would have guessed. Now that we are married, do you think we might try using one of the side doors?"

Dare ignited several candles. Shadows from the candlelight flickered across his handsome face. "Already losing your taste for adventure?"

"Never."

While she was attempting to catch her breath, Dare had already removed his frock coat and waistcoat. Regan stood up and reached around to unfasten the buttons on the back of her dress.

"Here." Dare walked over and finished undoing the remaining buttons. "If I may be so bold?"

"From you, I expect nothing less." She felt his fingers trace the nape of her neck as they traveled downward to the laces of her corset. Regan shivered in anticipation. "Does making love feel different when the lovers are married?"

"Let's find out," he murmured, nuzzling the curve of her neck.

Her corset loosened and slid to the floor. Soon her chemise, petticoat, and stockings were discarded until she was naked. It was terribly wanton of her to stand in front of Dare unclothed, but his hungry gaze gave her the courage not to run to her bed and dive into the bedding.

"Come with me." Dare took her hand and guided her over to a chair. With her sitting naked on his thigh, he leaned over and removed his boots and stockings. Willing to help, Regan finished untying his cravat. She unfastened the buttons of his shirt.

Regan struggled not to giggle.

"What?" he whispered in her ear.

"Until now, I have never sat on a gentleman's lap completely naked."

"It is a charming and decadent pose to be certain." Dare cupped her breast and lowered his head to kiss the soft, warm flesh. "I can assure you that Lady Karmack and your Miss Swann would not approve."

Dare groaned as if she was a wicked temptation that he should resist, but he was incapable of adhering to common sense. It made Regan feel powerful and mysterious. Then he lifted her off his lap and helped her to stand.

Well, this was not exactly how she envisioned her wedding night, Regan thought, feeling suddenly awkward. Perhaps Dare was not ruled by passion, after all.

Regan was about to reach for her discarded

nightgown when he muttered "trousers" and turned his attentions to the buttons at his waist. Minutes later, he carelessly dropped his discarded trousers on the floor.

"Is that a large bruise on your leg?" Regan asked, peering at the dark smudge on his skin. It looked rather painful.

"A minor incident at the club," he said, dismissively.

Regan arched her right brow playfully. "And what about your shirt?"

Dare hesitated. Her brow furrowed as he silently considered her request. "What if I told you that I have a few bruises under my shirt that match the one on my thigh?"

Concern clouded her face. "Let me see."

He leaned over the candles he had lit and blew out the flames, casting the bedchamber into darkness again. "No. Forget about the bruises."

In the darkness, she heard a whisper of fabric and a flash of white as Dare removed his shirt. Regan started when his arms circled her waist. He guided her toward the bed.

"What of my brother?" The back of her knees bumped against the mattress.

"Frost is very open-minded, but I would prefer not to invite him to watch."

Regan sat down on the bed and crawled backward until she could lie down. "Oh really? And what are you planning to do?"

Dare crawled up her body, bracing his hands on either side of her head. "Ravish you until we both collapse from exhaustion."

Oh, my.

Dare pressed her body into the mattress as his mouth slanted over hers. His tongue undulated against Regan's, a shallow pantomime of what he intended to do to her body. She reached down and caressed Dare's swollen manhood. The velvet flesh radiated heat against her palm. He moaned against her lips and ended their kiss. Straightening his arms, Dare widened the gap between their bodies so he could cover her hand with his.

"I do not want to wait."

Before Regan could ask him what he meant by this cryptic statement, Dare lifted his hips and fitted the broad head of his arousal against the opening of her sheath.

She felt his breath on her cheek.

"I should stop. I'm rushing this," he said, his arms shaking as he resisted the urge to end his torment and plunge his rigid length of flesh into her womanly sheath.

The realization that Dare was gradually losing his hard-won control was as intoxicating as brandy to Regan. "No . . . no," she murmured, parting her thighs, and inhaled sharply as his manhood eased a few inches deeper. "I want this, too. I need you, my—husband."

Dare slipped his hand under her buttocks and urged her body to take more of him. "I can no longer fight it," he said, sounding apologetic.

She arched her back just as Dare abandoned his restraint and thrust deeply into her. Regan did not have time to marvel at how perfectly they fit, because her lover was far from finished. Once he began moving within her, Regan slid her hands to his back and held on.

Regan could barely make out the details of Dare's face, but she did not need her eyes to recognize the man in her arms. The weight of his body, the feel and taste of his skin, and the scent of their combined arousal were as familiar as they were comforting. Stripped of all her senses, she would still know this man, for her soul cried out to his. Dare belonged to her, and he had ensured that she was bound to him as well.

She raked his back with her fingernails, silently urging him to quicken his pace. Dare groaned and nibbled at her chin before his mouth dropped to her shoulder. He cupped her breast and scraped her nipple with his beard stubble. She gasped and her legs tightened around him as he eased the slight burn by laving the tender bud with his tongue. There was no doubt in Regan's mind that Dare craved her body just as much as she wanted him.

Dare surprised her by pulling out of her. Before she could mourn the loss of his manhood filling her, he rolled Regan onto her stomach. "There are so many ways to take you," he growled into her ear as he stuffed a pillow under her belly and positioned her on her knees. "I want to savor them all!"

Cool air washed over her. Regan felt a little silly on all fours, until Dare covered her body with his. His fingers probed the drenched opening of her sheath. She bit her lower lip when he replaced his fingers with the firm, blunt head of his arousal. With a hand splayed on her hip, he adjusted her stance until he was satisfied with the angle. Then he filled her, sliding deeply. Regan clenched her teeth to keep from crying out.

It was a glorious sensation. Her womanly sheath

constricted around his manhood, coating the rigid flesh with her desire for him. Deep inside her body, her womb throbbed in anticipation for what was to come.

Regan did not have to wait long. Sensing her unspoken need, Dare began to move. Slowly at first, and then he quickened his pace. His hips slapping against hers, over and over, until she understood the rising madness that had overtaken her husband's control.

Regan cried out as Dare's fingers slid down her front and stroked the tiny nubbin of flesh between her legs. She choked back a ragged cry as colorful lights burst behind her closed eyes. The brilliant display reminded her of Vauxhall Gardens' fireworks.

Dare straightened so he could grip her hips. Without breaking his rhythm, he hammered his manhood wildly into the very heart of her with unflagging accuracy. Regan widened her stance on the mattress, drawing his thick, rigid flesh even deeper. Dare groaned and froze. And then with a sudden surge, he bucked against her buttocks as he found his release. Regan buried her face into the pillow as her sheath squeezed his manhood. Another wave of pleasure swept over her hot, sweat-slick flesh as she felt the final pulses of his seed fill her womb.

Even with her heartbeat pounding in her ears, Regan could have sworn that she heard Dare mumble something against her back.

It sounded awfully like "home."

Grim-faced, Frost stared down at the sleeping couple. He was not an artist, but his fingers itched, nonetheless, to capture the graceful lines of their naked bodies entwined, which disappeared beneath the curving folds of the sheet. Frost had stumbled upon an achingly beautiful scene, and his throat tightened in longing for something that he could not quite define.

Even in slumber, his friend protected his lover's modesty. One arm was wrapped around her, shielding Regan's breasts, while his other hand was splayed over the nether curls between her legs.

Frost gave Dare a pitying glance. Poor bastard. He wondered if Dare had figured out that he was in love with Regan.

His sister's eyelids fluttered open. She smiled sleepily at Frost, until awareness swept through her muddled brain like sunlight cutting through the fog. Her dark blue eyes widened in alarm. "Good grief, Frost!" Regan tried to sit up, and then realized that Dare was holding her. She frantically plucked the sheet covering her and Dare's legs, and pulled it up until it halted waist-high. If given the chance, Frost figured that Regan would have pulled the sheet over her head.

"Dare . . . wake up!"

It was tempting to laugh at his sister's predicament . . . until he noticed the topaz-and-pearl ring on the third finger of Regan's left hand. The muscles in his body coiled with so much tension, the bones in his jaw and shoulders crackled to relieve the strain.

"When were you and Dare married?" he asked, surprised by his mild curious tone.

Dare glowered at him while he tugged the sheet around his waist higher to ensure that Regan was suitably covered. "Last evening."

Frost felt the vertebrae in his neck pop one by one as he cocked his head to the side. "Regan is only twenty. She needs my consent to marry."

"Frost," Regan began.

"Quiet, dear sister," Frost said genially. Nevertheless, his sister winced at the edge he could not quite soften. "I believe Dare was about to explain how the two of you married last evening without my consent."

Dare held Frost's unblinking gaze. "Well, fortunately, you were generous enough to grant it."

"Ah, I see," Frost said, slowly pacing the length of his sister's bed. "And was the vicar satisfied with my letter of consent?"

"As to be expected, you were very thorough," Dare replied.

Frost's turquoise-blue eyes narrowed with feigned amusement. His friend had absconded with Regan, married her without Frost's consent, and bedded her in her family's home. He could not help but silently marvel at the man's cheek. If it had been any other chit, Frost would have lifted a glass of brandy in the gent's honor.

Dare had not moved an inch, but Frost was not fooled by his friend's nonchalance. "By the by, there is one more thing that you should know."

"And what is that?"

Dare cleared his throat and gave Frost a sheepish grin. "The vicar married us because he believes Regan carries my child."

"And does she?"

Dare chuckled softly and glanced at Regan. "Not for lack of effort."

The invisible leash that had held Frost in check

snapped. He had not been aware that he had lunged for Dare until he heard his sister begging him to stop. Anticipating his attack, Dare rolled off the bed and onto his feet with the grace of a fighter. It seemed to matter little to his friend that he wore nothing under the sheet.

Regan made a soft sound of distress.

Frost's eyes widened when he noted the nasty bruises covering Dare's torso and thigh. "What the hell happened to you?"

"Ruffians." He paused. "I believe we have already addressed the minor scuffle near Nox. I see no benefit in continuing the discussion."

"You neglected to mention the severity of your injuries." The bruises were in various stages of healing. "Though you seem to have made an almost miraculous recovery."

Regan frowned at his insinuating tone. "Frost, were you responsible for those ruffians attacking Dare?"

Frost was genuinely insulted by her accusation. "Aw, sister . . . You disappoint me. You know I like to deliver my messages personally."

To prove his point, Frost slammed his fist into Dare's arrogant chin. Regan screamed and gathered the sheet around her with some misguided thought to rescue her new husband. Dare staggered back and grabbed one of the bedposts to remain on his feet. It was one of the things that Frost admired about his friend. The gent could take a solid punch.

"Raise your fists and defend yourself," Frost demanded coldly.

"No." Dare found himself entangled within his

wife's protective embrace. "Regan, please . . . return to the bed. Your brother has every right to be angry with me."

Once he was convinced that Regan would not put herself in harm's way, Dare straightened and met Frost's hooded stare. "If you must, do your worst. It will not change the fact that Regan is my wife."

"Perhaps not, but I know I will feel better," Frost sneered.

It galled him that Dare had bested him. All in all, it was a bitter brew to swallow. Certain Frost would reject Dare as a potential husband for Regan, his friend had simply married her. Dare was gambling that only a coldhearted bastard would contest the union and drag his sole sister into a humiliating scandal.

While it was tempting to watch Dare squirm, Frost would never deliberately hurt Regan. It was obvious that his sister was in love with the man. She would never forgive him if Frost tried to have the marriage declared invalid.

Recalling the news that had prompted him to enter Regan's bedchamber, Frost decided to set aside his issues with Dare for the moment. The gent had bigger problems than a furious brother-in-law.

Regan bit her lower lip. "Frost, I suppose an apology is in order."

"I do not require one from you, my dear," he said, feeling generous. "Although I am disappointed that I was unable to see you married off properly." He shot a scathing look at Dare.

Frost crouched down, picked up the pillow that had fallen to the floor, and tossed it at Regan. She hugged it to her breasts. "When you both have dressed, I would appreciate it if you would join me in the library."

Frost doubted Regan and Dare would have much of an appetite once they heard what he had to say.

Chapter Twenty-nine

The pillow hit Dare in the face.

"Help me get dressed," Regan said breathlessly, rushing to her wardrobe to find the proper dress for what she perceived was his upcoming execution. Tossing the dress over a chair, she retrieved her undergarments from the floor.

"Regan, calm down," Dare said, though he could not shake the edgy feeling in his gut. "If your brother was plotting my demise, he would have done more than fracture his knuckles on my chin."

Not that he was making light of the facer Frost had just delivered, Dare thought, painfully aware of his throbbing chin. Regan's brother had fists of granite, capable of knocking the arrogance out of a man.

Regan stopped, and gaped at him. "How can you jest at a time like this?" She shuddered. "Frost knows what we were doing in that bed."

Dare squinted at her. "Sleeping?"

She was too rattled to appreciate his humor. "It is all the things we did *before* we went to sleep that will trouble Frost more. Good heavens!" Regan slapped her hand over her eyes.

"What?" Dare pushed aside the sheet and started collecting his clothing.

"My brother saw me naked!"

Dare did not bother reminding her that acquiring a brother-in-law was more upsetting to Frost than glimpsing a lady's bare backside, and that included his sister's. "No offense, love. Unless you possess some curious oddity like a third nipple or a large mole in the shape of our king's regal nose, I doubt Frost even noticed." He tugged his trousers over his hips.

Regan pulled her chemise over her head. "Lord Hugh Mordare . . . you tease me at your own peril!" She gasped when he walked past her to retrieve his shirt. "Oh, your beautiful stomach!" Her eyes grew suspiciously moist as she lightly caressed his abdomen. "And you call this minor. Are you quite certain my brother had nothing to do with this?"

Dare lightly touched his sore jaw and grimaced. "Quite. Though I would not have blamed him if he had sent a press gang after me that night. He is your brother, and I had upset you. I deserved a ruthless beating for my conduct." The tears shining in her eyes hastened Dare to put on his shirt before he took her into his arms. "Now, now . . . no more tears. It looks worse than it feels. Last night should be proof enough."

Regan blushed at the reminder. "Oh, I feel so embarrassed. I cannot believe Frost came into my bedchamber without knocking first."

Dare tucked the tails of his shirt into his trousers and fastened the buttons at his waist. "For what it's worth, Frost handled the news of our marriage better than I'd expected."

He had witnessed true fury in his friend, and the tap on the chin he had received was not it.

Regan frowned as she tied the tapes of her petticoat. "I have to agree. Something disturbed him enough that he felt the need to enter my bedchamber. It was not news of our marriage. I saw the shock on his face when he noticed the ring."

Dare shrugged. "We will know soon enough."

Despite his colorful bruises and his sore jaw, Dare was feeling very good. He had the lady standing beside him to thank for his high spirits. *His wife.* Regan sent him a grateful smile over her shoulder when he pulled her closer to tie the laces on her corset. He did not mind playing lady's maid for Regan as long as she allowed him to undress her later.

After their meeting with Frost, Dare had high hopes that he could lure the delectable lady back into bed.

When Dare and Regan strolled into the library, the tension in the room was oppressive. Instinctively, he stepped in front of Regan, using his body to shield her from the unknown danger that had inadvertently spared Dare from his friend's wrath about their sudden marriage.

"Dare, I do not know any kinder way to tell you," Frost said, smiling slightly as he took note of the man's protective stance. "So I shall be forthright and brief. Berus has brought news from Nox, and I confess it will be distressing to hear."

Regan threaded her fingers through his and squeezed, reminding him that he was not alone.

"My father?" he asked, his throat drying at the thought that his last words to his sire had been spoken in anger.

To Dare's relief, Frost shook his head. "No. As far as I know, your father is in good health. Dare, it is your brother, Charles."

Some of the stiffness in his shoulders eased. "So my father found him," Dare said grimly. "Where is he?"

Frost clapped his hand on Dare's shoulder. "You do not understand. Your brother Charles is dead."

Disbelief crossed his face. Dare released Regan's hand and staggered backward until his hand brushed against a reading chair. He sat down. "Are you certain?"

Frost poured a brandy and handed the glass to Dare. "Berus arrived about an hour ago with the news. Your father had sent two of his friends to Nox. They were ordered to find you, and to tell you that your family needs you."

Charles was dead. Dare nodded absently while he sipped the brandy. "Of course." He could not recall a time when his family did not need him.

Regan knelt beside his chair and gently stroked his hair. "Let me ride with you," she said, drawing both men's gazes.

The lines around Frost's mouth deepened as he scowled. "A generous offer, dear sister. However, this is a difficult time for the Mordare family."

"It is too much to ask," Dare said, his mind immediately dismissing the notion of dragging Regan into the state of confusion that always seemed to hover over his family like a dark cloud.

"It is not too much to ask of your *wife*," Regan said, letting her hand fall away as she stood. "Lest you both forget, I am a Mordare now."

Dare brought his hand to his brow. "Regan . . . ," he said wearily. It was a tempting offer, but there was Allegra to contend with. The woman was unpredictable even on her best days.

"What of your mother and Louise?" she persisted. Dare noted that she had not mentioned her new sister-in-law. "Your father will need you to take care of the details he is unable to face. I can help, if you let me."

Dare had only been thinking of his own selfish needs when he had married her in Lady Netherley's drawing room. He had not considered that he was binding Regan to his family as well. It was enough to almost make him regret that he had given in to his reckless desire to claim her for himself.

When Regan moved beyond his reach, Dare realized that she had misunderstood his silence. He rose from the chair and clasped both of her hands. The topaz-and-pearl ring sparkled as the morning sunlight danced across the surface. "My mother has always been fond of you. Perhaps the news of our marriage will ease the grief in her heart."

The brilliant smile Regan gave him confirmed that he had done the right thing.

Dare just prayed that he would not live to regret it.

Regan sat beside him in the coach. Attired in a pelisse-robe, her long black hair pinned and tucked into a bonnet, she had managed to look untouchable and quite beautiful. After Regan had announced that she wanted to join him, she had insisted on changing her dress before they departed for his family's town house. He had seen no reason to deny her simple request. If his brother was dead, Dare's tardiness would not change Charles's grim circumstances.

Dare glanced down at Regan's clasped hands, which were resting on her lap. She had sheathed her slender hands in lemon kid, which complemented her jonquil gros de Naples skirt and matched her half boots. No one staring at Regan would have suspected that she had spent most of the night writhing naked beneath him. The heat of last evening's coupling warmed the ice that had congealed in his gut since Frost had told him that Charles was dead.

"It is kind of you to come."

She seemed surprised that he had acknowledged her presence at all. "Think nothing of it," she said gently, her gloved hand reaching for his.

Dare folded her fingers within his and longed for the sanctuary of her bed.

"I cannot fathom what you must be feeling."

No, she truly did not comprehend his private thoughts. Even now, he was hesitant to share them out loud for fear that she would see the cold, ruthless scoundrel she had married. "You think I am mourning my brother?"

Regan's free hand stroked the leather folds of her tortoiseshell reticule. "I realize that your relationship with your older brother has been something of a trial for you."

"I feel nothing," he said bluntly.

Her dark blue gaze flew up to his austere face. "Surely you do not mean—"

"You have not misunderstood me. I cannot recall a year when I did not detest my brother." He saw her appalled expression, and sighed. Perhaps she would understand better if he explained the defining moment of Charles's cruelty. "Do you want know why my brother was so fascinated with Allegra eleven years ago?"

Regan glanced out the window of the coach. "I have spoken to Lady Pashley on several occasions. She is articulate, educated, and very lovely."

Dare shot her an amused look. He highly doubted that his sister-in-law would be so generous toward Regan. "Allegra's refined virtues are not what caught my brother's eye," he said patiently, using his other hand to caress the top of her hand. "Her most appealing asset for Charles was that she was the woman I loved."

Dare was taken aback when Regan's dark blue eyes filled with tears. "My dear, I did not mean to distress."

"No, no . . . I mean—" His gaze dropped to her breasts as she heaved an audible sigh. Regan glanced upward and hastily blinked away the moisture in her eyes. "What I mean to say is that you must have loved her very much."

He did not want to talk about Allegra. However, Regan was his wife, and she deserved the truth. Besides, his cunning sister-in-law might use the past to hurt Regan. Although she had not admitted it, Dare suspected there had been one or two occasions when Allegra had done exactly that.

"At sixteen, love is a difficult emotion to define. A young man's passions run hot. My love for Allegra was all-consuming. She was a fever in my blood, and I feared that I might die if I did not possess her heart and body."

"I see."

Her impassive response coaxed a faint smile from his lips. His wife was not pleased that another lady had once claimed his heart, but she was fair-minded and willing to hear him out.

"Charles had been away in London when I had declared my feelings for Allegra. She claimed to return my feelings wholeheartedly, and we dreamed of the day that we would marry."

"It sounds dreadfully romantic, like something out of a poem or romantic novel."

Dare gave her an assessing glance, wondering if Regan was mocking him. She did not seem particularly amused by his confession. In fact, Dare thought Regan looked a little pale. "Are you all right?"

"I am fine," she said politely. "Pray continue."

"Charles eventually returned to Rooks House. For a time, all seemed well. My brother had male friends and half a dozen local mistresses who demanded his time. I never suspected that he and Allegra were meeting in secret."

Regan turned her head, and her lips parted in surprise. "How did you learn of this?"

"I did not learn of their betrayal until months later." Dare removed his hat and smoothed back his hair. There had been no time to return to Nox, so he still wore his clothes from the previous evening. "For you see, I was blinded by my love for Allegra. While I made plans to approach her father, Lord Dyton, and offer for her hand, Allegra had been sharing my brother's bed."

"I do not know what to say."

"Neither did Allegra. She could have told me the truth about Charles. Instead, she began to make excuses about why she could not join me at our secret meeting place."

"Because she was meeting Charles," she deduced.

"Yes. It amused my brother to bed Allegra in the same spot that I considered hers and mine. Before long, she was carrying my brother's bastard."

Unconsciously, Regan's hand touched her stomach. Dare noted the telling action. Though he had deliberately lied to the vicar to gain the man's support, there was a chance his child was sleeping in her womb. He had not taken any measures to prevent such an outcome, nor was he inclined to now that she belonged to him. The notion of plunging into her clinging sheath, filling her with his seed over and over until she was heavy with their child, momentarily distracted him from his dark thoughts.

"Did Charles know?"

His delightful reverie burst like a fragile soap bubble at the mention of Charles's name. "Of course. My brother had planned it from the beginning. When he was quite certain Allegra was with child, Charles sent Allegra to me."

"Oh." Regan silently digested the information. "Did you?"

It was Dare's turn to glance away.

"Oh, I see."

"Allegra broke down almost immediately after we—we— I thought I had done something wrong. That I had hurt her without meaning to in my clumsiness."

Regan carefully separated her hand from his.

"Dare, I would prefer that you spare me the details of your night of passion. I have heard enough of Allegra and your great, fervent love for her."

Dare frowned. "That was not the point of the tale."

"Then what is your point?" she snapped.

Dare scratched his head. He was trying to explain something important, but he was making a hash of it. "Weeks later, Lord Dyton dragged Allegra into the front hall of Rooks House and demanded to see my father, because he had learned of his daughter's delicate condition. I knew that I was being given an opportunity to do right by Allegra. I naturally told Lord Dyton that I was the sire of Allegra's child. My father was furious. Charles, of course, laughed when I offered to marry her. That's when I knew . . ."

"That Charles was the sire," Regan finished his statement.

Dare clasped his hands together and nodded. "I only had to look into Allegra's tearstained face to see the truth. It was why she had sobbed the night we had been together. Allegra had fallen in love with my brother, Regan. She had been devastated when Charles had sent her to seduce me."

Regan winced, recalling her grand confession to Frost when she admitted that she had deliberately set out to seduce Dare. She was beginning to understand why Dare had been wary of his feelings for her even when she had been so transparent with her own.

"So you accused Charles of seducing Allegra?"

Dare chuckled. "Fool that I was, I was still willing to marry her."

"But you—then how did she marry Charles?"

"When Allegra realized that I was prepared to forgive her, and offer her unborn child my name, she broke down and confessed that Charles was her lover. My brother vehemently denied it. However, Lord Dyton was not interested in the truth. With pressure from my father, Allegra's marriage to Charles would make her a marchioness, and later a duchess. He and my father were satisfied with the outcome."

"Did Charles ever tell you why he seduced Allegra?"

Dare grinned at Regan, pleased that she understood what he was trying to tell her. "Charles wanted to take the woman I worshiped and reduce her to the level of a whore. He understood my chivalrous nature better than I did. He knew that when I learned of the child, I would marry Allegra. The notion of me raising his bastard as my heir amused him."

"What a horrid, evil man!" Regan declared, her hands curling into fists as if she was prepared to fight Charles on Dare's behalf. "No wonder you feel nothing for the man."

Dare placed his hands on Regan's face and pulled her close so he could kiss her lightly. Her lips were sweet from the hot chocolate she favored each morning. "You are such a fierce creature when riled. Remind me never to cross you."

"Too late. I have been vexed with you for days."

"Hmmm. It is a good thing that I came to my senses and married you." He indulged himself, and stole another kiss. "Do not fret, *mon coeur*. Charles did get his comeuppance when my father forced him to marry Allegra."

"How?"

"My niece's birth was difficult. Allegra almost died, and it took her almost a year to recover. Through all these years, she has been unable to conceive an heir for Charles."

"Poor Allegra."

"Oh, how she would despise you for your compassion." Dare placed his finger against Regan's lips before she could respond. "No, listen to me. Allegra has made her bed. She might have fancied herself in love with my brother, but the truth is, she married Charles for his title and the power that comes with it. Unfortunately, she failed to provide him with the one thing that made her useful to him."

Regan kissed Dare's finger. "His heir."

Neither one of them spoke for several minutes.

Dare could sense that Regan had something on her mind. He had become quite familiar with her body, and noted the subtle clues tipping him off that she was working up the courage to ask him something important.

"When you left the town house, Frost told me that you still loved Allegra," she blurted out. "Was he telling the truth?"

"Regan, I risked incurring your brother's wrath and broke the law to marry you. Does that not tell you anything about my feelings?"

A single tear slid down her cheek. "Gentlemen marry for many reasons, and most of them have nothing to do with love."

Dare shook his head in amazement. A lady's brain was a very convoluted organ that a mere gentleman could not hope to decipher. He had thought his intentions were clear as glass.

He captured both of her hands, and felt Regan brace herself as if she were awaiting a physical blow. "You deserve honesty, Regan, and I want to give it to you." He brought her right hand to his lips and kissed her knuckles. "I have told no one else what I have shared with you. I need you to understand this, too."

"Just tell me."

"For a long time, I was convinced that I was in love with Allegra," Dare confessed. "When she gave birth to Louise, Charles was furious that he had been cheated of his heir. He used the pitiful excuse to abandon his wife and infant daughter for months at a time. Gradually I found myself taking Charles's place whenever I visited Rooks House. My mother and father encouraged the friendship because Allegra was lonely, and there were moments when I could pretend—"

She silenced him by pressing two fingers to his lips. "I think I understand."

"Do you?" Dare nipped at her fingers lightly. Despite Regan's unconventional upbringing, Frost had done a damn fine job protecting his sister from the darker side of life.

"During those visits to the country, you could experience what your life might have been with Allegra if Charles had not ruined things."

Perhaps he had underestimated the depth of Regan's compassion and forgiveness. "Allegra had her own regrets. She longed for Charles to be the husband she had dreamed of, and every time she lost another baby, she withdrew further from her inattentive husband. In the early years of their marriage, both Allegra and I were content with our little fantasies. That is, until she crawled into my bed one night. I rejected her, and we had a bitter, hurtful argument. It was the first of many. By then, however, I had come to acccept that my love for Allegra had mellowed into a comfortable friendship."

Regan's head came up at his admission.

"I started to spend less time at the family's country estate." Dare gave her a roguish grin. "There were other women."

"Hmm, indeed."

Although he adored her dark blue eyes, he enjoyed the flashes of green. "Dozens . . . legions . . ."

"Enough!" She groaned as she realized he had been baiting her. "Now you are merely being obnoxious."

Dare relented. "There is very little left to tell. Allegra tried for a few years to convince me that Louise was mine. Her spiteful taunts gave me a few bad nights, but I saw through her games and lies. That is why I wanted you to stay away from her. Allegra has grown bitter, and increasingly jealous of everyone."

The coach slowed, and Dare realized he had spent the entire journey filling Regan's ears with some of his darkest secrets. It seemed unfair, but his heart felt decidedly lighter for it. And now he was about to drag her into the unsavory tangle that comprised his family.

The coachman opened the door.

Dare descended first. Before Regan could lean forward, he blocked the doorway to prevent her from leaving.

"Dare?"

A small smile teased his mouth. "Were you lying

to Frost when you told him that you were determined to seduce me?"

Regan blushed, plainly uncomfortable by his question. "It was a foolish game. Why does it matter?"

"Regan Alice, I just opened my heart to you," Dare said, placing his hand over the organ he thought long dead. "Can you not do the same?"

Her compassionate gaze shimmered with tears. For once, her tears did not trouble him.

She took a deep breath. "I—"

Someone in the house opened the front door. Dare glanced back to see Allegra standing in the doorway.

"Hugh? Where have you been? Something horrible has happened to Charles." It was difficult to look ethereal and tragic when she was infuriated at Dare for making her wait. "Is someone in the coach with you?"

"Go inside, Allegra," Dare ordered harshly, and turned away.

Allegra sputtered. "B-but Hugh?"

"Now!" he growled.

His sister-in-law slammed the door.

The lines of tension in his face faded as he stared at Regan. "You were about to say?"

The lady was nervous. Regan had an endearing way of tilting her chin when she was unsure of herself, and the telling gesture was obvious.

At least it was for him.

"We have no time for games," Regan said sternly. "Your family is waiting for you."

Dare rubbed the underside of his sore chin as he gave her a considering glance. "And I am willing to let them wait until I get what I want!" Regan yelped as he reached into the interior of the coach and pulled her against him. His voice softened to a low sensual purr. "However, Allegra is watching us from the window and I have no intention of making love to you in front of spectators."

"And some of us are truly grateful for your restraint, milord," the coachman muttered as he stood patiently behind them.

As Regan's lips parted in surprise, Dare cursed under his breath.

He had forgotten about the servant.

Chapter Thirty

The laughter that had welled in her chest at the coachman's sarcastic remark vanished when the Mordares' butler opened the door and beckoned them inside. Walking beside Dare, her stomach fluttered as she saw Allegra was waiting for them in the front hall. Louise stood next to her mother, her tearstained face conveying the girl's misery clearer than any words.

Dare opened his arms, and Louise ran straight to him. He wrapped his arms around his niece and picked her up.

"Papa is dead!" She buried her face into her uncle's cravat and sobbed.

"I know, little one," he murmured, his solemn gaze locking on Allegra. "I am so sorry."

The words were meant to soothe both mother and daughter. Allegra dabbed at her eyes with a crumpled handkerchief and moved closer. "We have been searching for you for hours. Your father has barricaded himself in his study. We believe he has been drinking."

"And my mother?"

Allegra made a soft sniffling noise. "Asleep. Hugh, she was inconsolable. The doctor dosed her tea with laudanum to quiet her. Where have you been? Most of the staff is still searching the streets for you."

Regan stood awkwardly next to Dare. She was an outsider, and the marchioness was doing her best to ignore her presence. However, she had not come for Allegra's sake. "Lady Pashley, please accept my condolences for your loss. I realize these are difficult times."

The marchioness stroked the back of her daughter's head. "Hugh, we are unprepared for guests, and this is a time for family. I know Frost is your friend, but it is presumptuous of him to assume that you want some young girl trailing after you when there is so much to discuss. Perhaps you should send her back to her brother where she will be more comfortable."

Regan marveled how the marchioness could make her feel so unwelcome without uttering a single word or glance in her direction.

Dare crouched down, allowing his niece to stand. He nodded to the butler. "Maffy, could you take Louise to the kitchen. I'll wager Cook has something special for her."

The butler stepped forward. "Aye, she does, milord." His expression softened with undisguised affection as he extended his arm to the girl. "What say you, Lady Louise? Shall we go spy on Cook?"

At her nod, the pair wandered off.

Dare waited until his niece's footfalls had faded away before he responded to Allegra. "Let me be clear. Regan stays."

The marchioness's face pinched at his harsh tone. "Be reasonable, Hugh. Our family—"

"Regan *is* family." The right corner of his mouth curved contemptuously at his sister-in-law's wordless exclamation. "Congratulate us, Allegra. Regan and I were married yesterday."

The color drained out of the woman's face. "No! Surely, you jest. Banns have not been posted. Your mother . . . she would have insisted on taking part in the wedding plans!"

Dare placed his hand on the small of Regan's back. "We were married by special license. My mother will put aside her disappointment when she learns that she has a new daughter to fuss over."

Lady Pashley looked at both of them in disbelief. "How could you?"

"You know how love matches are, Allegra," Dare said, amused by his sister-in-law's shock. "I could not spend another night without Regan."

Regan resisted rolling her eyes at her husband's arrogant tone. She was not going to give the marchioness another chance to call her childish. "Dare, perhaps it is best that we discuss our wedding later when there are less pressing concerns. If your father has barricaded himself in his study, we should make certain he has not come to harm."

To her relief, Dare nodded. "Yes, of course. Will you check on my mother while I see to my father?"

Regan smiled at him, grateful to have been given a task. "It would be my pleasure."

"I will take you to her," Lady Pashley said, finally recovering from the shock of Dare's announcement. "We have put Her Grace in another bedchamber."

The marchioness tittered at Dare's hesitation. "Really, Dare. You were the one who brought Lady Regan into our family. Give her a chance to earn her place." She inclined her head at Regan. "Come along, I am certain we can keep each other entertained while Dare visits with his father."

Dare despised abandoning Regan to Allegra's tender mercies, but he was confident that his wife would not be gulled by the other woman's lies. As he strode through the passageway, he was astonished by the silence. Allegra had not been exaggerating when she had claimed that most of the staff had been sent out of the house to search for him. With Maffy looking after Louise, the house was forbidding as a tomb.

The door to his father's study was locked. Dare raised his fist and pounded against the wooden surface. "Father. Open the door." He waited, his ears straining for proof that his sire was within the room.

Silence.

Dare pounded on the door again. "Father!" He was reluctant to attempt to break the door down. His body was already covered with enough bruises. If he went to the kitchens, he could procure a key from Maffy.

The sound of the lock mechanism clicking halted his departure. Dare opened the door and peered inside the gloomy interior. His father had moved away from the door and was standing in front of his over-sized desk.

"Father?" More silence. Dare entered the study. "I have heard the news about Charles."

It was not until he had stepped inside the room

that his nose caught the distinct stench of death. "Dear God!" He crossed the distance between them and saw what had caused his father to barricade himself in the study.

Charles.

His lifeless corpse was laid out on the desk. Dare had no love to spare for his older brother. Still, his throat swelled with emotion at his father's broken sobs.

"What happened?"

His hair unkempt and the front of his shirt soiled, his father did not look much better than Charles. "It was my fault," he said, his voice sounding hollow as he grieved.

"Frost was told that Char—his body was found in an alley." Dare's gaze strayed to his dead brother. Someone had stabbed him. The front of Charles's shirt was torn, and it was matted with filth from the street and drying blood. The considerable amount of blood indicated that his brother had lingered as his blood had flowed out of him. How long had he lay dying in the alley?

Awkwardly Dare touched his father tentatively on the shoulder. His father was not an affectionate man, but when a man lost a son, it warranted some attempt to comfort.

"I am sorry, Father."

The duke did not embrace him. Nor did he step away from his son's hand. "I have blood on my hands."

Dare slowly shook his head. "Charles always had a feral nature. You could not tame it any more than he could resist hurting the ones he loved."

His father glared at him. "No, you do not understand," he hoarsely rasped as he pounded his fist
against his chest. "I am the one who *murdered* him."

Regan followed Lady Pashley up the stairs. It was
perhaps too much to hope that the marchioness
would leave her alone with the duchess. The woman's
curiosity brushed against her like the sticky silk of a
spider's web.

"No one expected Hugh to marry," her sister-in-
law said, casting a glance over her shoulder at Regan.
"I hope the news will not upset Her Grace."

"My husband is correct," Regan replied, deliberately reminding the haughty woman that Dare was
hers. "The duchess has always liked me. I think she
will be pleased that her son has decided to give up his
wild ways and give her more grandchildren to spoil."

Lady Pashley halted.

Belatedly, Regan recalled the marchioness's barren-
ness and winced at casual cruelty of her statement.
"My lady, forgive me. I only meant to say—"

"I know what you were implying." They continued down a narrow passageway until they reached
the door at the end. "So Hugh told you about my
unfortunate condition."

"Only to explain why his brother was unkind to
you. And why he felt honor-bound to look after you
and Louise."

Lady Pashley twisted the knob and opened the
door. "Ah . . . so that is how he justified our rather
unique friendship." She offered Regan a guileless
smile. "Perhaps I should keep you company in the
private sitting room. It appears we have much to
talk about."

Chapter Thirty-one

"You are drunk . . . tired and confused," Dare said. The idea that his father had anything to do with his brother's death was too incredible to comprehend. "You do not know what you are saying."

His father shifted, turning to face Dare. "I had to stop him. The whores were bad enough. The local villages around Rook House are riddled with your brother's bastards. Over the years, I have had to settle with some of the more prominent families."

The duke was drunkenly recalling the sins of the past. "I know the story, Father. I was there. Lord Dyton was different from the rest. Not only because of his position in society, but because you considered him a good friend. He could not be threatened or bribed. So you forced Charles to marry Allegra." Dare glowered at his brother's corpse. "You speak of ancient history."

His father removed a handkerchief from his waistcoat pocket and pressed the linen to his damp forehead. "Not so ancient when your brother cannot seem to restrain his appetites! I thought he was getting better, but then that woman showed up at my doorstep, her belly bloated with another one of your brother's unwanted bastards. And then there was that other woman." His reddened eyes shifted in Dare's direction. "The one you wanted."

Dare went cold as his father's insinuation seized him by the throat with enough force to close his throat. "Mrs. Randall. You know for a fact that Charles approached her."

The duke squeezed his eyes shut, causing two tears to course down his weathered cheeks. "I warned him. A lady would never tolerate such roughness . . . I told him to keep to his whores."

"Christ!" Dare scrubbed his face with both hands. It troubled him that his brother had been aware of his interest in the widow. When Mrs. Randall had been found murdered, Charles had wormed his way into Dare's thoughts, and he had wondered. Still, murder seemed too inconceivable to seriously contemplate. "Are you certain? You violently defended him when I suggested a possible connection."

"What was I supposed to say?" his father shouted at him. "He was my son. My heir. I was trying to protect my family."

Dare opened his mouth, and then promptly closed it. His father was correct. Would he have done anything different? If his father was responsible for Charles's murder, could he bear to see him dragged in front of the magistrate?

"You claimed that Charles had disappeared. Was that a lie?"

"No." The duke shuffled his feet, moving closer to the desk to stare at his son. "You saw what he had done to Allegra. Charles was missing. I thought—" He cleared his throat. "It no longer matters what I thought. Charles had gone into hiding, and I had given up hope of finding him on my own when he suddenly returned to the house."

"Did he admit to strangling Mrs. Randall?"

"You know how Charles is when he gets in one of his moods. Churlish. Difficult. Stubborn. He brushed aside all civility. Someone had told him that you were searching for him, and he was furious, so furious that you had people hunting for him like he was a criminal."

Dare resisted pointing out that his father had done the same thing. Both of them had been concerned that Charles was too unstable to be left wandering the streets of London.

The duke reached out and stroked Charles's hair. "He wasn't making any sense. Somehow he got it in his head that with the help of your friends, you were setting him up for the widow's murder. He was convinced of it. Charles intended to murder you. I chased after him, pleading with him to rest while I summoned a surgeon. There was a fever in his brain. Anyone who saw him could see that he needed to be bled until the madness left his eyes."

"It wasn't your fault. I doubt anyone could have reasoned with him."

"Charles took one of the daggers from the wall. He brandished it in the air, and told me that I would be burying you on the morrow." His father lifted his gaze to Dare's face, silently willing him to understand. "I had to stop him. You would have never anticipated such an attack from him."

Dare was aware that Charles would have fought anyone who was foolish enough to stand in his way. "You had no choice," he echoed softly.

"I put my hand on Charles's arm, and he struck me across the face." The duke's visage reddened. "Can you believe it? A son hitting his own father? No man would tolerate such disobedience. In a rage, I threw myself at him and we fell to the floor. When I rolled off Charles, I saw the handle of the dagger protruding just below his sternum."

He brought his hands to his head and clawed at his hair. "It was so thoughtless of me to forget about the dagger. Christ, I murdered my own son."

Regan remained in the sitting room, obediently sitting on the settee while the marchioness slipped into the bedchamber to check on the duchess. The door opened minutes later. Lady Pashley brought her finger to her lips as she quietly shut the door.

"Her Grace is still sleeping," she said apologetically. She chose the chair to the left of Regan and sat down. "She was so upset earlier. It would be kinder not to disturb her sleep."

"I agree." Regan allowed her gaze to wander about the handsomely appointed room. On the floor next to the marchioness's chair, she noted that the duchess had left her sewing basket. "Why was Her Grace moved to another room?"

Although quite comfortable, this private sitting room was smaller than the duchess's.

"It was the physician's suggestion," Lady Pashley explained as she gracefully crossed her hands on her lap. "Everyone fears Her Grace might never recover from Charles's death. After all, he was her favorite. You have seen for yourself that she will take to her bed for even minor upsets. The physician hopes to break the duchess's predictable routine by having her wake in a different room."

Regan nodded politely, neither agreeing nor disagreeing. It was not her place, but she was not overly concerned by the duchess's desire to surround herself with comforting possessions when she was upset. She suspected the physician would not be invited back to the residence when her mother-in-law learned that he was responsible for her new bedchamber.

"Perhaps we should adjourn downstairs to the drawing room."

"With His Grace locked in the study with Charles's corpse, I predict that Hugh will be unable to return to your side for hours."

Regan's stomach soured. "Lord Pashley's body is truly—"

The marchioness nodded. "His Grace insisted that the body be carried into his study. The duke's grief is so acute, he refuses to leave Charles's side. As for me, I cannot bear to look at him."

"You may not believe it, but I am sorry for your loss." Regan had not lost anyone close to her. Her father had died when she was very young, and while her mother had been absent from her and Frost's lives for years, she had left nothing behind for them to grieve over.

The marchioness reached down and pulled out the duchess's sewing scissors from the basket. Idly she tested the point with her finger. "You must think me a cold woman for not standing and wailing over my husband's corpse."

Regan blinked in surprise. "Not at all."

Lady Pashley rose from her chair. "Charles was

not an easy man to live with. I suppose Hugh spoke of the difficulties in our marriage."

Regan glanced away.

"I see. Well, Hugh has managed to surprise me. That is twice in a single day." She trailed her fingers over the back of the settee. "He rarely speaks of what happened between us. I hurt him dreadfully, and then there is Louise."

"You are Charles's wife. Despite your differences, you are still his family."

"Yes, I am intimately acquainted with Hugh's bloody honor." She offered Regan a coy smile. "Although my feelings are really none of your business, I will tell you that my love for Charles was squandered away a long ago. I will wear mourning clothes out of respect for him and the family, but anyone who expects more from me will be sorely disappointed."

"It is not my place to judge you, Lady Pashley. According to my brother, very few people had kind words to say about your husband. For that, you do have my sympathies." Sensing the end of their civility, Regan stood. "I believe I will quietly pay my respects to the duchess before I go downstairs to find Dare. Do not worry; I have no intention of waking her."

Regan stealthily walked to the closed door of the bedchamber and placed her hand on the latch. She opened the door just wide enough to peer inside. With the draperies shut, the room was dark. Still, one thing was apparent.

Dare's mother was not sleeping on the bed.

The soft whisper of fabric caused Regan to glance over her shoulder, but it was too late. Lady Pashley gave her a hard shove that sent Regan stumbling into the empty bedchamber.

The attack stirred an elusive memory, but Regan did not have time to pursue it. Her shoulder collided with one of the bedposts, and she landed on her backside.

Regan glared up at the marchioness.

"You were the one who pushed me into the street traffic!"

"If I had known Hugh was contemplating marriage to such a silly chit, I would have pushed *harder*."

The older woman tackled Regan, knocking her onto her back. Although they were similar in height and weight, the marchioness was astonishingly strong for a woman.

Struggling for her freedom, Regan struck her opponent with her fists. One of her blows hit Lady Pashley in the eye. The woman howled in outrage, and reached for something that she had tucked into her bodice.

The duchess's sewing scissors.

"No!" Regan twisted and tried to buck the angry woman off her. She grabbed the marchioness's wrist and used all her strength to push the point of the scissors away from her face.

The scissors stabbed a section of carpet above Regan's head.

"Why did you have to ruin everything?" the woman seethed, lifting the scissors again.

Regan wildly punched at the marchioness's arm, sending the scissors flying.

Before she could savor her victory, Lady Pashley wrapped her hands around Regan's neck. "Why? Why? Why?" she screamed into her face.

Regan gasped and choked as she fought to pry the woman's ruthless fingers from her neck. Lady Pashley gritted her teeth and leaned forward to increase the pressure around Regan's neck.

Her blood was a roar in her ears as swirling dark spots appeared in Regan's vision. She was losing strength with each passing second. Regan could not break Lady Pashley's unyielding grip, so she aimed for the closest thing within reach. She punched the woman in the nose.

"No!"

Those merciless fingers withdrew, and Regan immediately replaced them with her own to prevent Lady Pashley from renewing her attack. She was so busy drawing air into her starved lungs that it took a few minutes to realize she was not alone.

Unable to speak, she watched Dare as he struggled to subdue his sister-in-law. Regan rolled over on her side, and the duke's face came into view. His lips were moving, but she could not hear anything above the roar of blood in her head. Maffy suddenly appeared in the doorway. Dare pushed Lady Pashley into the butler's arms and turned his back on her.

The rage and agony on the woman's tormented visage would haunt Regan in the days to come. The duke joined the butler, and the two of them managed to drag her out of the room.

"Regan!" She started at the light slap to her cheek. She must have fainted because she did not remember Dare pulling her into his arms. "Stay awake."

"Bully," she croaked, softening her accusation with a smile.

"Christ, Regan . . . I thought—" He hugged her too tightly, but she was in no condition to complain.

"What the devil did you say to Allegra to send her into a murderous fury?"

"I pitied her," Regan said, her abused throat causing her voice to crack and fade to a hoarse whisper. She had also underestimated the woman. "Trust me, I will not make the same mistake twice!"

Epilogue

The physician insisted that Regan remain in bed for a week.

If her throat wasn't bruised, she could have told the man that she rarely heeded orders, even well-intentioned ones.

Regan's compliance lasted the length of a nap.

She found Frost and Dare in the library quietly talking as they drank their brandies.

"You were supposed to remain in bed, Regan," Dare said mildly, his disapproval just as annoying as her brother's.

Frost must have guessed her uncharitable thoughts. "I suggest you tie her to the bed next time. Or beat her. It is the only way to handle a stubborn wench."

Regan stuck her tongue out at her brother. Frost was only teasing. He had never laid a hand on her, no matter how badly she had behaved. It was the marchioness who should fear her brother's wrath. When he had learned of Lady Pashley's attack, it had taken Dare, Saint, and Vane to stop him from marching down to the magistrate's office and throttling the woman with his bare hands.

The notion that Frost was willing to kill on her behalf was touching, though entirely unnecessary. The marchioness would suffer for her crimes.

Since the gentlemen were seated in two chairs, she pointed at the sofa to let Dare and Frost know that she planned to join them with or without their permission. Dare captured her wrist and shook his head. Instead, he tugged her into his lap.

Regan did not protest. Since Dare had carried her out of his family's town house, he had not strayed far from her side. He had glowered over the physician's shoulder during his examination, and his hand had poured that ghastly laudanum down her throat so she could sleep without seeing Lady Pashley's face sneering at her.

"Where?" she croaked, gesturing at the empty chairs. Before Dare had bullied her into taking a nap, Sin, Vane, Reign, Hunter, and Saint all had called on the Bishop residence. Like all good older brothers, they had taken turns cursing, offering sympathy, and fussing over her whenever tears threatened to ruin her composure. She wished that she gotten the chance to bid them farewell.

"They were only following the good physician's orders," Frost assured her. "Once they know you are receiving visitors again, I am certain we will be burdened with a lot of unwelcome guests."

Regan rolled her eyes at her brother. He could not fool her. Frost privately loved seeing their old house filled and bustling with life and laughter.

She glanced at Dare. "Your father?" she mouthed.

"At home with my mother."

He did not mention that his parents were preparing to bury their son.

Dare absently stroked her fingers. "I met with the magistrate while you were sleeping. Even if charges are filed against my father, the magistrate predicts that he will be acquitted. It is quite apparent that the Duke of Rhode was defending himself from Charles's attack."

"Your father did London a favor killing a murderous madman," Frost drawled, taking a sip of his brandy. "The French pox has claimed the sanity of more than one hapless gent."

The surgeon who had examined Charles's corpse had also insisted on examining Lady Pashley. He had concluded that the marquess was not the only victim of his reckless debauchery. When he had been trying to beget his heir, he had passed the incurable disease on to his beautiful wife. Charles had always been violent and irrational. No one had noticed that his marchioness had been slowly succumbing to the disease.

The duke had been so certain that Charles had murdered Mrs. Randall. Regan disagreed. She had experienced the brute strength of the madness growing within Lady Pashley. Although she regretted her attack on Regan once she calmed down, Regan thought the woman capable of murder.

Since it hurt too much to speak, she had written down her suspicions. Grim-faced, Dare had read her ideas out loud to his friends. Although she had no proof, it was a plausible theory. She and Mrs. Randall had one thing in common. Dare. Everyone knew of his interest, including Lady Pashley. When Dare had left the ball with the widow, Regan had not been the only one who had been distressed by their departure. Had the lady given in to her blind rage and murdered Mrs. Randall?

Regan's bruised and swollen throat had convinced the magistrate that the murders could be laid at Lord and Lady Pashley's feet. He was not particular which one took the blame. Charles was dead, and his wife would eventually join him after the disease ravaged her body. For now, she would live out the rest of her life locked away in an asylum so she could not harm herself or others.

In time, Regan would come to forgive Lady Pashley, who was as much a victim as the woman she had murdered. It was Louise who truly deserved her sympathy. The poor girl had lost her mother and father on the same day. The duke and duchess wanted her to remain with them, but Dare and Regan would be there for her, too. This was not the first scandal the Mordare family had weathered, but God willing it would be the last.

Dare's thoughts were wholly focused on her. "How are you feeling? Do you want me to carry you back to bed?"

Regan shook her head. If she was going back to bed, she would not be climbing back in alone. She quirked her right eyebrow at his askance look.

"Not fragile," she whispered in his ear.

Dare shivered and slid his hand over the curve of her hip. He angled his head and Regan leaned in to meet his lips. Her hand tightened on his shoulder as she savored the soft, worshiping caress of his mouth. No, her husband did not think she was fragile. He was holding her as if she was priceless.

Frost's low chuckle reminded them that they were not alone. "As much as I enjoy observing enthusiastic lovers now and then, I confess even I have my limits."

Without taking his hungry gaze off Regan's face, Dare said, "There must be some young pretty wench in desperate need of seducing."

"There always is, my friend."

Regan silently concurred as she watched her brother put down his glass of brandy and abandon his chair.

Dare winked at her. "Why do you not go find her?"

He and Regan were both remembering what had happened the last time they were alone in the library.

Frost bent down long enough to kiss Regan on the top of her head. "And with a little dedication, I shall find them all."

With a farewell wave, he closed the door behind him.

A testament to his strength, in one fluid move Dare transferred them from the chair to the floor. Regan wiggled her shoulders and stretched out on the thick rug as Dare settled between her legs.

It was fortunate that she still wore her nightgown. It would take less time for Dare to get her out of her clothes.

He collected a small length of her hair and blew on the ends. "So what now, my lady wife?" He tickled her nose with her own hair, making her smile. "Is seduction on your mind?"

"Every day, for the rest of our lives?" she said huskily, her feelings lending strength to her voice. "I love you."

His hands shook as he cupped her face. "Then I am the luckiest scoundrel in all of England!"